D0849993

BLACK DOG

Also by Thomas Laird

Cutter

Season of the Assassin

BLACK DOG

THOMAS LAIRD

CARROLL & GRAF PUBLISHERS
New York

Gigi

Carroll & Graf Publishers
An imprint of Avalon Publishing Group, Inc.
245 W. 17th Street
NY 10011
www.carrollandgraf.com

First Carroll & Graf edition 2004

First published in the UK by Constable,
an imprint of Constable & Robinson Ltd 2004

ISBN 0-7867-1350-X

Printed and bound in the EU

BLACK DOG wags his tail at Krystyna Green, my friend and editor. Thanks also to John Jarrold for his excellent advice and commentary on this book.

This book is also dedicated to Rick and Harriet Espinoza, with much love.

Finally, to Kris Lindstrom. My agent, my bud, my number one reader.

Here's looking at all of you kids.

Out – out are the lights – out all!
And, over each quivering form,
The curtain, a funeral pall,
Comes down with the rush of a storm,
While the angels, all pallid and wan,
Uprising, unveiling, affirm
That the play is the tragedy, 'Man,'
And its hero, the Conqueror Worm.

Edgar Allan Poe, *The Conqueror Worm*

Chapter One

Doc's problem was chest congestion, he said. Mine was the sinuses draining into my ears. But neither of us matched the problems of the corpse on the floor before us. She'd been gone for eighteen hours, Dr Gray the MD explained before he left. Cause of death was yet to be determined, which was not unusual, but the color of the vic's face was indeed a bit atypical for someone who'd been gone less than a day. She was white. And not a Caucasian white. White as in anemic. Bloodless. There were also needle tracks on the inside of her left arm. Junkie? She didn't look the type. Well-groomed. Apparently well dressed from the stuff in her closet. She was a flight attendant for International Air. In her early thirties, quite attractive – at least she had been some eighteen hours ago.

But the pallor was unnatural for a vic this fresh, Doc kept saying, and I had to agree. That was, I agreed when I could get him to talk loudly enough for me to hear him.

He wheezed and I just couldn't hear with all this juice from my sinuses draining into my ears.

'Someone's been bleeding her, Jimmy P,' Doc pronounced.

'You think so?' I grinned.

'I mean for real bleeding her. The needle tracks. Crude, James. My nurse at the doctor's doesn't leave black and blue marks like these.'

They were noticeable to the untrained eye of two laymen investigators without Dr Gray's expertise. But Gray wouldn't comment on the discolored punctures on Jennifer Petersen's left arm. There were at least four such welts that I could see.

1

The body was bagged and tagged after all the Crime Scene business was attended to. The photographs had been taken, and yet another mystery had been thrown our way.

This city never ran out of dubious deaths.

We sat at the far end of the bar with our two Diet Sprites. Doc was coughing and wheezing, and I had to keep asking him to repeat himself.

'I said, I'm going to retire this time for real,' my partner declared.

'You said that when you went off to finish your PhD. You were back on the job six weeks after you earned the doctor's. You're gonna die doing stiffs with me.'

He looked at me sadly. As if I just shot a nail into his soul.

'And this time you'd be incorrect, Jimmy . . . I'm not feeling right.'

'Then why don't you take some time?'

'I am. I was going to tell you. I'm taking a month's leave of absence.'

'You're going to leave me this white-faced stewardess on our plate? You're going to leave me do all that work alone?' I jabbed at him.

But he wasn't firing back at me. This was not the partner I knew and loved.

'I just don't get back up as easy as I used to, James. I'm getting old. Too old.'

'What?'

'I'm getting too—'

'I heard you, Doc. I just don't believe you.'

'Believe me, Jimmy P. Believe me.'

He had his gray-blue eyes aimed right at me. There was no mistaking what he was trying to say.

'You mean you're going to retire,' I told him.

'After the course of one month of down time, I'll make it final. But that's the way it looks from where the sun now stands. I am Chief Joseph of the Nez Perce: "I will fight no more forever."'

I wanted to blow him off the way I had a hundred times

2

before when he got into this retirement rant, but this time I sensed that he meant it. There was no joking around with Doc Gibron's end of an era. There was nothing vaguely amusing about losing my mentor, partner, and best friend. I just had to hope that he would reconsider. Before I retired I thought I'd dry up and blow away like a spent November leaf. And I always thought it would be the same for Doctor Harold Gibron of Homicide.

Doc was true to his word. He went on one-month leave and I was paired up with Jack Wendkos, an old partner of mine. He worked with Gibron and me on The Farmer case – the guy who created his own supply of human organs for the black market and the Outfit, Chicago's Mafia.

Jack was a much younger man than the two of us. He was in his late thirties and he'd been working Homicide for almost eight years. He was a solid investigator. Just recently married a near-victim of The Farmer's. She was a science professor at a university about sixty miles from the city. They were now living in Geneva, another far western suburb.

Dr Gray had us, Jack and I, at the autopsy for the overly pale stewardess we recently became assigned to. I filled Jack in on the way to Dr Gray's lecture.

I could see the frown form on Jack's Gentleman's Quarterly face. Wendkos would be perfect for that slick's cover if he hadn't had his nose squashed in Golden Gloves, back when he placed second, in high school.

'Pretty lady at one time,' Detective Wendkos whispered.

Cops always seem hushed, here in the autopsy room. It was like respect for the dearly departed, I imagined. But there was no one here who'd be disturbed by any kind of noise.

Jennifer's brains and internal pieces were lying inside stainless steel containers, near various parts of her corpse. Gray'd done the usual complete operation on her.

'This young woman died of severe blood loss. Must have taken some time, Jimmy. Jack. This young lady's down to her last quart of oil, if there's that much left in her.'

Gray removed his latex and looked over at us, across the slab of the remains.

'He did this with a needle?' I asked.

'He could have used a mortician's tools, Lieutenant Parisi. These needle holes are larger than the typical syringe that a doper would use. This guy may know something about mortuary science.'

'You mean a funeral mortician?' Jack asked.

'Could be,' Gray countered. 'It's just speculation. He wasn't very good with a needle, though. Or he just didn't care how brutal he was about inserting it. Hence all the bruising, the black marks on her arm. A good nurse would never have been that awkward.'

Gray turned off his recording tape near the slab where we stood.

'Anything else, boys? This girl was bled dry. Must have taken some days to do it. And the other remarkable item here is that there is no evidence of penetration. She hasn't been sexually assaulted, I don't think.'

'So all he wanted—'

'Yes, Jimmy.'

Gray walked away from Jack and me.

'Was her blood,' I finished when the good doctor was well out of earshot.

'Svenghoulie,' I told Wendkos.

'Who?' Jack asked.

We were seated in my office that overlooked Lake Michigan. The view was the only perk of this fraction of a cubicle.

'The guy on TV. "Creature Features." One of those cable horror shows,' I explained.

'Must be before my time,' Wendkos grinned.

You could see the neat little seam on the left side of his nose that extended to his left nostril. The scar was the result of the magna punch that laid his honker flat on his face, back from his Golden Gloves era.

We were about to leave to interview some people at International who knew Jennifer Petersen. But our trip to

O'Hare was interrupted when we got the call to a scene on the West Side.

The West Side was the barrio, the hood, of this city. This was gangbanger territory. Poverty territory. Homelessness. Street land and home of the yos and yoettes – young black males and females. They were the predators in this neighborhood, especially the black males. Too many uneducated yos and yoettes. It was too easy to look for a living in the streets. The schools couldn't compete with the corner crack barons. There were some Hispanics, the farther east and south you go from where we were headed. But it was one continuous barrio from the western periphery of Chicago almost to the Lake. It was a harsh landscape. Full of grays and browns and blacks. Dark colors, dark lives. The young males who were athletes might have had options about getting out of here, but the remainder of the hoodsters stayed put until the next drive-by slaying. We put kids on the meat wagon almost hourly, in these parts.

The apartment on the far West Side, here, was more like a flop in some sleazoid downtown hotel. One of those joints designed for the poor, the dudes with just enough coin to put a roof overhead. It was amazing they hadn't condemned this apartment building. But the inspectors probably didn't make their rounds around here too often.

The old man was propped up against the wall of his kitchen-dinette. It was a one-bedroom flop. Barely enough room to stretch your arms out sideways. Claustrophobic close.

The arterial spray was off to the left of his sliced-open throat. Black male. Probably in his late sixties or early seventies. The blood covered about eighteen inches of ancient wallpaper.

'Jugular,' Jack offered.

There was a pool of fresh blood on the once-white, now-gray tile beneath the old man. And in his arms was a tabby cat. The cat was gone also. Someone had sliced off all four of the feline's paws. The kitty's blood had soaked the old man's pants, on his lap.

'He figured he owed himself the cat too?'

5

Jack looked at me as if he were surprised.

Then a teenaged girl raced into the crime scene, past the uniforms who couldn't stop her. She was maybe seventeen. Didn't look like the typical yoette on these streets. Well groomed. No gang symbols on her anywhere. No tattoos. Cheaply but cleanly dressed. And a pretty girl, also. Reminded me of someone I used to be in love with, but Celia was much older than this teenager.

She didn't scream as I rushed toward her with Jack at my side.

'You shouldn't—'

She snatched her right arm back from me, but her right fist went to her mouth. Not a sound came from her. I was afraid she might be going into shock when I saw the size of her eyes. The whites seemed enormous, the eyeballs almost popped out of her head.

'You have to leave. This is a crime scene,' I tried to explain to her.

'Is he—' Jack asked.

'He's my grandfather,' the girl told Jack.

'You have to leave . . . What's your name?' I asked.

'Joellyn. Joellyn Ransom,' she said.

'This was your grandfather?' Jack queried gently. He had both her hands now and had managed to turn her around, away from the sight of the old man and the cat.

'Yes.'

Then the tears tumbled down Joellyn Ransom's cheeks. Jack walked her outside to the uniforms.

The Crime Scene Investigators snapped their photos and did all the dusting for prints. Dr Gray had already come and gone. This was another bleeder, I thought. The slash to the jugular had stopped Arthur Ransom's timepiece. And the cat's. I thought the coppers on scene were more shocked at what happened to the feline than they were to what did in Arthur Ransom. Human corpses were typical around here. Dead domestic pets weren't quite so everyday. It was rather ironic that animal life seemed more valuable than human life, but there it was.

6

The meat wagon came for Arthur. Jack and I made our last look over on this crime scene. He took notes for the two of us. I was not much for notebooks. It'd been my weakest link as an investigator. I relied too much on memory, and my memory would betray me eventually. I felt as old as Doc Gibron did when we watched them bag Jennifer Petersen.

We interviewed the people who knew Jennifer Petersen at International at O'Hare. I have always despised coming here to this circus of an airport. Too many frenetic people. Crowds. Everything jammed up. People running around in a frenzy. Pickpockets did a booming business here. There was a victim with a dangling wallet or purse everywhere. The security was a joke. You were on your own in this jungle. Cops hated working this place, and the security clowns were making minimum wage. They could give a shit if you got boosted.

We seldom had homicides on this scene, but we interviewed people here, from time to time. I almost got to interview O.J. Simpson, but I was diverted onto another case.

Someone at the *Tribune* got wind of the facts regarding Jennifer Petersen's demise, and now some writer was talking about vampires and bloodsuckers doing Ms Petersen.

All we needed were werewolves and goblins to complicate a murder case. Got people crazy. Bela Lugosi returned from the grave. Nosferatu and all that Transylvanian jive. It was hard enough unraveling a standard vic's demise without the papers making it go Hollywood. Next would come the tabloids and the TV media and their takes on the Petersen murder. The circus would have many rings.

We interviewed four employees of International. Three were sister flight attendants. They knew Jennifer only barely, they said. She kept to herself. Her home base was O'Hare, so she had a lease on an apartment a few miles away from the airport. That, of course, was where we found her.

The queries came to nothing, so Jack and I took lunch at the O'Hare Chili's. We both ordered Old Timer Burgers. Both of us were on diets, but Jack showed far better results than I did. I had fifteen pounds to unload.

7

'So he kept her quiet by strapping her mouth shut with the gray duct tape we found in her kitchen,' Jack repeated. 'He kept her immobile by also strapping her to her bed with the same gray duct tape. Apparently he didn't let her get up, since we found the fecal and urine stains on the sheets of her bed.'

I looked down at my newly arrived Old Timer Burger, and my stomach pangs had vanished.

'Thanks,' I told my younger partner.

'Sorry, Jimmy. But we do need to sort—'

'I know, I know. It's okay.'

I tried to bury the burger in condiments. It didn't help.

'So he had her there for two or three or four days,' Jack continued. 'The stains seem to support that theory.'

I took a bite out of my Old Timer Burger. My hunger and my empty stomach overcame the usual revulsion at case details. You gotta eat, no?

'They've already named this guy with Jennifer Petersen. Downtown they call him "The Count".'

'They got a name for the perpetrator of the poor old yo on the West Side?' I asked.

'He's not high profile enough to get a moniker. Just another yo, to some people.'

'Not to me. How about you, Jack?'

He smiled and shook his handsome noggin.

'I knew there was something I really liked about you.'

Chapter Two

My wife Natalie kept me going even with the weight of all that goo in my ears and the usual burden of being a homicide investigator. I looked at my young beauty of a mate and I consistently wondered how a middle-aged guinea like me ever became as fortunate as I was. I'd write her poetry if I had the muse. But I was poetically tone deaf, as Doc Gibron of the PhD in Literature would say. I tried to tell her I loved her at least once every day, but repeatedly forgot, and my shortcomings in that department haunted me. Time seemed very short with Natalie. We were always headed in different directions. She was in Homicide now, too, but we tended to work different shifts, so I rarely saw her on the job. We made as much time for ourselves as we could, but with two almost grown children – the oldest being away at a university – and two small fry, our baby girls, we still had commitments to the young people in our home.

My mother, Eleanor, helped us out a great deal of the time, handling the two young girls and keeping an eye on Michael, my only son, but Natalie and I liked to be for-real parents as often as work would allow us. And the parent thing did not allow us to be alone very frequently.

'A good thing it is too,' Natalie cracked. It was a Wednesday morning that found us in bed with a day off and the girls at my mother's house and Michael and the big girl at school.

We slept in. It was 9:07 a.m. and we both felt very much guilty about how good this all seemed.

'Why is it a good thing, Red?' I asked.

'You'd just knock me up again if we spent too much time together.'

'Flattering yourself, are we?' I smiled.

She was right, of course. I'd eventually get her into 'trouble' if nature took its course, and we had agreed that we'd produce no more offspring. I was getting too old – fifty-five this summer – and Natalie wanted to pursue her Homicide career without any more infants to nurse. We had our two girls together, as well as the two older ones who adored their new mother. Erin gave life to Kelly and Michael. They remembered their mother and loved her very much, but they took to the Redhead as if she'd always been a part of the Parisi mob. I missed Erin, but I didn't feel guilty about loving Natalie anymore. I hadn't removed my first wife from my life. I think I simply added on to it with the Redhead.

Retirement was not an issue. I had no hobbies. I liked to read but I didn't get much chance, other than to peruse the jackets of the vics I investigated. I didn't follow the Sox the way I used to, ever since the strike. The NBA was in shambles, even with an aged Michael Jordan on a team he shouldn't have joined. And football was dominated by 400-pound giants that have turned the NFL into a near-freak show. All Natalie and I did for recreation was go to the movies, and we had damn little time to do that.

But was I happy? As much as a man who earned his bread dealing with the dead and those who made them that way can be happy. Family was all I had, of course. But I didn't find it to be chains on my soul. I had not had the urge to take off in the midst of some mid-life crisis. You know, buy a Harley, run down to Mexico and live in a shack by the Gulf of Mexico with some mestizo *Mexicana* and start a new life collecting seashells.

Life had sent me a number of wounds to the vulnerable tissue. But the women in my life have kept my head above the surface of the roiling seas, as Doc might phrase it.

The Count had already made it to the headlines of two of

the bigger newspapers in the city. The tabloids had joined in the fun as well, and even though this guy was not a serial operator – yet – Jack and I had the sick feeling we'd be hearing from him soon. The problem was that since there was no series of murders, it became a bit difficult to talk about this cheesedick's tendencies. He had no track record yet. Fortunate for all the possible vics he could be acquiring, but unfortunate for homicide investigators who looked for patterns to predict behavior.

No one saw Jennifer Petersen latch onto a male partner after she landed at O'Hare seven days ago. She took a cab to her apartment, two miles from the terminal, and then she was swallowed into obscurity at her residence. No one ever heard from her again. Except, of course, for The Count, himself.

We tossed her efficiency apartment thoroughly. He left no sign. No fibers that couldn't be attributed to Jennifer herself. No fingerprints but the vic's. He cleaned up after himself as well as any organized killer can.

The only calling card that Jack and I could make was the awkward punctures he left on her arm. The black and blue remainders of the needle he used to take her blood.

'What's he doing with the blood?' Jack Wendkos mused on the way toward O'Hare.

We were again canvassing the various stores and shops and restaurants at the airport to see if anyone had seen Jennifer on her way out of the terminal.

'Drinking it. Naturally. That's what vampires do, you Polski,' I smiled.

'No one can drink the real thing, can they?'

'Some African tribes drink the blood of the animals they kill. Think I heard that in some history lecture in college,' I offered.

'That be bullshit, Lieutenant. I don't even want to think about it.'

'How about all that lovely au juice you swill down with the prime rib you so greatly love?'

'That isn't the same, Jimmy.'

'Well, I guess so. But it's from the blood of the steer, no?'

'Are you *trying* to make me heave, Lieutenant?'

We pulled into the grand terminal that is O'Hare Airport. We pulled up to the official no parking zone right near the United entrance, and we showed our badges to the uniform who was hustling toward us to get us out of the no parking zone. The badge did have a few perks. The black uniform cop smiled and waved and went back to his surveillance perch.

We started with the restaurants. Jennifer completed a flight from Seattle the day she vanished inside her own apartment. The Chili's manager directed us to his day manager who was on shift the day Ms Petersen was directed toward the ages. Middle aged, but very attractive, this day manager was. Forty, forty-five. But very ripe. The type of mature who still turned heads of males a decade younger than she was. Her name was Kori Whalen. No ring. I wondered if she was divorced. She was too fine to have been passed over.

We showed her the photos of Jennifer.

'Yes. She was in here. Late in the afternoon.'

Kori was a platinum blonde with a very fine root job. Not a hint. Jack had also noticed the qualities of this day manager goddess.

It wasn't supposed to happen. You were not supposed to strike gold on the first dig. The usual was to spend six or seven hours canvassing a site for someone who might be able to help a case. But here it seemed to be.

'Was anyone with her?' Jack asked the manager.

Kori had the full bosom, the lean waist, the tight rear end, and the muscular calves. She demanded one's full male attention. She must have been a real drawing card for this airport restaurant. I thought I was beginning to flush.

'No. She was alone. But she had lots of male patrons aware of her.'

I was thinking that it'd be tough competition if Kori were in the same room with Jennifer Petersen. Petersen was attractive. Kori, however, was the kind of woman who commanded your breathing patterns.

I reminded myself that I was married. Happily. I felt like reminding Jack Wendkos how blissful he was too, but we were both somewhere near a primal slobber.

'No one approached her?' Jack finally was able to ask.

This was becoming a very difficult interview. And none of it was the day manager's fault. It was just that God spent far too much time on some of his creatures.

'No. I didn't see anyone come up to her.'

'Anybody in that crowd appear strange?' I asked her.

'There are two or three million strange people in this terminal at any given moment,' she replied.

I was melting. I should have sent the Redhead to do this query. But I was a senior investigator, I told myself. I would regain my composure. Jesus, I felt like a rookie fresh out of the Academy. I squeezed my fists and struggled, and I was back under control.

'No one appeared more odd than usual?' I asked again.

She was ready to confirm what she already said, but then something stopped her.

'There was a guy . . . He stood out, I guess. He was in here when that poor woman was eating . . . I remember . . . I remember that he looked extremely pale. As if he had the flu. I almost asked him if he needed help. But he left just before the stewardess did. I recall it clearly. Yes. He left before she did. Never made a move toward her, that I saw.'

'What kind of pale?' Jack asked.

'Like I said. A sickly white. A fishbelly white. You know, kind of anemic.'

'Can you give us a fuller description?' I asked.

'He was about six feet tall. Thin. What you'd call gaunt, I suppose. You know, like almost caved in. Terrible posture. And he was dressed weird too. All in black. Black . . . Like those goofy kids – the Goths? Is that what they call them?'

'Yeah. Something like that,' Jack affirmed.

'He had very black hair. With a blue sheen. That's how you know it's really black. I watch people every day. To see if they try to run out and stiff us. To make sure they don't

13

rip off our servers by stealing tips . . . He never did anything off key that I remember—'

'How'd he pay for his bill?' I asked.

'Ask the cashier. She's working now.'

We had to fairly rip ourselves away from this stunning piece of handiwork – Christ, I was using Doc's language again. I must have missed him more than I thought.

Sheryl was the cashier. We approached her and displayed our credentials and then Jack told her about Jennifer Petersen, showed her the photo of the stewardess, and Sheryl remembered the guy with the black hair and the pale puss.

'He paid with one of those direct check cards. I can remember it because he startled me when I looked up at him. Jesus, what a spook! I mean we get crazies in this terminal all the time, but . . . He was exceptional. Yeah, I remember him.'

'Can you get the receipts from the day he was in here?' I asked.

'Sure. But you'll have to ask Kori. That's her department, old receipts.'

Jack couldn't believe our good luck. A credit card trail and another round with the blonde beauty who had us both under her spell.

It was a Visa number. During the hour he and Jennifer Petersen were in the restaurant, only five people used a credit card. Two were males. One of the males was seventy-two years old, which we found out when we put our technicians in Computer Systems to work. The other male was Anthony Mann, aged twenty-six, of 1231 River Canal Street. It was an Old Town Address. Jack was familiar with the hood there, having lived there during his first marriage.

We pulled up to the curb in front of the red-brick three flat where Mann resided. We got out of the blue Taurus and walked up the steps to where the doorbells were located. We rang Mann's flat three times. Finally he answered, buzzed us through the entrance door, and we ascended the three flights to his top apartment.

14

He was standing by the door, the entry way barely cracked open in front of him. All I could see was the top of his head and his gray-yellow eyes.

Trouble was that his hair was dishwater blond. No black to be seen.

He opened the door all the way when he saw our badges.

'Did you retrieve my credit cards?'

When he asked us, I felt like a groan was emerging forth from my deepest parts.

'Stolen card. So all we have is a description. Young Goth, The Count, perhaps, living on the proceeds of that ripped-off card,' I told Jack.

It was early October. Still warm. Indian summer. But I couldn't wait for the real fall to happen. I liked the big cool off. The crispness of the autumn air. I was staring out that perk of a window toward the beach. There were a few people walking the sand of the public facility. But it was too late in the season to be in the water, even though it was in the upper seventies.

'We need to hit the West Side before dark,' I told Wendkos. 'It's too much of a combat zone there after the sun goes down.'

'That's when The Count does his trade, isn't it, Jimmy? After dark.'

There was a smile on that handsome face, but it didn't contain any real pleasure at his small joke about the Count.

We took the elevator down to the parking lot, but this time I was driving. The traffic was moderate on the Expressway. I had the air conditioning on so that we could hear each other.

'We put the word out on that hot card. We know it the very next time Whitey decides to use it.'

'Jimmy, you really think he'll try using that Visa again?'

'Probably not. Not if he's as smart as the guy who left us that sterile crime scene. But then he might not know someone's seen him in Jennifer Petersen's presence. He might think he's an anonymous member of the crowd. Who knows? Maybe this Goth bastard is a wrong number. He left before she did. Maybe he's just a thief.'

Neither of us thought so, but we remained quiet all the way to the West Side crime scene.

We canvassed the neighborhood until the sun crept toward the horizon. We had two patrolmen accompanying us, but I really didn't feel safe. I don't think Jack did either. I had my usual nine-millimeter in my shoulder holster. The .44 Bulldog was in the inside pocket of my black leather, knee length jacket. And I carried the switchblade in my outside right pocket.

Nobody 'knew nothing.' That was about what we produced from two hours of walking the blocks of this hood. We got a lot of angry stares too, even though both of the uniforms were black. Regardless of their color, the black patrolmen were considered the enemy by a lot of the yos in this neighborhood. The African American coppers were aware of all this ill sentiment. They were visibly relieved when we informed them that they could go on back to their regular beats.

'Low profile,' I muttered, on the ride back to the Loop and my office.

'I hear you,' Jack said. He was the wheelman in the Taurus on the route back to the Lake.

'Drugs . . . It's usually drugs,' Jack offered.

'Yeah. I suppose. But Arthur wasn't a user. No trace in the autopsy. Not even an aspirin in his system.'

'He could be a procurer. A very old clocker,' Jack insisted.

'True. Or maybe he's got a story that's brand new. Everybody assumes because he's black and from the hood of hoods that he's in pharmaceuticals. Maybe getting cut up was strictly personal.'

'Could be, Lieutenant . . . How many of these kinds of cases do we close?'

I looked over at him. My eyes were heavy and I was very tired.

'Not nearly enough to call it justice, Jack.'

'Because they're low profile. Maybe a blurb in the papers if they get any newsprint.'

16

'Yeah. You are correct.'

'That don't make it feel any better. Christ, two of us and two uniforms as bodyguards. That ain't a fucking task force, Jimmy.'

I remembered the grief of Arthur's granddaughter, Joellyn. I remembered the pain I felt when I watched the light in Celia Dacy's eyes go out, a few years ago.

'We'll have to be a task force of two, then,' I told my younger partner.

Doc Gibron had to take two months' leave of absence after working a double homicide of a four- and six-year-old-pair of sisters on this same West Side. We almost lost him on that episode.

'A task force of two,' Jack muttered.

'Madness, ain't it?' I grinned.

Chapter Three

My son Michael moped around the house. I thought it was teenaged depression. He was a junior in high school, so I thought it was a little late for him to be going through what most adolescents leave behind them when they pass through junior high school. When I pressed him about his depression, I got silence. I was not used to interrogating my own family, but I had done so in the past when the situation required it.

'Is it a girl?' I smiled at him.

He was a handsome young man. Much better looking than the old man. Taller. About six one. Muscular without being bulky. He had my brown eyes, but he had a much less weathered face than I have ever had in all my years. He looked like he had guinea blood in him, but he also had some of the physical beauty that his mother Erin showed in her facial features. The nose was straighter than mine. The cheekbones a bit more pronounced with a hint of the Gael in them – my wife was Irish.

'Then what is it?'

'I'm not a suspect, Pa. Leave it alone,' he muttered.

'This isn't like you, Michael. The hell's wrong?'

It was a mistake to lose my temper. I tried to compose myself. Getting pissed was always a mistake with teenagers. To them it was a sign of weakness.

As suddenly as he had shut me off, he turned to me. And I could see the tears. I went over to him and tried to hug him, but he wouldn't let me.

'I need to talk to somebody, Pa. But it can't be you.'

'What're you talking about, Mike?'

'I need to talk to somebody. A counselor, maybe.'

'Don't you have them at the school?'

He was beginning to frighten me.

'Not that kind of counselor. Like a shrink or a psychologist. You know?'

The tears had ceased.

'We're not moving from this place until you tell me what the hell's going on. I'm your father and—'

'It isn't something at school. It's something that happened a few years ago. Back when I was at St Catherine's.'

St Catherine's was his old grade school.

'What happened at St Catherine's?'

'It didn't actually happen. It almost happened.'

I watched him.

'You know Father Mark.'

The heat raced toward my cheeks.

I nodded.

'I've been reading in the paper about all those guys who were . . . I've been seeing on TV about all those kids who . . . '

He choked up on me at that point.

'You're telling me this priest tried to pull something on you?'

'You remember when I stopped serving at the mass?'

I nodded again.

'I thought that was because of a conflict with—'

'It was because of Father Mark. He tried . . . He tried . . . You know what I'm saying?'

'And you waited . . . what? Five years to tell me?'

'I couldn't tell you. I have to talk about it to somebody. I have to make sure he's not . . . not doing it to somebody else.'

We were sitting in the living room of my Northwest Side home. All the females in the clan were somewhere else. It was one of the few times we weren't swamped with a female presence.

'You're a cop, Pa. I tell you and you go nuts . . . And he really never did anything to me . . . He tried . . . to touch me. I thought he was just messing around, you know? Like playing grabass in the locker room or something . . . But I could see in his eyes that he wasn't playing. And then there were two or three guys in my class he tried to do the same thing . . . If I talked about it, I thought everybody might think it was *me*. Like I was queer or something. That's why I stopped serving. That's why I never wanted to go to mass.'

I never forced my kids to go to church. Not when they became old enough to make decisions like that on their own. Michael had always been stubborn about attending when he was in junior high, but I never knew why until—

'I need to talk to somebody, Dad. Just to get things okay inside me.'

'But you said he never actually—'

'He tried to touch me, Pa. He scared the hell out of me. I still have dreams. And then he's still a priest, somewhere.'

Father Mark had been transferred from St Catherine's about a year after Mike graduated grade school. I could find out where.

'I don't want you to do anything,' he told me.

'What're you talking about? You can't let that guy get away with—'

'This is my problem, Pa. I want to talk to someone. I want to make it be over with, inside. I want to stop the bad dreams.'

Then I embraced him. I had bad dreams too. About the death of my father. He fell twenty-six steps to his death in our family home. The bad dreams came from the fact that my mother pushed him. And I suffered over whether she meant for the old man to break his neck on that fall down those twenty-six steps. I spent a lot of hours with the Department's shrink.

Now Michael had nightmares. About a priest laying hands on him. And even though the worst hadn't happened, my son imagined what might have happened.

And he had bad dreams.

After we broke off the embrace, I looked at him.

'We'll get you some help . . . But I can't let it slide, Mike. I've got to find out where this guy is. He can't be doing this to anyone else again. Ever.'

'I should've told you. But I was afraid. You were a cop. And the whole thing would've—'

'I know. I understand. But I have to look into it. You understand, don't you?'

He tried to smile. It didn't come off, but it was the son I knew again. Not this morose, haunted kid who had suddenly come to live with me.

All those cases made me look away from my own son. I didn't pay attention to him. I wasn't watching him, seeing his mood turn to dead serious. I was too busy dealing with strangers, murderous outsiders, and I wasn't looking at my own boy.

I wondered what I had missed with my eldest daughter Kelly. Had she been stricken with something terrible like this, and had I been too busy with the messes I was paid to clean up?

I wanted to take the .44 Bulldog and stash it in my coat pocket. I wanted to find Father Mark and place the snub nose of my piece in his mouth. I wanted to get him on his knees and have him feel as helpless as Michael did when this prick with a collar made a move on my kid.

It wasn't possible. Then I would become the criminal this reverend was. I knew that. But I wondered where the church was hiding this guy. They were beginning to feel the heat in the media about pedophile priests, but the old Roman arrogance was still in control of them. They took care of their own – even their twisted brethren.

I thought about all the years he'd been keeping this thing from me. Was he afraid I'd shoot the bastard? Didn't he know me better than that? Maybe he thought I was like some of the other members of our family, the members who turned left and went wrong. I have relatives who are members of the Outfit, Chicago's version of the Mafia.

I could get them to take care of Father Mark. All it would take was a phone call. They'd make sure he'd never be seen again.

There was no chance. I had dirtied my hands by reaching out to them before for information. But that was as far as it went – information. They'd made their turn in life, and I'd gone another direction.

But the thought was more than tempting.

And what if this priest had actually molested my son? Not just attempted to, but molested him? Would I let the dogs loose? Let the Ciccios, the mob division of the family, have this limpdick priest?

I couldn't face my boy if I involved them. Could I face him if I stuck that nub of a barrel down the priest's throat?

He would get the counseling. But I'd have to meet up with Father Mark, if I could locate him. I was certain the church would not be forthcoming about any embarrassment of theirs who they had 'transferred'.

I hugged my son again. It wasn't something we did very often, and now this was the way we were thrown closer together.

'We'll get you some help, Mike. I'll take care of everything.'

The tears were hot and acidic on my cheeks, but I didn't let Michael see them.

When I told Natalie, she didn't cry, but I could see the scarlet anger cloud over her face. With a redhead, a blood-red rage was easy to spot.

'We should shoot him.'

She was coldly serious.

'But we're coppers,' she added.

'I'm going to look into it,' I told Natalie.

We were in bed. It was dawn. Dawn was usually the best time for me with her because I could see her lovely face rise out of the dark.

'Me too.'

'No. Let me. I'll keep it low profile. Please, Natalie. Let me.'

'I know. He's really yours and not mine—'

'Don't say that. Don't *feel* that way because it's not true. He loves you and he's connected to you . . . Just let me handle this one. The main thing is we get him some professional help.'

'I know somebody, Jimmy.'

'Yeah? Who?'

'His name is Dan Jenkins. He deals with victims of pedophilia. He knows all about self-image and all the stuff Mike is going through. I know him through Children's Services. I sent him several referrals when I was a street cop.'

'So you can set it up,' I told my wife.

'Really?'

I held her tightly to me.

'Goddamn it. Goddamn it. My son has bad dreams. Goddamnit, Natalie.'

I felt her fingertips press into my shoulder blades as she held me even tighter.

We continued to canvass the West Side to find out if anyone saw someone coming out of Arthur Ransom's building on the night of the murder, and we again had two black patrolmen accompanying Jack and me on the streets of this dangerous hood.

We rang the bell on the three flat directly across the street from Ransom's place. A very old woman answered the door.

She was wearing a purple men's shirt and she had bib overalls on as well. We showed her our badges and she asked us inside – a first for these West Side interviews. Jack looked as surprised as I felt. The uniforms stayed outside to keep an eye on our vehicles.

'Your name, ma'am?' Jack asked as we sat down across from her in the living room.

'Dilly,' she said. 'But my real name is Dorothy.'

She sounded pretty well educated. Another new twist for this barrio.

'Used to be a schoolteacher about six blocks up the street. That was back when you didn't need a bodyguard to go to the grocery store.'

She smiled, and I saw all the gold of her dental work.

'We're here to ask you about the killing of Arthur Ransom,' Jack told her.

'I thought as much. Was wondering when you'd get around to me.'

'You live alone here?' I asked.

'Rufus!' she called out toward the kitchen.

We heard the furious thumping of an animal charging toward us. I was almost inclined to reach for a weapon, but the huge malamute flopped down at Dilly's feet like a docile poodle. The animal must've gone 150 pounds. He was more wolf than malamute.

'Got no cats on this block,' she told us. 'Rufus can't abide felines. I keep him inside as much as possible, but there's always some damn fool tomcat that comes a little too close to my man here.'

'And then what happens?' Jack asked.

'That dog is as gentle as a lamb to human beings. But he's torn the heads off six cats that I know of.'

We looked down at the huge canine/lupine animal, and I could see him dismembering an unwitting pussycat.

'Rufus keeps people from bothering me. I take him every-where with me, and even the bangers don't want to mess with this dog.'

She petted him lovingly.

'But you wanted to know about this Arthur Ransom?'

'Yes,' I answered.

'You thinking it was drug related?' she asked.

'That's what we were trying to find out,' Jack replied.

'That's what the po-lice always assume around here,' she grumbled.

'You don't think it had anything to do with drugs,' I said.

'No. I don't. I didn't know Arthur Ransom well, but I know he was a decent man. Took care of that granddaughter that he was ever so proud of. She was over there all the time. Her mother was no good. Now there was a crack baby! But she's dead now, and the girl lives with her father. I hear he works at the racetrack, but he's no doper. Arthur bought her her clothes. Made sure she kept up school. I think she's supposed to graduate next spring . . . I heard all this from Arthur himself. He went to the same laundrymat as I do,

24

'bout four blocks up the street. Rufus took a shine to Arthur. Arthur was good people, Lieutenant. He didn't deserve what he got. Neither him nor his pet cat, from what I hear.'

'You see anybody go in or out of his building on that night?' I asked.

'No, but this dog of mine was all anxious that night, I remember. He kept going to the front window there. Every time I looked out, there was no one around. But I go to bed early. My blood pressure medicine makes me tired. You know?'

'Had he been having problems with a neighbor?' Jack asked her.

'Everybody has problems with neighbors here, Detective Wendkos,' Dilly smiled. I thought I detected a little sarcasm in her grin.

'You mean gangbangers?' I asked.

'You need to talk to your tactical friends,' she said.

'You know tactical?'

'Yes, Lieutenant. Everybody in this neighborhood knows the tacticals. They're out here often enough. There just aren't enough of them to hang out twenty-four, three-sixty-five.'

Again she gave me the sly smile.

'You think some of the locals might have done Arthur,' I said.

'Sure. Nothing new. That's how they get blooded.'

She meant initiated.

'You think Arthur's death might have been part of a gang initiation,' Jack said.

'Nobody knows except Arthur and the bitch who did him,' Dilly spat.

Her grin had turned to anger. I wondered how she had survived this environment for all these years.

'Life is cheap on this street. Arthur should've had a dog like Rufus. Bangers don't like dogs. They'd shoot my man if they ever had the chance. That's why I keep him inside. Arthur is what those tacticals call a low profile killing, isn't that right, Lieutenant?'

'I've heard the term. But it doesn't make any difference to me, Dilly. I'm not into profiles. I want whoever did

Arthur. All murderers are equal to me. I'm real democratic that way.'

She smiled again, but there was no snideness in her gold streaked dental work, this time.

Chapter Four

The Count chose Jennifer Petersen. She wasn't random. That was the way Jack and I were going to play it. He had to know she lived alone. He had to know he'd have her alone in that apartment and that he wouldn't be interrupted doing what he was going to do to her.

The blood was the angle that we took in pursuit of this killer. All that blood, and he had to have some reason for draining her damn near dry. Sex wasn't the issue according to Dr Gray. There were no signs of any recent intercourse. No semen, no bruising from rough entry. It had to be that red serum he was after. Why kill someone when you could knock off a Red Cross blood bank? It was a lot less risky than murdering a live victim.

Ritual. I had my son Michael on my mind. I had had nothing but Mike on my brain since he confessed the thing about the handy priest. The Roman Ritual. Body and the blood of our Lord. But there were other rituals.

'What have we got in the files about these Goths that the women at the O'Hare restaurant were talking about?' I asked Jack as we stood in the hallway outside my office.

I was referring to that one particular white-faced spook that both the manager and the cashier remembered seeing the day Jennifer Petersen was removed from the living.

'I don't know much about them, Jimmy. I've heard that they're mostly harmless freaks who enjoy the shock effect of their appearance. I don't know that I've ever come across them in one of our criminal jackets.'

I cracked the top of the Diet Coke. I'd been holding it so long it was warm.

'Who'd know about these people, then?' I asked my younger partner.

'The shrinks in psycho might know something.'

Dr Nelson Creiger was one of our Department psychiatrists. His office was much larger than mine. I almost felt slighted.

'These kids – and they're mostly kids – tend to grow out of it when they finally mature,' Creiger smiled. 'But not all of them fade away. Some of them get involved in more serious stuff.'

'Like?' I asked. Jack stood next to where I sat. Jack never seemed to sit when he could stand. I wondered what his blood pressure read.

'Satanism, for one.'

'Devil worship?' I asked.

'Black sabbath. Ritual torture, sometimes ritual killing. Usually just animals. But not always.'

'What kind of vic do they look for?' I asked the shrink.

'Children, sometimes. If they're the worst kind of hard core, I mean. The real psychotics have been known to abduct and murder kids, but they'll victimize women also, if that's where all this is leading, Lieutenant,' Creiger said.

'That's where all this is leading, Doctor.'

His jaw dropped just slightly, but then he clamped it shut.

'We are talking about the Jennifer Petersen case, I take it.'

I nodded at the psychiatrist.

'You think some Goth-looking perpetrator might have been involved?'

'We're entertaining that notion,' I told him.

'You have a sighting, so to speak?'

'There was someone in Petersen's vicinity on the day she was murdered. We have a couple of eyeballers,' Jack told him.

'As I said, these so-called Goths tend to be harmless teenagers and some college kids. I might look into something a bit more sinister, if you're playing the ritual angle, as you said.'

'What's more sinister?' I queried.

'There are known cases that involve vampire cults,' the Doctor said.

'Vampires? As in Dracula?'

'No. Psychotics who imagine they are vampires, naturally. There's nothing supernatural about them. They're very real nutcases. Sorry I didn't use something more technical, but that's what they are. They use blood in their rituals. They've even killed to gain their supplies. They're rare, but they're out there.'

'They bite people?' Jack smiled.

'Yes,' Creiger stated.

Jack's smile went limp.

'No shit,' he told the shrink.

'No shit,' Creiger responded. 'They even have fangs implanted by dentists who apparently are as strange as they are.'

Jack went pale.

'Of course the fangs don't work the way Bela Lugosi's did in the movie.'

'We had a case of these self-proclaimed vampires in 1997. I can loan you the jacket,' Creiger told me.

'Please,' I replied.

He went over to his file cabinet and retrieved the jacket.

'These people are very shy, Lieutenant. They're going to be very difficult to locate. They don't exactly advertise. They're a very small clique.'

I nodded, rose, and walked out of his office with Jack just a step behind me.

'They have these exotic clubs. They cater to people with very special tastes.'

The speaker was Sergeant Don Mahoney. He was the Homicide who worked the Mary Handley murder in 1997. She had died as Jennifer Petersen had. Drained of most of her blood. Strapped to her own bed. Mary Handley was a single bank teller with no family. There was no one to check up on her, just as Jennifer Petersen had no one to interrupt what had happened to her. Two women who were alone and disconnected.

The exotic club which was involved in the 1997 case was a spook bar on the periphery of New Town. They catered to Goths and Satan Cults and weird groups and clubs and cults on that order.

So when we left Don Mahoney downtown, Merlin's was where we were headed.

Merlin's was never open during daylight hours, Mahoney warned us with a smile before we'd left him. They opened after dusk, after the last rays were gone. That was sort of a trademark of theirs, Mahoney supposed.

Jack and I got there about 10:00 p.m. long after the sun had gone down.

The bartender looked more like a standard biker. I showed him the artist's rendition of the Goth who'd been close to Jennifer Petersen at the O'Hare Chili's.

'Looks like most of the males who come in this place,' the long-haired barman smiled. I didn't see any fangs, but he was missing his left front tooth. He had tattoos on both his forearms. He was massive. He wasn't cowed by cops, apparently.

'You on probation?' I asked him.

'Is there some beef, here, Lieutenant?' the bartender pleaded.

'Take a better look at the drawing,' I told him.

Merlin's was dim inside, as you would expect. There were a few for-real Goths lurking at the tables away from the bar. They all wore their uniform black clothing and they all looked like they had slathered white pancake on their faces. It was tough to tell the males from the females.

'I'm telling you, Lieutenant, this guy has a lot of identical twins in here.'

'You sure?' Jack asked.

'Look. If I recognized him, I'd tell you. Thing is, I am on pro. Can't afford to lose this part-time job. My PO doesn't know I work here nights. Can you cut me a huss? I mean,

I'll give you a call if anybody like this shows up here. I mean, really . . . '

The biker bar guy looked sincere. He was doing a good job of making us believe he didn't know the face on our rendering sheet.

'You got any hard cores in this place?' I asked.

'How do you mean?'

'I don't mean these assholes with the chalky faces and the hands up their girlfriends' thongs. I mean hard core.'

'You mean like black sabbath dudes?' the barkeeper answered.

'Yeah. That's what he means,' Jack said. 'Devil wor-shippers. Blood ritual types.'

'We get them from time to time. But they're not much for sharing the wealth. They keep very quiet. Even in here. It's dangerous to talk, more dangerous to be overheard.'

'You're on Don Mahoney's pad, no?' I asked.

'How'd you—'

'I'm not here to hassle you . . . what's your name?'

'Leonard. Leonard Bliss.'

Jack almost let out a guffaw. I saw him cover his mouth.

'Listen. Leonard. You can make some fazools if you con-tact me or my partner if you do hear anything about the murder of that flight attendant that I told you about before. You reading me, Leonard?'

'Sure. Sure, Lieutenant. I'm glad to be of help.'

'I don't have to tell you that I'm happy to keep your moonlighting job a secret from your PO.'

Leonard frowned when I squeezed his nuts, just then.

'Leonard. We're buddies, no? Keep your eyes open. Listen around. We'll scratch your back, yeah?'

Jack and I went over to a table and sat down with the Diet Sprites we'd ordered when we first encountered Leonard Bliss.

'Do we have to stay, Jimmy?' Jack grinned nervously.

'Just long enough to make our presence known. Maybe we can stir somebody up enough to have them be overheard by Leonard when we leave. Who knows what fucking evil lurks, Jack.'

There were paintings on the wall which neither of us could recognize. They weren't prints, certainly. Looked like crude originals. Cheerful stuff. Like nude females being crushed by pythons. Nude males and females being tortured by the demons I read about in Dante. That kind of thing. We didn't see any pastoral scenes on Merlin's walls.

One female Goth was dancing in front of the table where her male partner sat. He wasn't watching her. She danced in a lazy sort of swirl – it was hard to make out very much in this dim lighting. But we saw her crawl under the table and disappear beneath the blood-red tablecloth. The male Goth's head jerked up as if he'd been electrically shocked.

'That's a relief,' Jack declared. 'At least they're into blow jobs.'

'Either that or she's changing his oil via his dick.'

Jack frowned.

'Can we go home now, Dad?' he asked.

We got up and managed to find our way out to the street and the navy blue Taurus which was our unmarked vehicle.

There were a few other bars that these Goths frequented. We made a stop at the joint called Dire, and later we checked out The Ninth Concentric Ring. Both of which were a load of genuine grins. Anyone inhabiting those two saloons had to be on the lower pole of bi-polar. Dark, gloomy, morose. Morose would be putting a happy face on them. No one in either establishment had ever sighted our boy.

After the third stop at The Ninth Concentric Ring, our shift was over. Another murder on our plates would probably seem light-hearted compared to our tour of hell in Chicago on a Wednesday night. I was sure we'd both be happy when the sun rose. And rise it did just when Jack and I pulled out of the downtown lot, headed, both of us, for home.

Some killers like to use familiar hunting grounds. Jack and I gave the O'Hare concourse a shot on the next night, Thursday. It wasn't likely that our pale-faced Goth would try to hit on another flight attendant. How he chose Jennifer troubled me more and more. How did he know that she lived alone, that she had no one to check up on her from time to time? No current boyfriends. No family. Both of Ms Petersen's parents were deceased.

He must have had access to personnel files. He must have researched her. Did he work for International?

We walked O'Hare for three hours and came up as empty as I knew we would.

Jack and I went into the corporate office of International Air on Friday. We went to personnel and checked out the employees. No one remotely fit the description of the white-faced Goth who'd been spotted at the restaurant.

'Maybe he was just a credit-card thief,' I admitted to Jack as we walked out of the International office.

'You don't really think so,' Jack told me.

'He felt right.'

You couldn't prosecute on feelings, gut instincts. Evidence was what our prosecutors demanded, of course.

But the blood ritual angle and the weirdness of the Goths or the vampire cults or at least some variety of spook seemed righteous to me. It resonated inside, as the poets claimed.

We stood over her. She was strapped to the bed just as Jennifer Petersen had been – with gray, all-purpose duct tape. And Dr Gray had uttered the same lamentation over this female corpse. Her name was Madelyn Meaney. She wasn't a flight attendant. She was an insurance adjustor for Holiday Insurance, a downtown outfit. Lived alone, no family to check on her. Almost the same profile as Petersen's.

At least we wouldn't have to zero in on O'Hare Airport any longer. He wasn't stuck on stewardesses. His choice would be random if it weren't again for his vic's disconnected life.

How did he know? How did he find them?

'Where can you research people, find out about their lives?' I asked Jack in the Taurus as we drove once more to the West Side to interview the homies about Arthur Ransom.

'The library?' Jack smiled.

I didn't look his way as we drove on.

'Social security? The Feds? Credit people?'

Then I turned and looked right at my partner as we plodded our way through midday cross-town traffic.

Chapter Five

My daughter Kelly is a replica of my first wife Erin. She is the same height and approximate weight. She has the same green eyes. And she has a slightly twisted grin that emerged on Erin's face whenever something struck her as ludicrous or damned fool silly.

It almost shocks me how much she's like her mother, but it's a gift to have all that remembrance in her daughter's carriage and general behavior. What they call one of life's 'tender mercies'.

I don't talk to Kelly nearly often enough. Especially now when she's a woman on her own at the university. But I felt like I neglected her too when she was little, since I worked all those different shifts. Getting to her activities was difficult. Erin was the present parent at too many of her things. I was busy cuffing assholes who did murder while my girl was becoming the young woman she is today.

But I don't think she held it against me. Her mom was my apologist. She made it clear that it was the nature of Daddy's work, not that Daddy didn't want to be there at her various performances, athletic and dramatic.

Kelly Parisi is a natural actress and an equally gifted singer. She sings mezzo-soprano and actually made the Archbishop of Chicago weep with her rendition of 'Ave Maria'. It was at her high school's Christmas mass a few years ago. She's majoring in theatre and voice at the U, currently.

So I made it a point that we would go out, just the two of us. It was in the middle of all this trauma about Mike and the priest, and again, I felt I was ignoring my eldest.

I took her to lunch at one of those soup and sandwich specialties. But all she went for was the soup. Onion with mozzarella cheese on the surface.

'I've been lonely for your company, Big Girl,' I told her as I perused my soup and ham sandwich combo.

She shot me her mother's scraggily grin. Her green eyes were always intense when they watched you. I had to believe she was a terror to most of her would-be boyfriends, with those piercing eyes.

'You feeling guilty about Michael, Daddy?'

There was very little pretense about her. That was a given.

'Why do you say that?'

'Because you've been spending a lot of time with him now, and maybe you think it was your fault you weren't around to protect him.'

She'd make a great interrogator. But then she'd never make anybody cry with the 'Ave Maria' again.

'You're right. I do feel guilty. About Mike, and about slighting you, all these years. Because of my job.'

'I never felt angry about it, Daddy. You were there every chance you got.'

I tasted the chicken noodle. It was a bit salty.

'How much of both of your lives did I miss, Big Girl?'

'You're feeling sorry for yourself. You're terrible at self-pity, Daddy.'

'Oh. I flunked my screen test – or my audition,' I smiled.

'You couldn't have protected him – or me – any better than you did. You can't be with your children every time they go out of the house.'

'I used to watch witnesses on shift. No one ever got shot. Not on my watch.'

'Were you supposed to follow Michael into the sacristy? Were you supposed to catch Father Mark in the act?'

I smiled again and put my spoon down.

'I get no huss from you, darlin'. You're just like your

Momma that way. She would not tolerate whining. From her students in that classroom she loved so much to her own family. I never saw her exhausted with life. Not even when she was in chemo or radiation. She lost her hair, but it didn't seem to make much of a dent. I was sure she was going to beat it. There was no doubt she was going to go into remission . . . and then it took one month to kill her. She went into the hospital and never came out.'

She reached across the table and clutched my hand in a painfully strong grip.

'You are not going to go maudlin on me, Daddy. We all made our peace with Momma, I thought.'

She kept on squeezing my hand, but the pain didn't seem to bother me. It was as if my hand was detached from the rest of me.

'This is all because of what happened to Michael, isn't it.'

'Not all, Big Girl. You're in there in a big way too, you know.'

'I know you love me. Never been in doubt, Daddy. And I'm not mad at you for missing a recital or a volleyball game—'

'We never get them back, Kelly. We never get back the day you walked into Confirmation in that white dress and veil. Down that aisle at St Pat's. You were a heartbreaker then and you'll do it all over again when I have to give you away.'

'You'll never give me away to anybody, Daddy. Quit being such a romantic.'

'Me?' I grinned. 'Jesus, I never been accused of that one before.'

'It wasn't your fault. It was the priest's. Don't let him throw it all on your back, Daddy. Don't let him get away with that, too.'

Out of the mouths of babes. But Kelly was far from a child. I thought of her at her Confirmation again, with all those other little girls in cloud-white dresses, and I choked up and couldn't stop the streams that erupted onto my cheeks.

Kelly squeezed my hand even harder.

'Jesus! You pumping steel at the U?' I grinned.

I commanded my waterworks to cease and desist.

'It was not your fault, Lieutenant Parisi. Sir. Daddy. It was *not* your fault.'

I took her hand, this time, and I kissed it. She blushed at the buss.

Then she gave me that snaggily-assed grin of her mother's, and she went back to finishing her lunch.

There was nothing to do but go after murderers. It was what I did.

Jack told me he was looking into credit card personnel, since The Count had already made use of someone else's Visa. It didn't seem likely he'd hold a federal job since they do screen people. You would suppose a white-faced Goth wouldn't have much chance working with a federal agency, but we would check around anyway.

There had to be some place The Count was finding these women. It was a serial thing now. A series, even though it was still at two. Two was enough. At some point their lives intersected – although it was speculation that The Count had done them both.

What we had was that both vics lived within four miles of each other. And that was where any similarity at all ended. Two very different women, except for their disconnected lives. No families. Few friends. No current lovers. Both had dwelt in tiny efficiency apartments. How was he finding them? It was like gnawing on a canker sore in your mouth. You knew it would hurt to test it, but you did it any damn way.

Where was common ground for young women?

Hair stylists? Health clubs? Analysts?

We would have to look into it right away or there would be another dried up, bloodless young female duct taped to her mattress inside her one bedroom efficiency. That much I thought I could predict about The Count. And Mary Headley's murder resurfaced. We'd see if there was any connection to Jennifer Petersen.

I took Michael to the gym where we recently purchased a

membership. I was supposed to be using the facilities to lose weight, and Mike was into the weight room. But tonight we decided to play one-on-one basketball.

Which turned out disastrously for me because I'm terrible at hoops and my son isn't bad, as I said before. So after I take three straight pastings in the one-on-one, we decide to cool off in the pool. We changed into our suits and went into the water for about a half hour. I was becoming a lot more accepting of joining a health club about the time my overheated, sweaty guinea ass hit the cool of that club water. I felt relaxed for the first time in an age as I side-stroked a lap or two in the four-foot-deep pool.

I sat in the shallow end, on the steps, submerged to my chest. Mike did about ten laps effortlessly. He was a better swimmer than I was too, but I was better in the water than I was on the hardwood court. I lettered in high school for our swim team. Even had a school record in the freestyle.

Mike waded toward me as I soaked myself on the steps that lead into the pool.

He sat beside me on those steps. There were only three other swimmers here with us.

'I heard you had a talk with Kelly,' Mike said.

'Talk?' I asked.

'She said you talked with her . . . about me and Father Mark.'

I watched the other three swimmers do laps without pausing for rest.

'I talked to her about you. Yeah.'

'She said you said you felt like responsible for what the priest did to me.'

'Yeah. It's the way I do feel, Mike.'

'Then don't.'

'I wish it were that easy, bud. I know it was Father Mark's fault. I know I can't be with you wherever you go.'

'Then you shouldn't feel responsible—'

'I am responsible for you, Mike. That's what being a father's about. Being responsible when no one thinks it's your fault. I used to get up in the night to see if you and

Kelly were breathing. I was terrified of that SIDS business. Or I thought you'd get tangled up in something in the crib and . . .

'Well your mother broke me of it. One night when I came back to bed, I found her lying face up with a grimace on her face that told me she wasn't breathing. I kept calling her name, but she wouldn't unlock herself. But when I finally touched her, she blew out a load of air and started laughing at me. I was really pissed at her, but I remember how relieved I was when she let go and started mocking me.

'She was showing me instead of telling me.'

'Showing you what, Pa?'

'That I couldn't be there for every breath all of you took. I couldn't be on surveillance for you all for twenty-four-seven. Your mother was a master teacher, padna.'

I splashed him with some water.

'There's nothing you could've done, Pa.'

'You can talk and talk. You can even remind me of your mother's lesson for me. But you'll never convince me. If she couldn't, neither can you, Mike. You're just going to have to learn to live with me, the way your mother did.'

He watched me for an extended moment. Then he splashed me in the face with a wave of his own.

'You aren't gonna lose any weight sitting on the steps in the shallow end, Pa. C'mon. It's getting late. Do a few laps.'

My son Michael went back into his previous lane and began the freestyle. He moved well in the water. Smoothly.

I got up and watched him go, for a while, and then I dove back in and headed toward the far end of the pool.

The better part of a month passed, and we had nothing new on either case. But we probed everywhere we could. Nothing shook loose.

Both of The Count's vics were members of the same health club – Women's Fitness. It was on the Northwest Side. The computers downtown came up with a winner, finally.

Kelly was back at the university. Michael was in high

school. And my mother Eleanor ran herd over our two toddler daughters. Natalie was busy with her own full caseload.

We drove up to the entrance of Women's Fitness and parked the Taurus. Jack was driving. It was now in the middle of November and Indian summer was history. It smelled and felt like it might flurry.

When we got to the receptionist, I asked for the manager.

Her name was Wendy Carrigan. She seemed very fit, herself. Jack gave her the usual once-over that didn't disappear simply because he was a married man.

'We'd like a look at your personnel files,' I explained to Wendy.

'Those documents are confidential,' she replied.

'This is a homicide investigation,' I told her.

That seemed sufficient for her. She led us into her office. We sat down as she retrieved the personnel jackets.

'Is there someplace we could look these over?' Jack asked her.

'Just use my office. I'll leave you alone,' she smiled.

Very pretty manager.

'Christ, this shouldn't take long,' Jack grimaced.

Women's Fitness must have been a pretty lucrative venture. We had thirty files apiece.

It was about fifteen minutes in when Jack found him.

'Albert Finnegan.'

No one I had looked over had even resembled the Goth described by the women at the O'Hare restaurant where he'd been sighted.

The photo didn't show him in pancake or whiteface. But it did display a pale thin young man that fit the rendition our department artist had drawn. Dead ringer.

Twenty-six years old. Not married. Lived in the New Town district, not far from some of those Goth/vampire bars we'd scoped out.

Jack went through the other four files he had remaining, but Albert was the only winner in either of our personnel jackets.

'Get us some help, Jack.'

41

I meant back-up. He took out his cellphone and called the downtown office. They were sending a few uniforms to Albert Finnegan's address in New Town.

By the time we got to the site, it was flurrying and it was dark. Late afternoons in November strike me as eerie. Odd. Out of sorts. Something that I can't lay my finger on. This time of year the sun disappears early.

It must have been Albert's favorite time on the calendar, I thought. He lived in a three flat. Top floor apartment. No one was home in the bottom two flats, but there was dim wattage apparent from his front window.

The uniforms had still not arrived. We heard a crashing noise from above, where Albert lived. We couldn't wait for the back-ups, now. The Count might be bleeding a new vic while we waited, I thought. We went to the entrance, but we didn't ring Finnegan's bell. We did it the illegal way. Jack jimmied the entrance door's lock with a tool that Wendkos had borrowed from Doc when Gibron went on leave.

'The door was already opened,' I told my partner.

'That's the way I saw it too,' he grinned.

'We have probable cause?'

'I think so, Lieutenant.'

'There it is,' I responded.

And we started up the stairs.

There was loud music blaring inside Finnegan's apartment. We knocked and Jack called out, '*Police*!!' two or three times. And then Jack put his foot to the door.

It was no deadbolt, so the door exploded inward. We had our weapons drawn. I had the Bulldog out because it was far superior to the Nine in stopping power. Jack carried a Colt. 45 automatic which was not standard weaponry at the CPD. But he also carried a nine-millimeter Beretta that was kosher. You carried an extra gun in this business because there were occasions just such as these.

The wattage was indeed dim in the living room that we'd entered. No one was here, at least in this room.

'Take the bedroom. I'll check the kitchen,' I told my partner.

He nodded and headed toward the door to what was apparently the bedroom.

There was only the hallway toward the kitchen that remained in this small flat.

I passed Jack on my way toward the back. Jack waited until I got by, and then he opened the door slowly.

I was in the kitchen, then. No lights. I tried to adjust to the dimness, but my eyes were too slow. Just as I reached for the nub of the kitchen light switch, I felt the slash and the electricity of the blade that cut into my left forearm. I had the .44 in my right hand, and I fired a round blindly into the blackness of the kitchen. The loud music still blasted from somewhere in the living room as I saw the kitchen door flung open and a black figure bolt through the exit on his way out. I let loose with another deafening round, and by this time Jack was racing toward me. He flipped on the kitchen fixture overhead and saw that I was bleeding heavily.

'Go! Go, go!' I yelled at him.

But he stood still and began looking about in this grungy kitchen. He found a dishcloth and he made a tourniquet and expertly cut off the little shower of blood I was making on the grungier gray tile on the floor beneath us.

The uniforms arrived too late to lay hands on Albert.

'You should've gone after the prick,' I bitched. But it was a half-hearted complaint because we both knew Jack might've saved my life. Albert had cut me to the bone and nicked an artery, and I might've run dry like Albert's two victims.

'No sir,' Jack declared. 'We'll find that little cheesedick later. You're going to the hospital, Lieutenant,' he told me.

Chapter Six

I was lucky that Jack knew how to use tourniquets. I could've bled to death if he hadn't shut off the flow, the ER surgeon let me know when I was released from the hospital.

I went home to a wife, two very noisy and small daughters, and a mother who could barely restrain herself from anger. But Eleanor had been the wife of a Homicide – my father Jake – and she knew how to control her emotions. My father had been shot twice in his career, but neither wound had been life threatening. My cut could've been worse if Jack hadn't been there with his first-aid magic, but I have never been shot, like my old man.

'You can go home, Ma, if you're tired,' I told Eleanor.

She looked at me with dismissive eyes.

She knew this family was hurting. Michael was at school now, but he would come home with his demons still intact because he had only begun his therapy with the counselor Natalie had set him up with.

'I'm in this until the termination,' my mother smiled tiredly. It was her World War II V for Victory grin.

Natalie was holding my good hand.

'This guy cut you?'

'Yeah. That's why I've got all the funny wrapping paper,' I told her.

She tried to show me some teeth, but it was too much effort.

'Well, I'm home for a few days.'

'You have to stay home?'

'Medical orders. The Captain says I can't come play at Homicide for four or five days. Have to have a doctor's release, Natalie.'

She reached over and touched my good right arm.

'What's going on, Jimmy? It's like there's a black cloud over us.'

'Yeah. Looks that way, doesn't it.'

Then I felt tired enough to collapse.

'But we shall persevere. Those two little females of ours, and the two bigger ones, have needs.'

'Yes, Jimmy.'

'Eleanor's on top of everything. Don't worry.'

'I hate to have her do all this work. It's not fair—'

'She loves those kids. All four of them. And only two demand her constant attention. Anyway, I can spell her. I still have one good hand to lay the wood to them.'

Now Natalie smiled. She knew I'd never hit any of my children. Ever. Erin hadn't used corporal discipline and neither had I. Natalie was just as much the non-physical kind of parent that my first wife was.

'I'm tired, Red. Any room for me in this bed?'

She grinned raggedly and sat on the bed with me. It was a queen-sized mattress, so there really was enough space. I lay down next to her with my clothes still on, my left arm in a sling. I felt her cool hand on my forehead, and then I didn't feel anything else. My lights finally went out.

The four days passed, and I felt much better.

Michael was still visibly shaken by those near-incidents in junior high.

On the fourth day, the day before I was to return to the job, I visited St Catherine's. Father Mark hadn't been there for several years, but I thought I might pick up some information regarding his current whereabouts. My previous inquiries at that church had fallen on deaf ears, it appeared. There had been no word from them.

My arm was out of the sling, but the stitches were barking

45

at me. The family doctor told me to take Tylenol or some over-the-counter painkiller for the irritation. I wasn't to scratch at anything, the doctor explained. The stitches might be coming out in a few more days, so I was ordered to endure.

We still had no leads on the whereabouts of Albert Finnegan. We had no clues about the guy who did Arthur Ransom. We tried to look up Joellyn's father without success. Jack had informed me about our caseload over the phone only after I had made the call. Wendkos was sincerely trying to let me rest.

I drove up to the entrance of St Catherine's in the family van. Eleanor was again watching the baby girls and Michael was off to school and the big girl Kelly was on campus at the U.

Father William Kelly was the pastor of our church. He was a fine homilist – never went past the eight minute mark – and a generally decent human being, it seemed to me in the few encounters we'd had previously.

His secretary, Agnes Tilson, walked me to his office, here in the St Catherine's rectory.

She shut the door behind me.

Father William looked up from his desk.

'Jimmy Parisi?'

He didn't look too certain.

'Yes, Father . . . I came here because you didn't return my calls.'

'You called here?'

'Several times.'

Kelly had that flaming red nose that you'd associate with lifetime drinkers. But I'd never heard anything about this priest being a juicer.

'I'm sorry, but I never heard that you'd called, Jimmy. There. Have a seat.'

He motioned for me to sit across from his desk. His thin blond hair was wispy and he sported the long strand of hair across a basically bald pate. So Father William suffered from vanity, just as most of the rest of us did.

'I'm here about my son, Michael.'

A light seemed to come on inside him.

'That I do know about. There have been several complaints about Father Mark . . . our Bishop is trying to deal with Father Mark and two other priests in this diocese.'

'I'd like to talk to Father Mark myself.'

'I really don't know where he is, Jimmy.'

'Then find out from the Bishop.'

He sat forward, his elbows on the table, his hands clasped.

'Is this part of some criminal investigation? I know you're a policeman—'

'It's personal, Father William.'

'I see . . . Are you planning on getting some kind of revenge from this priest?'

He cut right to it. He wasn't playing throw and duck with me.

'I'm not seeking revenge. I want to know where this man is, and if he's still a priest, I want to know why.'

'The Bishop is currently preparing a public—'

'I don't give a shit what the Bishop says.'

Father William sat back in his chair.

'I'm not used to talking to a priest like this, you understand. I was raised to respect anyone with a collar. But your brother priest crossed the line, like a number of other reverends we've been hearing about lately.'

'It's a scandal, Jimmy. I can't lie to you.'

'And you really don't know where they've put this man.'

'I can't say.'

'Or you won't say.'

'Both, Jimmy.'

'Then you're part of the problem.'

'You shouldn't become personally involved in this. You're a cop. You know you don't investigate something personal like this. You can't be objective.'

'You're right. But I don't see anything happening unless I find out where he is. And I'll be happy to involve several people I know from the city's newspapers.'

'That sounds like blackmail, Jimmy.'

47

'It sure as hell is, Father.'

He clasped his hands again, not in prayer but in anxiety, it appeared.

'You might want to try the five o'clock. At St Pat's. All the way out in Glenbrook.'

It was all the information I was getting from him, so I stood and then left him sitting with his hands squeezed tightly together. His knuckles appeared bone white, just before I turned and walked out on him.

Father Mark did the five o'clock, that next Saturday night. I was slated to return to work the following Monday. Tuesday the stitches were to be removed.

I arrived at 4:00 p.m. for confessions. St Pat's was a small church in this big suburb, Northwest of Chicago.

I walked into the confessional and shut the door behind me. I sat down next to the screen that you talked through. The flap opened and I saw a faint outline of a face.

'Father Mark?'

'Yes?'

'My name is Jimmy Parisi.'

'Yes?'

'My son's name is Michael Parisi.'

'Yes.'

'You recall the name?'

'No.'

'I think you're lying, Father.'

'Pardon me?'

'You know who Michael Parisi is. You had him as a server at St Catherine's before they moved you because you couldn't keep your hands off little boys.'

'I'm sorry but—'

'You're not sorry about any goddam thing. That's why you do the things you do.'

'I think you might want to speak to someone who's—'

'I want to talk to you, Reverend. You didn't get my son to play with your dick. But you left him with scars anyway.'

I heard him getting up.

48

'You leave this confessional and I will shoot you in the head, Father. Do you hear me?'

I clicked the hammer back on the .44 Bulldog that was now in my right hand.

I heard him slough back down in his chair.

'What you are doing is not only immoral but illegal,' he said.

'You're absolutely right, Father. But the good news is that I haven't blown the top of your head all over this nice confessional. But I wouldn't put it past me to change my mind.'

'All right. All right . . . I remember Michael Parisi.'

'He sure remembers you.'

There was silence from the priest's side.

'So what is it that you want?'

'I want you to resign. Quit. Now. Before the Bishop finally gets around to shit-canning you.'

'I can't do—'

'Yes you can. Your brethren of the cloth who've been caught at that shit have given it up, with help or without it. You're going down that road with a little shove from me.'

'But this is blatant—'

'I know what it is. I'm a cop. I don't care what you think. I don't care what anyone else thinks. You want to call for help? Go ahead. You want to call someone downtown and try to squeeze my nuts? Go ahead. There are a hundred ways I can make you dead, Father. That doesn't mean I'd resort to something as drastic and as immoral as that, but I just wanted you to know I could.'

He didn't respond.

'Did you catch all that, Father Mark?'

'Yes.'

'There are worse things that could happen. You could wind up in the shithouse with a gorilla who takes a liking to your backside. You hear what I'm saying?'

'Yes.'

'It's been a real pain in the ass looking you up. You've given my son nightmares. If our little talk has done anything

49

to inspire bad dreams in you too – well I'm just happy we've had this little conversation. Now I'm going to try and find a real priest who I can confess all this shit to.'

I got up and slammed the confessional door behind me on my way out. I could hear the noise reverberating all throughout the church here at St Pat's.

Doc was tired of fishing. He was tired of his time off. But he was taking another month-lone leave of absence because his mind wasn't right yet, he said.

'I like hanging around the house. With Mari and our girl.'

Mari was his pediatrician wife. The girl was his adopted, black, teenaged daughter.

'You going to make this holiday permanent?' I asked him.

We were sitting on his deck in back of his suburban home in Palatine.

'You look like you could use a longer rest, Jimmy.'

We both sipped at the expensive exported beer he'd served in frosted mugs. It was chilly out on his deck, but it was a clear afternoon and it was comfortable sitting with my partner.

'How's it going?' he asked.

I shook my head.

'That good?' he smiled.

'Even worse.'

'You never let anyone cut you before, Jimmy.'

'Yeah. The Redhead has made me aware of it in no uncertain terms.'

'Good for her.'

He laughed and looked out at the barren woods behind his pretty house.

'We both slowed up sometime back, Jimmy . . . Didn't you notice?'

Chapter Seven

We received the call about two hours into our days shift. Dilly Beaumont had been shot to death. She was the interview with the large dog. They shot the dog as well. We saw the two of them, woman and malamute, in Dilly's living room in her apartment on the West Side, not far from Arthur Ransom's place.

The woman had been shot twice – once in the chest and once through the forehead. The dog had been shot at least four times, as far as we could make out on first appraisal. Apparently they did the dog first. He was positioned in front of Dilly. He most likely went down first. But the Crime Scene people seemed to think someone else bled on Dilly's living-room carpet. There was a pool in front of and underneath the malamute, and there was Dilly's blood around and near her. And there was another trail, going from the living room with the two bodies out to the front door of the apartment and then down the steps toward the entrance. There the trail ended. The Crime Scene people would have something for us shortly, regarding the third party's presence in Dilly's apartment.

'They shot her because they thought she put us on to them,' Jack said in the Taurus as we sped toward the Loop. Jack was driving which was why we were at a high speed. I didn't believe in high m.p.h., whether it was during a pursuit or on the way to the dentist's. I was convinced that the tortoise knew how to run the race. Half of the issue was just getting there.

51

'It seems suspicious, doesn't it,' I agreed.

'Gang related?' Jack posed the question.

'It seems that way, also.'

Our next move was to become friendly with the Gang Tactical people.

'The Vice Kings are your probable perpetrators, in that neighborhood, Jimmy,' Lieutenant Dan Kray of Tactical told us. 'They'd be the dirt I'd dig on this one, if it really is gang related. No one else walks those blocks at night. They own that hood. Have owned it for the past eighteen months.'

'They killed her for talking to us about the Arthur Ransom murder, I think,' I told the sandy-haired Tactical cop.

'They kill people just to lower their inventory of ammo, Jimmy. You know the types,' Kray said.

He was a big man – six five and about 250 pounds of well-honed muscle. Kray was an avid bodybuilder. I'd previously seen the numerous trophies in his office where we sat. He wasn't overly bulked, however, like an Arnold the Austrian movie guy. He was just ripped.

'To me . . . I'd guess initiation, for Ransom. Insurance, for the woman.'

'I was thinking along those lines, too, Dan,' I told him.

'Good luck trying to substantiate any of it. None of the yos know nothin'.'

'We've heard that one about thirty times,' Jack affirmed.

'I'd be looking at a kid. A new inductee. I'll see if I can come up with any names for you, Jimmy. But like I said, I can't promise much. We mostly try to keep the fucking lid on. We don't prosecute many felons in that neighborhood. Never any witnesses. I didn't see nothin', you know?'

He rose when we did. We shook hands and headed back to my office.

We found Arthur's granddaughter at her part-time job at the branch library some six blocks from where Ransom was sliced to death along with his cat.

'I'll get in trouble if I don't keep busy,' Joellyn told us.

She was replacing books back onto the shelves.

'We talked to Miss Irving,' I told her. Miss Irving was her supervisor in this small but clean branch of the Public Library. 'She said it's okay to talk to us for a few minutes.'

'I don't know what I can tell you,' she said.

Jack handed her a copy of *Les Miserables* by Victor Hugo. He took it off the top of her stack on the four-wheeled cart.

'We have an idea that this killing had to do with a local gang. Your grandfather didn't have anything to steal and we can't find any connection to drugs,' Jack said.

'Of course it was them.'

'You mean the Vice Kings?' I asked.

'They're the lords of these streets, ain't they?'

I could see fear in her eyes. It was only natural. These bangers were lethal, and everyone in this vicinity knew it. The few merchants who did business around here paid tribute to them, Kray had already explained, and anyone who didn't make payments got relieved of his or her existence.

'You can't get to them, Lieutenant. But they can get to us. You know?'

'They can be had,' I told her.

'Yeah? And who's going to mess with them?'

'I am,' I explained.

'Ain't no Tactical has made a dent in that bunch,' Joellyn snapped back. There was plenty of sarcasm laced within her words. It sounded obscene coming out of that pretty face.

'They know. I know. But that doesn't mean we can't make an arrest.'

'You even gonna try?' she smiled bitterly.

'Yeah. We are,' Jack shot back.

'Well, you let me know when five-oh solves a kill in this hood.'

Five-oh was the po-lice. Us.

'I'm going to do whatever I can.'

'No offense, Lieutenant, but we heard all that before. Like I told you before. My grandfather was no big man. He didn't have no weight. He's what those Tacticals call "low profile", when it comes to being some po-lice investigation.'

53

'Yeah. Some detectives sort their cases like that. We don't
. . . Look, we need your help. Someone has to talk. That's
the way most of these things find closure. You hear anything,
or anyone you know hears anything—'

'This is D and D territory, Lieutenant Parisi.'

'Deaf and dumb,' Jack answered.

'That's exactly the way it is. Ain't no one gonna talk to
me. Not since I was his granddaughter. They ain't stupid,
you know.'

Jack handed her a copy of *On the Road* by Jack Kerouac.

Her eyes went down onto the floor.

'You know I'd say something to y'all if I knew anything. I
don't care what they do to me. Ain't getting out of here
anyways.'

'You might beat some odds,' I suggested.

'This game is fixed, Lieutenant.'

She grabbed three books off her portable cart.

'Go back and ask those Tacticals to give you some help. I
can't help you,' she said.

She pushed her mobile cart up the aisle and left the two
of us standing there.

The scar itched where the doctor had removed my stitches.
I was under orders not to scratch.

We sat at Garvin's in Berwyn. Doc's favorite bar/haunt.
It helped me remember my old partner, and Wendkos didn't
mind being subjected to the stench of tobacco, urine and beer
that permeated this saloon.

Garvin was in the hospital having kidney stones zapped
by laser, and Garvin's second wife, Arlene, was running the
place. She had an orange bubble of a hairdo that smacked of
the 1960s, but she was pushing seventy herself.

She put the Diet Cokes on the oak slab in front of us.

'Doc was fond of the *ambience* of this hole,' I told Jack.

'Yeah. It has an aura, all right.'

Tactical had come up with three names. Rico Perry,
Ronnie Jenks and Bobby Howard. They were the new blood
that had just joined the Vice Kings, according to Kray's

intelligence. They were between thirteen and fifteen years old, the Tactical copper had informed us. He had addresses on the three, so Jack and I were headed back to the West Side after the lunch of brats and Diet Cokes here at Garvin's.

Rico Perry lived only two blocks from Arthur Ransom. The apartment building might have been a double of the place where we'd found Ransom's remains.

We had two new African-American uniforms with us once more. We tried to get different coppers each time we canvassed because we knew how these patrol cops hated this duty.

We rang the bell and walked up the flight after someone in Perry's apartment at the top of this three flat answered us.

I knocked on the door. The entry cracked open. It was a small young male. He couldn't have been older than four.

'What y' all want?' the little voice asked.

'Your mama home?' Jack asked.

'Naw,' the child replied.

'Your brother or sister here?' I asked.

He shut the door. I thought we had lost him, but someone else opened up. This time it was an older young male. Probably Rico's age.

'You Rico Perry?' I asked.

I showed him the badge and the ID.

He opened the door and let us in. Apparently he didn't want the lower neighbors to hear what we had to say.

There was virtually nothing inside that door. A kitchen table in the small kitchenette, two chairs in front of a big screen TV. Numerous cables that hooked video games to that TV – and nothing else. The two bedrooms were off to the left down the hall that led to the bathroom, it appeared.

'Do you have a parent, Rico?' Jack asked.

We were surprised the teenager appeared to be non-hostile. We weren't used to that kind of feedback from an interview.

55

The young boy was positioned in front of the 40-inch big screen. He was playing some 007 James Bond game wherein the idea was to murder off *everyone* who appeared onscreen.

'Got my auntie. She at work. Works downtown.'

No big smiles aimed at us. But this kid was totally cool and collected.

'You know a man named Arthur Ransom?' Jack asked while we watched the child slay bad guy after bad guy on the video game.

Rico looked like an athlete. A real greyhound. Sleek, built for speed. Would have been handsome except his right eye drooped. It gave him a hangdog appearance.

'I heard that name, yeah.'

'What did you hear about Arthur Ransom?' Jack wanted to know.

'Somebody burned him, is all.'

'Burned him?' I asked.

'Yeah. You know. Waxed, burned: somebody did him.'

'You hear why?' Jack queried.

Rico turned and stared at the video game on the big screen.

'You want to answer the detective?' I said.

'Nobody know *why*,' he replied. There was still no hint of adversity or snideness in his voice. It was almost as if he were enjoying this interview.

'We could continue this talk downtown, but then we'd all have to walk out to the police car and you and little bro would have to take the long ride through the hood. And everybody'd see you with the five-oh, Rico,' I warned him.

'No one need to do any of that,' he spat. Now there was a dose of bile in his words.

We waited.

'Why you come talk to me? I ain't the only number in town.'

'Tactical says you just got some blood work done,' I told him.

'What you talkin' 'bout?'

'You're blooded now, Rico. You did the old man to make your bones,' I said.

'You been watchin' too many TV shows, Lieutenant.'

'Let's go. Turn off the TV and take the kid along, Jack.'

Wendkos walked toward the little brother by the tube.

'Awright, awright, goddamit!'

'You have something to tell us?'

'Yeah. I'm a member of a crew. So? Ain't nothin' illegal about that, is they?'

'You a member of the street gang called the Vice Kings?' Jack wanted to know.

'Ain't nothin' wrong wid it, is they?'

'Did you walk into Arthur Ransom's apartment and cut his throat and slice up a pet cat of his?' I asked him.

The directness set him back, but it didn't stop him. He wasn't afraid of either of us. He wasn't afraid of the law, the system of justice, the courts, the prisons – he wasn't afraid of any of us.

'I don't know nothin' about any of that,' he said evenly.

'Somebody gonna squeal, Rico. Then they might try you as an adult,' Jack told the teenager.

'I think we might call the Department of Children about your little bro, Rico,' I warned him.

'I told you. My auntie at work.'

He pronounced auntie more like 'awntie'. Not 'ant'.

'They can sort it all out,' I said.

'You do what you gotta do,' Rico hissed.

'If you were there, Rico, and even if it wasn't you who cut the old guy, it'll be murder one, and they'll burn you down just like the guy who actually did the killing.'

'You want to talk anymore, I want a lawyer,' he declared.

Someone had already schooled him on dealing with the five-oh.

'Next time we talk, you might need a counselor,' I smiled.

I motioned for Jack to come on out of there, and we left.

'Going to call Children's Services?' Jack asked me on the way out to the Taurus.

'If I don't keep my word, that young man's not going to believe me the next time I predict his future.'

57

We got to the unmarked squad and got in. I waved to the two uniforms as they pulled away from the curb. They were given their freedom, and I knew they'd be happy to be the hell out of here.

It was getting too late into the shift, and we didn't have time to visit the other two names on our list from Tactical.

We would encounter the other two young blooded bangers in the morning. Joellyn Ransom was right. We weren't about to receive any aid from the indigenous personnel in this barrio. By the time we got to Rico's partners, they might have both disappeared underground, somewhere in this concrete, blacktopped netherworld called the West Side.

Chapter Eight

Howard and Jenks, the other two banger friends of Rico, were invisible. No one had sighted them in over a week, Tactical informed Wendkos and me.

The Count had two vics under his bat cape, and we had no idea where he'd vanished to. We tried Leonard Bliss at the club Merlin's once more.

'Hello, Leonard. Have you heard from your PO lately?' I smiled.

'Hey, Lieutenant. If I had anything for you I woulda called.'

Leonard looked nervous at the mention of his PO – parole officer.

'Has Albert Finnegan been in this bar lately?' Jack asked. And before Bliss could whine that he didn't know any Albert Finnegan, Jack shoved the photo at him.

'Albert Finnegan's The Count?' Bliss asked.

'Maybe. That's why we'd like to get close to him. See, he cut the Lieutenant here, and that makes me very mad,' Jack told him. 'And you can imagine how it makes Lieutenant Parisi feel.'

Jack was about nose to nose with the biker as he leaned over the bar toward Bliss.

'So if this son of a bitch has been in here recently and you haven't told us—'

'Okay . . . all right. I seem to remember he was in here, maybe a week ago.'

'Did he have friends?' I asked.

'All these fucking Goths travel in packs, Lieutenant. Shit, I didn't know he cut you.'

'So?' Jack continued.

'He was with a woman. Or a kid. Christ, it's hard to tell how old these fuckers are, with the make-up and everything.'

'You catch a name on the woman?' I asked.

'No. But she comes in here all the time. I mean like every night. He's not as regular, just once in a while.'

'How come you didn't tell us all this the last time, Leonard?' Jack wanted to know. He was leaning toward the bartender again.

'I can't be talking about clientele and keep my job. You understand, don't you, Lieutenant?'

He looked over at me for help. Jack was almost nose to nose with the tattooed barkeep.

'Jesus, if I'd known he'd cut you—'

'When does she come in, usually? About what time?' I asked Bliss.

'Like ten, ten-thirty. Has a couple of wine coolers and waits for the other bloodsuckers to show up. Sometimes she hangs with the guy on that picture, but not always. These bitches sleep around. I wouldn't fuck any of them. They probably got AIDS or some shit.'

It was only 9:35. We'd have to wait outside in the car. Jack and I would never fit in with Leonard Bliss's 'clientele'. So we walked out to the Taurus, and then Jack parked us across the street and down the block aways. These Goths had no use for the po-lice either. Just like Rico and his boys in the Vice Kings. The Goths weren't known for criminal behavior, but we were the Establishment, of course, and weren't to be trusted.

When I did stakeouts, Doc was usually at the wheel. He always brought along his portable radio with the headset, and he invariably listened to an all-night jazz station out of Evanston. I would watch him bob his head to the rhythms of Charlie Parker or John Coltrane or Ramsey Lewis or Ahmad Jamal. Jack preferred to sit in silence. He only spoke when I talked first.

My scar was itching. I had some lotion with me to assuage the annoyance, so I took off my leather coat and rolled up my sleeve and I applied what the doctor had prescribed. That prick Albert Finnegan would have chosen the night I was wearing my good suede jacket. The suede was ruined. But I could've bled to death, so I tried to look at it that way.

My mood had declined, suddenly. I felt tired. Worn out. Maybe even beaten-up.

When you got older, death became proximate. When you got sick, it took much longer to rebound. It was harder to find the bright side in anything. Homicide did not lend itself toward a bright and sunny attitude. We dealt with human misery, human loss. All day every day. You tried to separate yourself from the misery on the streets, but it became more difficult as the years burned away. I couldn't recover, the way I used to. I took all the unsolved cases too hard, too personally. I wasn't following my own experience of letting go of the killers we couldn't catch.

But Albert Finnegan laid hands on me, and even though no one would ever connect humiliation to me because he cut me, *I would*. It became absolutely personal when someone drew blood. Finnegan crossed the line. Being cut by a punk is something, I thought, that I never would have allowed to happen ten or fifteen years ago. I would've sensed him in that kitchen with me or I would've at least heard him breathing. Smelled his presence, at the very least. But I had done none of the above. I'd been cut to the bone and had to be helped by my partner, and his stopping for me had cost us a collar. And it might cost us another murder, now that Albert roamed freely.

It was ten-twelve, the next time I looked at my watch. Jack hadn't said a word in all this time.

'There she is,' he said. It shocked me upright. I was almost dozing off.

'You sure?'

'It's dark, but she fits the general description.'

'So now we wait for real.'

We weren't going to follow her into the bar. We were going

61

to follow her on her way back out. She might lead us to Albert. If she didn't we could always question her later.

'Your turn,' Jack said. He meant that it was my turn to try and get some sleep. Merlin's had a four o'clock license, and neither of us figured this Goth girl would be an early riser. So she wouldn't be leaving until closing. More than five hours.

I leaned back and shut my eyes.

'Jimmy. Wake up.'

'What time is it?' I asked Jack.

'Four. Closing time.'

'What? Why the fuck didn't you wake me up?'

'You looked like you were all done in, Lieutenant.'

'I don't need a fucking nanny, Jack.'

'It's all right. I wasn't sleepy.'

She came out with the rest of the Goth crew.

'Slow night. Only saw ten or twelve of these *whatevers* walk through the front door.'

Their back exit was chained up. We'd noticed the chains when we talked to Leonard the first time. It was against the law to do it, but we weren't there to bitch about fire codes.

She came out with two other females. They could have passed for sisters, from a distance, but Albert's squeeze was taller than the other two. Albert's lady was almost six feet tall, it appeared. So it wouldn't be tough picking her out of a crowd of these neo-zombies.

They walked down the street to a blue Camaro. Albert's lady wasn't driving. So we followed the Camaro through New Town and found that the women were headed east.

They dropped our subject off all the way out at the Gold Coast. Apparently she was a monied Goth. A doorman let her into a very high-rent building here on Michigan Avenue.

Jack and I parked at the entrance to her building when she'd made it inside. We both got out and walked up to the doorman. He had the red cap and the gray uniform and the whole doorman's outfit.

'Gentlemen?' he asked.

Jack showed him the badge and the ID.

'Oh. Yes sir. Can I do something for you?'

'Her name?' Jack asked.

'Pardon?' the doorkeeper asked.

'The white-faced ghost who just checked in. C'mon. We don't have all night,' I told him.

'She's . . . Her name is Janet Meyerson. She lives with her parents. On the sixth floor.'

'Good. You did fine – what's your name?'

'Richard, Richard Friar.'

Jack smiled at me. The doorman was quivering. He apparently didn't have to deal with gendarmes too often in this hood.

'Does Oprah live near here?' Jack asked him.

'Why, yes. Three blocks down, as a matter of fact. Are you investigating her?'

'No,' Jack replied. 'But I like Doctor Phil a whole lot.'

We were tired of messing with him, so we walked back to the car.

'Twenty-four-seven surveillance on her. It starts now. We need to find out everything we can about her. She may get lonely for her boyfriend, and we want to be there for the two of them.'

The next day we received the fruits of Jack's labors, late in the afternoon. While I caught up on routine paperwork, Jack had done the intelligence work. Goth girl, alias Janet Meyerson, was a sometimes student at Columbia College in downtown Chicago. Sometimes because she had a habit of dropping classes and then returning for a semester or two. Her father was Philip Meyerson, a rich banking investor who worked in the Loop. Celeste Meyerson, mommy, was an heiress connected to real estate in northern Illinois. Going to college was just a hobby, it appeared. Staying out all night with goblins like Albert Finnegan seemed to occupy much more of Janet Meyerson's time.

We had surveillance on her, just as I'd ordered the night we followed her home. Jack and I were the team on her tonight. There were four teams of surveillance on her, six-hour shifts for each of us. The lucky teams were the daylight cops. Janet was very still during daylight. She only started to rock and roll when the sun was down. Around about the witching hour was her peak of activity, you might say.

She was headed to Merlin's again. This time Jack and I only had to wait until 12:45 a.m. when she emerged from the club. But she came out alone. She drove a black Lexus. Brand new. Immaculate. It would be no problem picking her out in the scarce traffic past midnight.

She turned east. We thought she was headed home. But she turned left onto the Outer Drive, Lakeshore Drive, and we were pointed north. She got off at Fullerton and proceeded to go west. She apparently didn't spot us because she drove conservatively and slowly all the way to her destination on Fullerton and Park Streets.

It was a three flat in an upscale northside address. We stayed well behind her, but we saw her walk up to the apartment building and buzz at the entrance way. She got a return buzz and entered the dwelling. There was only one light on among the three floors, and it was on in the middle apartment.

We didn't know if it was Albert Finnegan, of course. She could have been visiting any of her friends or lovers. But Leonard Bliss had been rather convinced that Janet Meyerson and our boy were a couple.

We sat and waited. Jack got out and checked the names by the doorbells. The second floor was occupied by B. Jenkins, Jack told me.

We didn't have grounds for a search warrant. Judges wouldn't let you kick doors down on a hunch. But Ms Meyerson was the closest thing we had to a lead on The Count, so we would have to be patient. We couldn't show ourselves to the girl yet, either. If this were someone other than Albert Finnegan, our lead would immediately dry up.

She stayed inside for forty minutes. Then she got back into the Lexus and drove farther west until we arrived at Fullerton and James, about two miles west. She got out of the car, went to the entrance and again buzzed for entry. She was inside another three flat. This time Jack found out the name was M. Martinez.

'You think she could've made us, Jimmy? And now she's just leading us around?'

'I don't think so, Jack. We've kept a pretty good interval.'

'Yeah, but Albert could've warned her someone might be following her. He hasn't been sloppy yet.'

Janet came trotting out of M. Martinez's building and hopped into the Lexus. Now we had two more names to add to the inquiry.

She drove out to Western Avenue and headed south and pulled into a White Castle.

'Good. I'm hungry,' Jack smiled. 'But I guess we won't—'

'What the fuck. I'm hungry too. Let's go inside with her.'

Jack looked at me as if I were joking.

'Naw. Let's get close and personal with this bitch.'

So we got out of the Taurus and entered the White Castle.

Janet was sitting with three other Goth females in a booth. They were smoking and sipping at black coffees. None of them even looked up at Jack or me as we sat at the counter. I ordered four cheese sliders and an order of rings and a Diet Coke. Jack ordered a half dozen plain hamburgers, fries, and a black coffee.

They were in a booth to our right, near the exit door. There was a plate-glass window next to their booth, and suddenly I looked outside, through that rectangle of plate glass, and I saw him. Six feet two, perhaps. Black leather jacket that was cut to the thighs. A white face that made me think of Halloween. Albert Finnegan was staring at the four girls or young women, and then they looked out the window and found him. I turned back to Jack who was working on his black coffee.

'Don't look around,' I whispered. 'The prick himself is outside on the grass, looking in.'

'What'll we do?' Jack whispered back.

'Wait and see if he's coming in . . . He never saw us in the light, I don't think. I don't figure he'll recognize us, and we aren't getting into a gun battle with all those young ladies sitting there. Even if he isn't armed, which I doubt, someone could get hurt. Go into the john, nice and casual, and call in for back-up. Be real laid back here, Jack.'

Jack sipped his coffee again and then slowly rose and made his way toward the men's room which was off to our left.

I ventured a glance toward the window and saw that Albert was staring at the quartet of lady Goths and that they were silently staring back at him. What were they doing? Communing? Reading each others' thoughts? What the hell was the story with this goof? Was he coming in or not?

Our man broke the deadlock with his apostles or whatever the hell they were and he started to walk around toward the entrance. I wondered if Jack had made his call for back-up. I turned back to my plate of high cholesterol fast food, and I waited.

Albert Finnegan walked through the door. He glided toward the four women, and then he sat down.

I put my hand inside my black leather jacket, and I clasped the handle of my .44 Bulldog.

C'mon, Jack, I thought. Get out here. C'mon.

I squeezed the handle of my squat, potent pistol, and I waited.

The girls were giggling at something Albert said. But it was a brief chuckle. Then the five of them went silent, and I saw Jack walking toward me. His hand was inside the pocket of his flight jacket, and I knew he was palming his piece also.

I turned toward the five Goths and Albert Finnegan turned his attention toward Jack and me.

Then he smiled, looked over briefly at the four women, and he bolted toward the entrance.

Jack and I rushed toward the door, and it was then that the four white-faced females shrieked in unison.

Chapter Nine

Albert Finnegan must have had some experience at track, because he burst down the block and left the two of us a half block behind him. By the time the back-ups arrived, Jack and I were both out of gas. The squad car that arrived first caught up with us about two blocks down from the White Castle. We got in and the two uniforms gave us a ride back to the parking lot of the restaurant. Then we got into the Taurus and began to search for Albert in this Northwest Side neighborhood. A total of four squad cars accompanied us, and we went over twelve square blocks before we decided that Finnegan had submerged.

The first item I had grabbed for when we first took off after The Count was the switchblade in my left coat pocket. I had the knife palmed in my left hand as we sprinted after Albert. I don't know why I didn't go for one of my two pistols, but I had a sneaking notion that I wanted some payback for the slice job this Goth had done on me. Being vindictive was not one of my better qualities, but I figured I owed the little prick something as a token of my concern for his welfare.

'I slowed you down,' I told Jack.

'No you didn't.'

'Don't stroke me, Jack. I slowed you down.'

'Okay, you slowed me down.'

But he was smiling.

'He would've outrun me too if it'd gone any farther, so fuck it, Jimmy. We probably should've used the car in the first place.'

'He would've cut through the yards. We would've lost him anyway.'

'Where do we go next?' Jack asked as we cruised this Northwest Side in vain. 'We interview the four brides of Dracula,' I told him.

Janet Meyerson was first on our list of interviews.

Her face was almost a bone white with black lipstick and black eyeshadow to create the effect of bloodlessness. She might have been a very pretty young woman if it hadn't been for the garish cosmetics. She had silver hoops the size of tennis balls in both ears. There were silver studs in both her eyebrows, and I saw the silver ball that was in the middle of her tongue when she spoke.

'This is a murder inquiry,' I told her.

'Yeah?'

She reached for a pack of smokes.

'Uh uh,' Jack warned her. 'No smoke zone.'

She huffed out a reply and stuffed the pack back into her black leather bag. There was nothing of color on her person.

'Tell me about Albert,' I asked her.

'I love Albert.'

'Really? Are you two engaged or something?' I asked.

'No. But we are committed.'

There was a slight emphasis on the word 'are'.

'You know your boyfriend murdered two women . . . At least two we're aware of,' Jack told her.

'That's false. Albert couldn't kill anyone.'

'You lie to us and there'll be repercussions,' I warned her.

'Repercussions?' she smiled vaguely.

'A shitstorm on top of you,' Jack explained.

'Why would I lie?'

'Because your boyfriend's a murderer,' I said.

'That's false. I told you he couldn't do anything like that.'

'He tied them down like cattle and bled them for a few days and that's how they died. As white-faced as you are now,' I said.

'That's disgusting. And I told you, Albert wouldn't—'

'So why'd he run from us?'

She looked at Jack. She had gray eyes. Like a she-wolf. They seemed almost hypnotic.

'He's had trouble with the cops . . . But nothing like . . . this. He's been charged for chickenshit stuff. Like credit-card theft and ATM things.'

'So you think he's just a thief.' Jack asked.

'I know he never killed anybody.'

'Where'd he get the blood from, then?'

'What blood?' she shot back at my partner.

'You know. The stuff you all have been snarfing at your little get-togethers,' Jack smiled.

'We're not into that.'

'You aren't?' I asked. 'What are you *into*, then?'

'Goth is a way of life, Lieutenant. But we don't go around hurting anybody.'

'There's no blood ritual involved, here.'

'No,' she said.

I was convinced she was lying and that she was becoming more and more agitated as we asked her about that blood ritual.

'If you're involved in any of this with Finnegan, you'll be going away for a very long time,' Jack explained. 'You'll cop conspiracy and maybe two or three other counts – all felonies. Your daddy on the Gold Coast won't be able to save you, Janet. No more make-up, no more blood cocktails. No more Albert, of course.'

'I have no idea what you're talking about.'

She licked her lips, and we spied the glint of the silver bulb implanted in the middle of her tongue.

'You can go,' I told her.

She looked surprised.

'I can go?'

I nodded. Then she slowly rose. She was a tall young woman, as we had noticed before. You took away the white puss and the silver spikes in her face and you had an attractive female. Now, however, she was the living dead she wanted to be.

We interviewed the other three and came up with nothing.

They were on the periphery with Finnegan, it appeared. They knew him through Janet and had only been around him a few times. It appeared that Ms Meyerson was the primary squeeze for The Count. The other three were just along for the ride. Apparently they liked to be around someone who was dangerous, and Janet had delivered Albert to them at the White Castle.

The information we got at Women's Fitness about Finnegan had all turned up dead end. He had lied on the job application, but no one at the club had verified anything he'd told them. He had shown them a driver's license with the name 'Albert Finnegan', but when we ran that name through Vehicles, no one popped up on the screen except for an Albert Finnegan who was sixty-six and very unlike the image of The Count we'd seen running away from the White Castle.

But 'Albert' had left a full set of prints on the window where he'd gazed at the four brides of The Count. We were hoping that he'd had a record.

And he did. Maxim Samsa had done a stretch at St Charles, the boys' reformatory in the city of that name, for car theft and aggravated assault. We pulled his file from our brethren in Juvenile. The information told us that Maxim had broken out of St Charles when he was sixteen and had been missing in action for six years.

The assault charge grabbed our attention, however. He had beaten an elderly man and had stolen his wallet. But the interesting part was that Maxim had bitten his senior citizen victim. In the neck, the file read. The old guy apparently thought Maxim was trying to drain a quart before he was able to fight him off and before a couple of street kids on scene helped scare Maxim off.

Naturally Samsa spent some time in psychiatric at St Charles. They seemed baffled by him, according to the report. Couldn't put any of their usual labels on him. Sociopath was the closest they could come to a description, but they were a bit confused about the biting incident.

He spent only a year at St Charles before he broke out. But no one ever discovered just how he had made his escape.

The best they could figure was that he found a way through the fence that surrounded the facility, but there was no hole or cut-out portion of fence to indicate that that was his mode of departure.

'Maybe he stretched his batwings and flew over the fucking fence,' Jack suggested.

I slowed my partner down in the foot pursuit of a murder suspect. I got myself cut by a punk dressed up for Halloween. My sinuses were still loading my ears and I had trouble hearing. Everything was giving out on me. The next thing to go would be my libido.

I sat down on the bed, next to Natalie. I was too weary to take my clothes off.

She sat up and took my head in her hands and brought me to her and kissed me. There was a healthy heat to her lips. I kissed her again, and then she lay back.

'Tell me about The Count,' she said. Her eyes looked very tired.

'Nah. It'll just keep you up tonight.'

I tried to smile, but the effort was too much.

'That bad?' she asked.

She smiled warmly at me.

'You feeling sorry for yourself, Lieutenant?'

She was trying to goad me. Get me angry instead of self-pitying.

'You bet I am. If I don't, who will?'

'Michael's thing is bothering you, too.'

'Oh yeah.'

'You shouldn't have threatened the priest.'

'You're right.'

'You should've capped him,' she grinned.

'Then you'd be a widow or at least the wife of a con.'

'I know. I'm glad you just loosened his bowels a little. Maybe I'll shoot him.'

'No you won't. Look into that bedroom with those two small, smiling faces.'

I was referring to our younger daughters.

'I know. But I can fantasize.'

'Michael still has bad dreams.'

'Yes, Jimmy. I remember clearly.'

She ran her palm over my left cheek tenderly.

'You *will* catch this little cheesedick, my love.'

'Are you trying to seduce me, Red?'

'There it is.'

We drove to St Charles to interview a teacher who dealt with Maxim Samsa at the reformatory. His name was Justin Fennell. The guy was an ex-heavyweight wrestler at Michigan State. I couldn't imagine any of these punks messing with him.

'You'd be surprised,' Justin told Jack and me. 'They'll test anybody. Some of these little fellows are fearless. You might be too if you came from their sad fucking lives. It almost makes you sympathetic toward some of them . . . almost,' he smiled.

The man was a veteran of all this. He was no romantic when it came to rehabilitating America's youth gone wrong.

He had an old-fashioned flat-top haircut and he reminded me of Dick Butkus, the former Chicago Bears middle linebacker – except Justin was much bigger than Butkus. And even meaner-looking.

'Tell me what you can about Maxim Samsa,' I asked as we sat down in their faculty lounge. I gave him the file we'd received from Juvenile.

'I remember him. He's the kid who bit the old man. Tried to pull a Dracula on him until a couple of homies came up and broke it up . . . This kid'll surprise you with his intelligence and charm, Lieutenant, Sergeant. He's nowhere near stupid. It's just that his form of intelligence is sort of the perverse variation. Maxim was always looking for an angle, even with the other inmates here. They still aren't sure how he got loose. But that's the kind of smarts he had. Survival smarts. I'd say he was a very dangerous adolescent. I can imagine he's become an even scarier young adult.'

'Yeah. We like him for at least two murders,' Jack added.

'Christ,' Fennell muttered. 'Why am I still always

surprised when one of ours goes out and pulls this kind of shit?'

'This guy's full of surprises,' I told the reformatory teacher.

'Apparently. You talk to his parents?'

'I see he has a father. Lives in Skokie,' I said.

'I talked to him just once. To try and get an idea about Maxim, you know. The old man is more evasive than the kid. He did twenty at Joliet. Maxim grew up with an aunt.'

'Yeah? That we didn't know,' I told Fennell.

'Did you know the aunt died of "suspicious causes"?'

'No,' I answered.

'Official cause was heart failure. I read the file on her. The interesting detail came right at the end of the case file.'

'Yeah?' Jack asked.

'His aunt – named Jean Greene – had numerous bite marks on her neck and upper torso. And there was a significant loss of blood, the coroner wrote in his report. They were never able to pin it on Maxim, though. The bite marks didn't match his dental report, so he walked away from that one.'

I knew the shudder was arriving, and I tried to stave it off, but it ran clammily up my spine in spite of my concerted effort to thwart it.

Chapter Ten

We found Ronnie Jenks and Bobby Howard with their faces blown off in an alley a half mile from Arthur Ransom's crib. Tactical discovered them and gave us the call. It was a Thursday night in late December. The city had been hit by an ice and snow storm, so everything was crusted over, white, and glazed. We couldn't speed to the site of their murders because the city guys hadn't salted the streets at that point. We slid and skidded our way through city traffic, but the traffic thinned out when we arrived on the West Side. Apparently the yos had sought shelter inside on this early evening. Jack and I had just gone on shift when we received the call about the two bangers we thought were involved with Arthur Ransom's slaying.

We slid to a halt in the alley. The Crime Scene people had already set up, their portable lights and generators already hummed and made a whiter glare of this site.

The Tactical cop, Dave Galley, stood next to the bodies.

'They're all yours, Lieutenant,' Galley said.

There was no smile on his face. Just relief that he'd be able to escape the cold now.

Jack and I put on the latex. Dr Gray still hadn't arrived. It was probably this bitch weather that slowed him down, like everyone else tonight.

I turned over Ronnie Jenks. I only knew it was he because Galley pointed to him and gave me the name. He pointed out Bobby Howard, who lay to the right of Jenks. Neither was recognizable.

'Sawed-off shotgun. Close range, point blank,' Jack suggested.

I had a real concrete notion that he'd be proved right by the specialists on site.

There were no noses on either of them. Jenks had no chin, either. There was a mass of twisted cartilage and bone, but not much flesh that I could make out.

'Two out of the three suspects we liked have been eliminated for us, Jimmy,' Jack said.

It wasn't the way I liked to clear the table. But he was right.

All that remained was Rico Perry. I didn't want him to wind up this way only because it wouldn't satisfy my idea of justice, or of closure. I wanted a live one in the hole. I wanted a tangible perpetrator to spend his life in a cage for what he'd done to Arthur Ransom. This kind of end was just too goddamned easy. I knew they were only fifteen years old, but they did an adult crime. It was cruel and brutal, not something a human teenager would do. This was something hardboiled and emotionless, what had happened to Ransom – and to the old lady, Dilly, as well. They were executed. Not murdered. Executed. As in the military sense of the word. Arthur's and Dilly's deaths were as stone cold as they came.

Someone breathing still needed to pay. The last I heard, Rico Perry was still sharing oxygen with the rest of the world.

I moped around the house. I moped around Natalie, who was becoming obviously anxious about my depression.

I was gaining weight. Every time I thought about my two cases, I got lower, and every time I got lower I sought instant gratification – which was food. Either something very salty or very sweet. I ate lots of junk food.

Natalie caught me struggling to button my collar button before I went to work. 'We're going for a walk when you get home,' she declared.

'A walk? In the dark? In this cold shit?'

'Yes.'

There was no look of arbitration in her eyes. She never demanded anything of me. She got my cooperation via other means. Natalie wound up usually getting exactly what she wanted.

When I came home from that day shift at 5 :00 p.m. on the evening before New Year's Eve, she was waiting for me. In full Arctic gear. She held out my hooded winter coat and I knew that we were indeed headed out of our warm home for parts unknown.

'You feel weak,' she said.

I watched the white, chilled fog come out of her lovely lips. The frost and ice had not melted on the grass and most of the sidewalk. The streets appeared black and slick because of the tons of salt the city men had spread with their trucks.

'What?'

'C'mon! You've been moaning and whining like a puppy for months, Jimmy! You think I don't hear you?'

'I didn't realize I—'

'You better *realize*. It isn't at all like you.'

I felt my face flush.

'I didn't want to rag you in front of the kids . . . about your weight, I mean.'

'Now I'm fat?'

She looked over at me. We were both snorting frosty breath, like a pair of horses.

'Yes. I'm fat,' I admitted. 'I gained twelve pounds and my pants and collars are tight, goddammit.'

'You're letting things get to you, yeah?'

'Yeah. I suppose.'

'Maybe some gym time'd help with the stress.'

'The gym'd beat the hell out of these cold-assed streets, Natalie.'

She threw her arm around my waist and we turned back toward our house.

Michael had been to the psychologist's four times. He said

he was feeling better, but I didn't ask if he was still having nightmares.

I went to his basketball games when I could. He was a reserve guard on the varsity at St John's High School, an all boys Catholic secondary not far from our Northwest Side address. Michael wasn't a gifted athlete, but he made the club because he was tenacious on defense. He'd claw your throat out to retrieve a loose ball. He'd hit the floor and get himself a new floor burn during every game. And he was fearless on the court. Which got him more than a little playing time.

Natalie was home on one of her vacation weeks with the young ladies, our daughters. Kelly was at the U as usual. It was early January now, and Michael was back to school as well.

He got into the van with me after St John's lost a double overtime on their home court by three points. Michael had only played about ten minutes of the contest.

'They could've used your "D" in that overtime,' I told him.

'I'm not good enough to play the crunch,' he said matter-of-factly.

'The hell you're not! You're a fucking animal out there! Excuse my fucking French. Catholic school. I forgot.'

The well-worn joke didn't work, this time.

He looked over at me with the saddest eyes I've ever beheld from my son.

'I felt helpless.'

'During the game?'

'No . . . with Father Mark.'

'Did you tell the counselor that?'

'Yes.'

'And what did he tell you?'

'He told me that I'm deeper inside than my flesh, on the outside. He said it was something like being a rape victim. The rapist could never touch what I wouldn't let him touch.'

I had heard that advice before when I was in uniform and had to deal with sexual assaults on the street. I'd heard the rape counselors say exactly the same kind of thing, and now someone had uttered those words to *my son*.

'He's right, this counselor. He could never reach—'

'I know he didn't actually do what he did to the other guys I went to school with. I shouldn't have the right to feel the way they do.'

'Yeah. You have the right.'

'Why?'

'There are more ways to abuse someone than just the physical way, Michael.'

'I know.'

'Do you? I never got any serious wounds in the war, but what I saw left its marks. Here.'

I pointed to my head.

'But they've gone away, haven't they?'

'Why, Michael? Just because I don't scream in the middle of the night? I get cold sweats all the time. My breathing becomes irregular. My heart palpitates. I have anxiety attacks like you wouldn't believe. I have to get up and walk around before they'll leave me alone. I'm not trying to make your problem look smaller than it is, because it's a big deal. But this counselor was right. You have to learn to live with your pain. And you can't let it hop on your back like a goddam jockey, Mike.'

He looked straight ahead, out the window of the van.

'I'm getting better, Pa . . . I really am. It's just sometimes . . . '

'Yeah, that sometimes is a bona fide bitch, ain't it.'

I tried to smile, but my face wouldn't allow it. Michael kept watching the traffic ahead of us on this salted, sloshy Chicago boulevard.

Rico Perry was still in the pink. We brought him in for questioning the first week in January about the murders of his two bro yos, Ronnie Jenks and Bobby Howard. We were sitting in the downstairs interview room, here in the Loop.

'You shoot your two main men, Rico?' Jack asked.

The kid's slow eye or droopy eye was looking at me and

his good eye was planted in Jack's general vicinity. The split stare was almost unnerving.

'Hail naw!' he laughed.

'Don't kill your own kind?' I asked.

'This a roust. I want mah lawyer.'

'You make that call and we'll be here the better part of the day,' I explained. 'You'll have to wait til that shitbag attorney of yours drives all the way down here—'

'Aw right! What you want?'

You put this kid in any kind of athletic uniform and you had a blue chipper. He just looked like a natural jock.

'We want you to tell us why you killed Arthur Ransom and the old lady, Dilly.'

He saw that I was serious, that I wasn't playing with him the way coppers always had. He'd been questioned before. Rico was an old pro at fifteen.

'You admit to what you did, and the prosecutor might go juvy with you.'

'I ain't did Arthur what-the-fuck's-his name. And I ain't did none of that old bitch, either.'

I slammed the palm of my hand against the back of his chair and he flew forward and almost hit the table in front of him with his face.

'You can't lay no hands on me! I know my—'

This time Jack slammed the back of his chair. He was taken unawares yet again, and that bad eye seemed to be gathering moisture after he nearly met the surface of the table once more.

'I want my lawyer! Now!'

'Sure. You can go,' I told him.

'For real?' he asked.

He wasn't buying his good fortune.

'You gon' whack me in my fuckin' haid if I get up, ain't you.'

I nodded and smiled.

'You cain't *do* none of that shit. I *know* my motherfuckin' rights!'

'So get up and leave,' Jack told him.

'This ain't right. All y' all doin' is trying to motherfuckin' *coerce* me into saying I done the old man and old woman.'

'The Constitution gives you your rights, Rico. You can leave,' Jack repeated.

'For real?' he asked.

For the first time in the interview, he sounded like a frightened little boy.

'For real, Rico. G'wan. Get out.'

He rose slowly. Then he saw we weren't going to come at him again, and he regained his West Side strut and left the interview room.

'We don't have jack against him. Not even his two buddies to flip him, Jimmy.'

'You're right. But at least he knows we like him very very much.'

Natalie had us signed up for a fitness center in one of the Northwest suburbs. It was so expensive that we couldn't afford not to go regularly. We took the toddlers with us because they offered free child care – and that removed a load off Eleanor, who was becoming a bit too familiar with our girls.

I'd been doing weights and running. I'd also stopped looking for instant gratification. The Redhead did not buy junk food for our household any longer, and it had mightily pissed off Michael, who seemed to be getting just a fraction better after each of his counseling sessions. But Natalie bought fruits to replace the chips, dips and salted snacks. Michael had given in and now ate apples instead of Fritos.

I'd lost six pounds in two weeks. My collar was getting looser and so was my waist button.

But she didn't sign me up primarily because of my weight gain. Natalie was too sly. She had another agenda. She was trying to run me out of mid-life burnout, and we both knew it. Red had spied the black dog running loose in our household, and she refused to let that dark canine feast on my self-pity and depression.

But she had never suggested that I go back to the CPD shrink. I'd been there and done that.

She was trying to help me sweat out this evil that had crept inside one of my weak spots, one of my apertures. She was trying to draw it out, the way you'd lance a boil. You either did a little cutting and draining or you learned to love the sheer agony and misery of self-defeat. I knew all that without having her explain it to me, and I knew that she knew that I knew it.

All this vile shit on my plate. The Count, Arthur Ransom and Dilly, the four Goth princesses. Low and high profile vile shit. The business that I was born to labor at. Murder. And the faces that attended each of them. It was as black as the black dog itself.

Run, Jimmy, my wife was telling me. Run it off. Swim it off in the Olympic-sized swimming pool at the club. Lift weights that'd take the place of the real weights that burdened me. Keep moving, she begged.

Don't look back. Do anything else, but for Jesus Christ's sake, don't look over your shoulder. There was no retreating in the homicide business. The only way out was straight ahead.

Chapter Eleven

I didn't want to think about him. I didn't want to bring back any memory of the connection he had to my life.

Abu Riad. He was the gangbanger chieftain who was responsible for the death of Celia Dacy, the black woman from Cabrini Green who lost her son, and then tried to take her revenge out on Abu Riad himself. Three of his henchmen had been responsible for Celia's son Andres being shot in a drive-by situation in front of Cabrini several years ago. Celia finally went after the head of the snake himself, and she was shot to death for her trouble. We were in love at the time, and although it could have cost me my job – you don't get involved with anyone involved in your cases – I had thought about marrying her. It was that serious.

Now he came back to haunt me with Arthur Ransom, Dilly Beaumont, and two faceless bangers, dead in a West Side alley.

'Why didn't you bring him up before?' Jack asked.

I explained about Celia and her son Andres.

'You think he might be behind all these killings?' Jack wanted to know.

'I think he's behind most of what goes on in that neighborhood. He hides behind his version of Islam. He pretends to be a religious neighborhood champion. Black rights. But he's a gangbanger and he's always been nothing but a thug. And I didn't want to bring him into play for personal reasons and I was wrong, Jack.'

Wendkos nodded.

The ride to the West Side was becoming routine, but it was never without tension. As always, we were accompanied by two black uniforms.

Abu Riad – real name, Charles Jackson – resided in a fine brick ranch home. The West Side used to be prime property a half century ago. Now it resembled Berlin in 1945 when the Allies marched through a blown down scene of devastation. The West Side was pretty close to a double of Berlin at the end of World War II. The buildings were just slightly more vertical than the German dwellings of almost sixty years ago.

'Hello, Charles,' I said as he opened his front door for the two of us.

I was surprised. Usually you saw his two bodyguards before you were allowed to be in his presence.

I called him Charles because no one was allowed to call him by his legal name.

'Lieutenant Parisi.'

'This is Sergeant Jack Wendkos,' I informed him.

'What happened to Gibron?' Riad wanted to know.

'You remember my partner?'

Riad nodded.

He was shaved bald. It was the fashionable thing to do in the hood, these days. He was a shade taller than five eleven but he always claimed to be six one on his sheets at the police department. He had a handsome face. Very black, very African. He'd been a fair athlete in high school – football and basketball. Abu Riad had been All City in both sports. But the call of the streets was stronger for him than the lure of the college athletic recruiter, so he made his living in the hood off the misery of others. He portrayed himself as a civic minded member of the community. The CPD knew him as a criminal, but he hadn't been caught to date. He was teflon, nothing stuck to him no matter how hard the city or the federals tried to make a case on him. Abu Riad always managed to have someone else shoulder his weight.

'We're here to ask you about those two dead boys in the alley. You know? The ones minus their faces?' I asked.

'You know I don't have anything to do with violence. Especially in my own neighborhood.'

He spoke very grammatically when he was in the presence of cops and reporters. When it was just another yo or yoette, he could talk that talk just as easily.

'They were two of your own. Two little Vice Kings,' Jack said.

'I do not affiliate with any street gang. You both know that.'

Hell, he ran them. We both knew it. He knew that we knew it. It was the little game we played.

'We think those two and a kid named Rico Perry were responsible for the murders of Arthur Ransom and Dorothy Beaumont.'

'I don't know those two names,' Riad explained.

'I'm sure you don't. But you gave the order on them both. You had Arthur burned because that was their initiation. Then you had the old lady done because you heard she talked to Jack and me.'

'That's absurd, Lieutenant. Are you trying to make head-lines by connecting me to some gangland killings? If you didn't come after me, they'd just be—'

'Low profile,' Jack offered.

'Yes. Indeed. Low profile. Indeed,' Riad smiled at my younger partner.

'There ain't no such thing, Charles. You will fall, one day. It'll make the biggest boom this forest ever heard. Just wanted to let you know we were thinking of you.'

'How many years that bitch been gone now?' Riad smiled.

I lunged, but Jack got between us.

'You ever refer to her by that word again and I'll tear your eyes out.'

Jack pulled me back from the still-smiling banger.

'Been so nice to see y'all again.'

Then we were out the door as he slammed it behind us.

'He ordered it. There's no doubt in my mind.'

'You should've let me in on it sooner,' Jack said as we drove east on the Eisenhower Expressway.

'I didn't want to bring it back to him. I knew it all along, but I didn't want to have to deal with him again. It got too personal, with the way Celia Dacy died.'

'I understand, Jimmy. But shit. This is a homicide investigation. Don't leave me out of the picture again, all right?'

'I'm sorry, Jack.'

'Okay. It's okay. Just consider me the way you would Doc.'

'All right. That sounds fair.'

Jack smiled, and we headed for the Loop.

We went after Janet Meyerson with everything we had. She was the only link we had with Maxim Samsa – aka Albert Finnegan. We set up an interview with her downtown, but she insisted on having a lawyer with her. His name was Terrence Raddigan. He was a very expensive downtown mouthpiece who rarely litigated. I'd known him for almost twenty years. He specialized in druggies and Outfit members. The guy wore a ponytail and was a throwback to the late sixties. Thought of himself as a radical.

'My client is here in order to cooperate in a murder investigation,' Raddigan announced as we were seated in the interview room that we Homicides used.

'Very nice speech, Terrence. Your client is a solid citizen,' I smiled.

Janet Meyerson wasn't wearing her black uniform or her white pancake face this afternoon. She looked like the affluent Gold Coaster she really was. Well-dressed, well-groomed. Clean and squeakily so.

'Where do you suppose we could find your friend Maxim?' Jack asked.

'My client has no knowledge of Mr Samsa's whereabouts.'

'You want to let her answer for herself, Terrence?' I asked.

He nodded, and then he swished his chestnut brown ponytail as if he were a stallion swatting flies.

'Where would you look if you wanted to find him?' I asked again.

She was a pretty girl, but not a beautiful one. She was too gaunt, too razor thin.

'He always contacted me. I never sought him out. He lived

85

in that apartment where you went after him. I never knew of any other place where he crashed.'

'You don't have a phone number, then?' Jack asked.

'Just the one at the old apartment.'

'Does he have other friends?'

'I never heard him talk about anyone,' she told me.

'But you told me you were committed to him,' I said.

'Yes, but that doesn't include ownership, Lieutenant.'

She never smiled. I don't think I ever saw her teeth to date. I wondered if she had any of those implanted fangs where the canines ought to have been.

'So this guy shows up whenever it's convenient for him, and you're supposed to be on call like some doctor whenever he wants to see you,' Jack told her.

She didn't answer. The lawyer's ponytail swished again. I very badly wanted to take my switchblade and remove that redundant hair with one slash. But I controlled my desires.

'If your client winds up being much more involved than she's let on, I'm going to open up the flames on her soles, counselor,' I warned him.

'My client, Ms Meyerson, has been nothing but forthright and cooperative. Is that all, gentlemen?'

'What'd you do with all that blood, Janet?' I asked.

It seemed to surprise her.

'What'd you do with all that blood he took out of those two women? Was it a ritual? Some kind of blood rite?'

If it was possible for Janet Meyerson to appear even more pale than her natural complexion, she had now achieved a bloodless, deathlike pallor.

'I don't know anything about . . . My God! What are you talking about?'

I began to wonder if she was simply Samsa's rich-bitch squeeze. Something from the outside. I wondered if she might not really be unaware of what Maxim had been up to during the two killings.

'He drained almost all their blood, Janet. He must have had some reason for doing it. He must have had some purpose for—'

She tried to rise, but she swooned, and her lawyer caught her before she crashed onto the tile floor below her.

'Jesus! Did you have to go that far with her?' Raddigan bellowed. I thought he was truly angry for maybe the first time in his career.

Jack helped her sip some water. She regained her consciousness and her composure as Jack attended to her, and then we let her go.

'You think Samsa's partying with other folks with this blood ritual?' Jack asked as we sat in the cafeteria at the downtown headquarters.

'Either that or Janet Meyerson's the finest little actress I've ever seen.'

'She was good, wasn't she.'

'Better than good. She was being real, Jack. Nobody's that good.'

'So Meyerson's a dead end.'

'No. Not really. We have her phone tapped. We have her surveilled. I think maybe Maxim has something in mind for her and maybe for her three other girlfriends too.'

'You think he wants to create some more personal blood banks?' Jack asked.

'I wouldn't think it was beyond reason. He knows there's pink flesh beneath that playhouse make-up they wear.'

'You want the other three to have taps and shadows?' Jack asked.

'We can afford it. Remember, this is the high profile case. Just ask the boys at the *Tribune* and the *Sun Times*.'

The newspapers had both been running a series on The Count and his two victims.

'You read a word about Arthur or Dilly or the two faceless bangers?' I asked.

He shook his head. But I wasn't happy I'd won the argument, if that's what this was.

Vampire cults. Satanism. Hoodoo and voodoo. There weren't too many places to go to do research.

I tried to do what my father Jake, the homicide copper, taught me. To think the way my enemies thought. That was a very old Sicilian adage. But it was a matter of survival too. You didn't put yourself in the other guy's shoes, you'd be receiving a size ten toe tip in your ass end. You had to try and jump one move ahead of the other guy. The opponent. The enemy. The perpetrator. It didn't matter what you called him. He was the opposition, and this was a lethal contest.

The Captain was unhappy. The Captain was unhappy because his superiors were unhappy. And everyone downtown knew that shit flows downhill.

'You got anything?' the redheaded ex-Army Ranger asked.

'We're tapping the phones of those Goth girls that we saw him with before he ran away,' Jack explained.

'But you don't like this Meyerson woman as a real tie to Samsa anymore?' the Captain asked me.

'I think he's got other playmates, but we haven't sighted them yet.'

'When do you plan on making contact, Lieutenant?' the Captain wanted to know.

'Unknown at this juncture. Wish I had better news, but the truth is what we've told you.'

'And we've got four fresh corpses on the West Side.'

He surprised me by bringing them up.

'It's Abu Riad,' I told him.

The Captain groaned.

'Ah shit, Jimmy. You're not going down that road again, are you?'

'I tried not to. I tried to keep it local, with the bangers who did Beaumont and Ransom. But it'd be a lie if I let go, Captain. He's behind it. He's the mastermind.'

'You're not letting something personal get involved in all this West Side stuff, are you?'

'Sure it's personal. He was responsible for Celia Dacy and her son Andres, and he fucking got away with it. How's it not supposed to be personal?'

'Then we take the two of you off that case. Stick to The Count.'

'I don't think it's necessary. We'll do Abu Riad by the numbers, Captain. I won't let my own feelings about the prick get in the way of a clean collar. I give you my word.'

The Captain studied me with his intense green eyes.

'All right. I'm going to remember you said all that and you better remember you said all that too. Will you keep an eye on the senior investigator, Jack?'

'He's a big boy,' Jack said.

The Captain eyeballed my partner.

'Okay, yeah. I'll keep an eye on him.'

'Go out and get the bad guys, then,' the Captain concluded.

Chapter Twelve

Madelyn Meaney's great-aunt wanted to talk to me in DesPlaines, a western suburb. The second vic's relative was one of the few who attended the funeral. Jack and I were in attendance as well because it was standard procedure to be on hand at an unsolved murder's burial ceremony. Sometimes perpetrators liked to show up and join in on the misery. There was that kind of cruelty in them. It was like a second opportunity to feed on the grief they'd caused.

We checked out the people at Madelyn's funeral, but no one stood out as a possibility.

Jack and I drove to the DesPlaines location on a Friday morning around 10:30. Mrs Dianna Meagher lived alone in a brick ranch home. Tasteful from the outside – no lawn ornaments. You know, the deer or the little black coachman that irritated African-Americans. The usual vulgar shit. We pulled into Mrs Meagher's driveway, and then Jack and I headed for her door. Wendkos rang her bell, but it took her some time to respond because she was eighty-seven and fully arthritic. So fully arthritic that she had to use two canes. I was surprised she didn't employ one of those geezer, omnipresent walkers.

She invited us in. Her hair was silver and she was bent at the waist from what time had accomplished against her, but her eyes were violet and reminded you of someone much younger.

She instructed us to sit, and we did, on the sofa opposite from the white loveseat she lowered herself onto.

'What can we do for you, Mrs Meagher?' I asked.

It was pronounced Ma-her, I'd found out at Madelyn's funeral.

'I found something odd at my great-niece's grave. I visited Madelyn just the other day.'

'Something odd?' Jack repeated.

'This.'

She handed me a piece of rolled up, parchment-like paper. It must have been a standard sized piece of expensive typing paper that people used to use for correspondence before computers took over. I think they called it 'onion skin'.

I unrolled it. On it was typed verse:

> *The soul shall find itself alone*
> *'Mid dark thoughts of the gray tombstone –*
> *Not one, of all the crowd, to pry*
> *Into thine hour of secrecy.*

'Do you have any clue what this might mean, or who might've written it?' I asked the old woman with the sparking, stunning violet eyes.

'Not a clue, Lieutenant. Not a hint,' the great-aunt of Madelyn Meaney told us. 'But there isn't a signature. And that was what disturbed me,' she continued. 'I remember you explained to me, Lieutenant Parisi, that murderers frequently go the funerals of their victims. I just thought this might have come from the monster who killed Madelyn.'

'It's a possibility, yes,' I told her. 'We'll certainly look into it right away.'

She offered us coffee, we refused, and the old girl looked relieved at getting rid of the two of us and the mysterious verse that someone had laid on her great-niece's final resting plot.

The call from Jennifer Petersen's first cousin came the same afternoon that we returned from Mrs Meagher's DesPlaines address. The first cousin – Renee Dumont – lived in Hickory Hills, a southwestern suburb. She'd been difficult to locate.

Petersen had no living mother and father, and most of the rest of her clan resided on the East Coast. There were even fewer attendees at Jennifer's ritual than there were at Madelyn Meaney's. It was very sad – just a few friends of Ms Dumont's and a couple of homicide investigators.

We pulled into the Hickory Hills driveway at about 4:40 p.m. that same day. We were invited in, and the cousin, who was a large, big-boned woman in her middle thirties, showed us a nearly identical piece of rolled up onion skin that bore yet another mysterious verse:

> *Be silent in that solitude,*
> *Which is not loneliness – for then*
> *The spirits of the dead who stood*
> *In life before thee are again*
> *In death around thee – and their will*
> *Shall overshadow thee: be still.*

The large-bodied woman, cousin of Jennifer Petersen, had no explanation for the poetry, either. She, like Mrs Meagher, had found the parchment paper underneath a single yellow rose.

'Don't look at me. I flunked poetry,' Jack laughed as we drove back to the Loop.

'You don't think I'm an expert on this esthetic shit, do you?' I asked the junior partner.

'How about the good Doctor? How about Harold Gibron, PhD?' Jack smiled.

We drove out to Palatine after our shift was far gone. We were on our own time, then. Doc lived in a burb, but he was supposed to reside in the city, as old city employees on the force were compelled to do. So Doc used his mother's address on the north side instead of his own, but he was never worried about getting caught and being canned from the CPD. He had that lofty PhD to fall back on, he kept reminding me. My partner never once called in sick since he returned from the leave of absence when the two young black girls were shot to death in a drive-by.

I never called in sick, but I had had a few leaves of absence over my career. But my mailing address was in the city proper, so I was in the clear from that out-of-city rap.

It was too cold on this early February day to sit on Doc's back deck, as I had the last time I visited my partner. We sat in his cheery living room, a fireplace fully employed at this moment with a blazing fire. The flames leapt upward at Doc's apparently effective chimney.

He gave us each the obligatory exotic beer from his collection of micro-brews, and then I handed him the two rolled up sheets of poetry.

Doc never even blinked or needed a moment.

'It's Edgar Allan Poe. "Spirits of the Dead". Some of his better stuff. Hard to believe the same guy wrote that piece of shit "Raven".'

'Yeah. Hard to believe,' I replied, my jaw still dropped open at his speed at solving the mysteries of these poems' source.

'What the hell do you suppose I did to get that degree, Jimmy P? You think I balled my female profs, eh? We read all kinds of stuff. Poe's lyric poetry included. He might have made a great poet if he'd stuck to lyrical only.'

'Really?' I asked.

Jack was as awed as I was. But Jack was awed by most everything Doc Gibron pulled out of his ass to remind you of the true enigma this man had always been. A Homicide with a doctor's degree in Literature. How many of those *rare avis* do you suppose manned the police forces in this country or any other country?

'You think I'm making it up? Let me find a collection of his verse.'

We followed him down to his gorgeous, oak-paneled basement. It was his library. And there were enough volumes to supply a real library on Doc's walls. Most of it was fiction. Doc had published stories in literary magazines. I could understand none of his tales, but I could tell they were intellectual pieces. He was working on his novel. He was always working on his future great tome that would surely free him from the burden of being a homicide copper.

He went immediately to a shelf on the left-hand side of the wall behind his wet bar, and he withdrew a volume bound in leather. Doc didn't go in for paperbacks.

'Here. Have a look,' he told us. He handed the volume of Poe to me.

'I don't like this, Doctor,' I told him after I perused the two pages that contained 'Spirits of the Dead'.

'You didn't even read the damn thing,' he cracked. 'I know because I would've seen your lips moving.'

'No. I don't mean that.'

I handed the Poe book to Jack.

'I'm not talking about the quality. I'm referring to the number of verses,' I said.

'What about them?' Wendkos asked.

I looked at Doc carefully.

'There are five verses. The first two victims of The Count each received their own stanza or whatever. That means he's figuring on doing at least three more.'

Jack handed the Poe back to Doc Gibron, and then our senior colleague returned the collection back to its resting spot on the shelf.

'The son of a bitch doesn't seem that literate,' I protested at Garvin's.

John Garvin had returned from his kidney laser surgery. It was as if MacArthur had waded back onto the Philippine Islands in World War II. But we both knew Garvin was a veteran of the European Theater with General Patton. The barman had been severely wounded at the Battle of the Bulge.

'Why? Because he's not formally educated?' Jack asked.

'Yeah. You heard what that teacher said at the St Charles Reformatory.'

'Maybe he thinks poetry will help him collect women,' Jack added.

'It could very well be. All we've heard about him is about

94

his survival skills. He knows how to fit in, and the group he's fitting in with lately are our pasty-faced friends.'

'The Goths,' Jack said.

'Where does he find them? He doesn't frequent the bars they go to all that often. He must be hooking up with them somewhere else if he's been accepted into their merry little society or cult or whatever the hell they consider themselves to be.'

'Let's try the Internet. We found The Farmer that way,' Jack suggested. 'Maybe he's cybering with these lovely, overly-white white girls on the ether.'

We put Computer Services to work once again. I was computer ignorant and Jack was barely more conversant with the machines than I was.

Wally Garrity was our resident guru. We kept these young men for a while, and then we usually lost them to big companies about the time these youngsters were ready to marry and have little computer geeks of their own.

Wally was short and gangly. Looked like an ex-high school flyweight wrestler. He was lean, not bulky. That's why I would've pictured him at the lower weights. He said something about winning the City Championship at his weight his senior year in secondary, so that was why I connected wrestling to him. He had the slight stoop that all jocks seemed to be cursed with.

'They like to meet in chatrooms.'

Wally had helped us find the crazy priest-psychiatrist who murdered women by trying to 're-birth' them by wrapping them in plastic wrap. We'd found Dr Null over the Internet, just as we'd made first contact with The Farmer via the cybernetics.

'Just like most other disconnected sods,' Wally smiled and said with a phony Brit accent. He was a big fan of R.D. Wingfield and the Inspector Jack Frost series of mysteries. I didn't read many mysteries, myself. I liked stories that didn't take any brains at all to figure out. Natalie was always taking me to chick flicks and was constantly amazed that I didn't bitch about going.

'It could take some time, Lieutenant.'

It was Wally's stock disclaimer.

I gave him a copy of the first two stanzas of Poe's 'Spirits of the Dead'.

'Ewww. A cryptic message from our boy, no?'

'They were left on the two graves of his first two vics,' Jack told him.

'There are three more stanzas, Wally. Quit fucking around and find him,' I said.

Wally colored and his scrawny frame tightened up.

'Just fucking with you, Wally,' I smiled.

'I never know with you, Lieutenant. You shoulda been a poker player.'

'What makes you think I'm not?' I smiled again. Then Jack and I left him to his state of the art machinery.

'Happy hunting,' Jack wished him.

'He has a stiffy for Poe,' I told my wife.

Natalie was doing sit-ups on the floor next to our bed. She was laboring, so I thought I'd talk her out of continuing.

'No. I'm fine . . . go on,' she huffed as she started stomach crunches. Her left elbow to her right knee, and then her right elbow to her left knee. She was still struggling, but it was a no-win argument with the Redhead.

'He left a stanza for each of the first two.'

'Yeah? Maybe you ought to start hanging out at coffee houses. Aren't these Goths the new Beatniks? Sort of?'

She grunted and went back to the exercises.

I checked out the newspapers. We hadn't heard from Wally in two days. I found a number of listings for open mike evenings at the big book chains, but I couldn't picture Maxim Samsa showing up at such a well-attended and public venue. I figured him for a much more low-key kind of setup.

There were bookstores that catered to those who didn't fit what Doc called the mainstream. These were bookstores that sold way out kinds of literature. Doc called them the 'zines crew'. And they had very selective interests. The occult was one such specific 'interest'. I found three listings in the *Tribune* Sunday book section that I thought might be possibilities for Samsa and his friends.

I also did some research on Edgar Allan Poe at the downtown library. I read some fragments from biographers about him and found out that he went to West Point and then left because of some petty gambling debts his stepfather would not pay. I read that he married his cousin, Virginia Clemm, and that she would've been considered jailbait these days – Mr Poe might've gone up for statutory rape if not for an incest rap . . .

But what interested me most was what the biographers claimed was a constant theme in the poetry of Edgar Allan Poe – the death of a young woman. Nothing seemed to fit all Poe's esthetic concerns as much as the demise of a young female. Nothing was more melancholy, more sorrowful, and it showed up in his poems time and again.

Our man Samsa had already done two young women. Now he was taunting me with his literary messages or whatever they were. I was convinced Maxim Samsa had left those two scrolls for me. He knew they'd end up with me eventually.

He was telling me his shop was still open and he was ready to do business. He was challenging me to come find him. The old movie cliché: 'Stop me before I kill again!' Cliché or not, his message was received.

There were still three stanzas remaining in 'Spirits of the Dead'. He was letting me know that there were three more sad chapters to finish in his personal poem. Three more attractive young females were going to die slowly. Their lives would be drained from them in a more than deliberate fashion via The Count's needle.

No, Samsa surely wasn't going to disappear. He felt invulnerable, like a drunken teenager behind the wheel just before that final heartstopping crash that he never saw coming.

I was going to meet him in that lethal intersection before he could count to three.

Chapter Thirteen

I had been to therapy sessions before, but they had always been for me. Going to therapy with one of your own children was a far different experience. I had a lump that was wedged in my throat on the ride over to the therapist's office, and I hoped my voice wouldn't betray what I felt when we arrived.

Michael was in control. It never appeared as if he were on the verge of some emotional breakdown. He wasn't a weeper. None of the members of my family – except for the two female toddlers – were criers. There would be tears from time to time, but no one in our family enjoyed bursting through with the waterworks. It seemed like cheap theatrics to me, but I never queried Natalie or Kelly about how they felt about emotional outbursts accompanied by raging waves of teardrops. If Natalie and Kelly wept, they never did it in front of me. Certainly Michael hadn't burst forth since he was a very little boy. As I said, my son seemed very tough. Not the type for public displays or outward rants.

The doctor's name was Dan Jenkins. Natalie knew him from some referrals that had been made when she was in uniform. His office was in Evergreen Park, a Southwestern suburb. The office wasn't lush. It was more military-looking – what you'd call spartan. No extras. No ginchy prints on his walls. Just a plain green wallpaper. This guy didn't spend any money on overhead, apparently.

We sat in leather chairs. Comfortable, but not something you'd kick back and go to sleep in.

'We're having this session, Mr Parisi, because Michael wanted you here.'

I looked over at my ever-growing-taller son. He was truly a handsome young man. He must have got the looks from his mother Erin, because I was much shorter and much more olive-complected. He was already getting too many calls from girls. There weren't any females at his high school, but they had a sister Catholic high school four blocks away from the all-male secondary Mike attended. He wasn't much of a talker. I heard him mumble a lot as I passed him on the blower in the hall between our kitchen and living room. We weren't going to put a phone in his room because we'd done that with his sister Kelly, and then we had never seen her for weeks while she burned the hours on her telephone. Not to mention the horrific bills she piled up on the blower.

'He wanted me here?' I asked.

I was looking at Jenkins. He was a tall, lanky man with chestnut brown hair. He must have been in his early forties, I guessed.

'Yes.'

'Did you, Michael?'

'Yeah, Pa. I asked the doctor if you could come with me today.'

'He wants you to know what's going on and he wants to hear what you have to say to him about it.'

I looked at the therapist. I'd been in therapy before, as I said, and I thought I knew how these sessions tended to run.

But I was at a loss to begin. I looked at Michael for help, but he just looked back at me as if I were supposed to answer some question he had already posed.

'Let me see if I can help get us started,' Jenkins smiled.

He had a notepad, but the ballpoint remained on the coffee table next to his chair.

'Michael feels as if he doesn't match up to your expectations of him.'

'You feel that way?' I asked my son.

'Well, yeah. You never seem to be able to tell me if I'm doing okay. You know? You never seem to talk to me and

99

tell me when I'm screwing up, either. You just don't seem to say much to me at all, and it makes it hard to know . . . '

His eyes began to tear up. After all that convincing pep talk I gave myself about how my son wasn't a weeper. Yet he wasn't bawling uncontrollably. He was just gaining small globes or droplets in the corners of his eyes.

'You're saying I don't let you know how I feel about you?'

He nodded his head.

'Michael is having trouble with his self image. Something I'm sure you've heard about before, Mr Parisi.'

I wasn't used to being addressed as a 'Mister.'

'You mean like eating disorder self image problems?'

'I mean the general kind. It's not just anorexics and eating disorder patients. It's not always about food – whether you're overweight or underweight. Michael doubts his self worth because the priest made him feel ashamed.'

'But he never actually—'

I looked into Jenkins's eyes.

Then I looked at Michael, whose tears were now streaming down his face.

'You didn't tell me what really happened, did you, Michael.'

He shook his head.

'Tell me what really happened.'

'Mr Parisi—'

'*Tell me what really happened*!'

'He . . . Father Mark made me touch him . . . And he . . . he did oral sex on me, Pa.'

He dropped his face onto his hands and he began sobbing.

'And was there anything else, Mike? Did he do anything else?'

'Mr Parisi—'

'He said . . . He said if I ever told anyone, he'd spread the word around that I was gay and that I had made the move on him, on Father Mark. He told me I'd be humiliated in front of all the guys I knew. At school. At church. Everywhere. He was angry because I told him I wasn't going back to that church. So he made me promise to be quiet. If I didn't say anything, then he wouldn't.'

I was numb. I must have sat mute for at least two or three minutes. Michael had stopped his tears. Now he sat stoically next to me. Jenkins stared at his notebook.

'I'm sorry I lied to you, Pa. I'm sorry.'

I got up and went over to him. I bent down and I hugged him tightly. Then I grabbed hold of his head as he shot an arm around my waist and held me just as firmly.

'You should've told me, Michael. I wouldn't have been mad at you.'

'I didn't want you to think—'

'I know, Mike. I know.'

Then I sat down again. Jenkins handed my son a box of Kleenex. Michael took two tissues and then handed back the box. He gave his nose a strong blow, and then he palmed the tissue.

'It's not just about self-image,' Jenkins continued. 'It's about Michael's sexual identity, too.'

'I'm not . . . I'm not—'

'No one ever thought you were, Mike,' I told him.

'He told me he would spread it around if I didn't. He said something like this doesn't have to be true, you just had to say it to someone and all of a sudden it would be true whether anything had really happened or not. He didn't give me any choice, Pa. He said he would tell everyone.'

'It's okay. I understand. It wasn't your fault, Michael—'

'I should've *done* something, Pa. I should've hit him in the mouth and run away, but he was a priest. I *liked* him. And then he threatened to . . . '

'It's not your fault, partner. It really isn't your fault. Don't you believe me?'

He looked at me and nodded very slowly.

'I'm a Catholic too, Mr Parisi. So we all know about guilt, I assume.'

'He isn't guilty of a damned thing. Except being young and helpless and in the presence of a predator, back then.'

'We know that. All three of us know it. But in Michael's head he's taking responsibility for allowing this thing to happen.'

'Responsibility? It was that son of a bitch with the collar who—'

'I know, Pa. My head knows that . . . but I can't convince the rest of me that I didn't let it happen.'

'Oh Michael. How can you think it for even a second? These guys that I hunt on the job are the causes of the misery they create. Lots of them try to lay the blame on somebody else. They like other people to help carry the load they made. So they cop a plea and say that society made them do it, or mommy didn't breastfeed them long enough when they were kids. You aren't responsible. It was *him*, Michael, and no one else. Don't you try and grab part of the burden he put together when he did you and all those other young boys. Don't you carry his weight.'

Jenkins looked down at his blank notepad.

'I don't use the goddam things either,' I told him about the pad. 'I'm too vain. I think I can remember everything. And the problem is that I *do*.'

I looked over at my son. Apparently his therapy was just beginning. I tried to stop the racing of my heart and pulse, but I didn't care about my hypertension at that moment. This wasn't about me; it was about the young man sitting next to me.

'You're going to be all right, Michael. You're going to be okay. I guarantee it.'

He looked at me as if he'd caught me in a lie. But then his eyes shifted over to his therapist.

I wasn't a drunk. My father took care of that affliction for the Parisi family. I was raised in the house of an alcoholic. He wasn't an out-of-control drunk, but he had to have his drinks after every shift. My father, Jake, who wasn't my biological father. My Uncle Nick, Jake's brother, had impregnated my mother, Eleanor, after it became apparent to my mother that Jake Parisi was shooting blanks. Jake had mumps in his teenaged years, and doctors believed that it could cause sterility.

The picture was much more complex, of course. Nick had been in love with my mother, but he left town to try his hand

102

at the petroleum business in the Southwest during the thirties, but by the time he returned to Chicago, brother Jake had given Eleanor an engagement ring. It fractured any bonds between Jake and Nick, but Nick backed off graciously and let them live their lives. Until the boozing and until it became clear that Jake would father no offspring. Eleanor pleaded her case to Nick, the story went. She wanted to be a mother if she could enjoy nothing else in their marriage, and Nick could supply the seed. It would give my mother some sense of family after being married to an alcoholic homicide detective who wasn't home much.

Nick gave in, and I was the by-product of my mother's deal with a not-so-devilish ex-lover. Jake knew I was not his, and there was always a sense of disconnectedness in our relationship.

I couldn't bring friends home to the house if I knew Jake was there. He wasn't an abusive drunk, as I said, but I couldn't bear to think my male friends or any of my girl-friends would see him and smell him after a three hour session at his favorite saloon owned by The Greek.

Michael couldn't tell it to me. He had to tell it to a stranger. I always thought of our home as a sanctuary. Things like this simply didn't happen to us. Especially since I was a policeman. I could protect my children and my wife. I almost lost the Redhead to The Farmer. But I never thought that danger extended to my children. Natalie was a police officer, a Homicide, more recently. She could take care of herself. But I was supposed to build an impenetrable wall for the rest of us. He was twelve when the priest did this to him. He was going to turn sixteen in a few months.

I sat at the bar of Garvin's alone. It was after my shift had concluded. It was midnight, and I was on the four to twelve. There was only Garvin and me in this west suburban dive of a tavern.

I wasn't here to get drunk. I wasn't a rummy, I told myself, and it was a little late in life to start up any new vices. I didn't really have any vices – except for being a workaholic. The job was the only fix I ever needed. When personal things, traumatic occurrences, happened I went to another case. Another unsolved killing. Another murderer in a world stocked plentifully with murderous thugs. I'd never run out of business. There'd never be a recession or depression in my line of business.

I took out the .44 Bulldog and laid it on the bar. There was no one here to see my weapon unsheathed. Then I took the nine-millimeter out of my holster and laid it next to the snubnosed .44. Finally I took the switchblade out of my other jacket pocket.

All my weapons were on the bar slab, in a neat, tidy row.

I couldn't protect my own son. I couldn't keep him from the evil in this world. It was as if I were as impotent as my two pistols when they were unloaded. It was as if my knife's blade were broken in two. It was as if, I thought, my maleness had gone south as well. Now I was an old man. The object of derision. The geezer who had his social security check snatched away from him when he was en route to the bank for a deposit.

I felt weak. As if the flu were coming on. I felt my forehead, but it wasn't warmer than usual. I looked at my arsenal, lying there on the bar slab.

A train went by on the tracks just outside Garvin's, and the whole bar shuddered and rattled as it sped past us. It was past the witching hour on a week night. The next patrons of this tavern wouldn't be in until 7:30 a.m. or so, when the deadman's shift was over.

I should have gone home. Natalie would worry if I didn't check in or if I was late coming home. She could call me now since I had a cellphone. Something I'd fought against for two years. But the damn things had become as much a part of our lives as fast food.

'Jesus, Jimmy. You expecting a war?'

He shocked me upright. I had been leaning over the bar, looking at my two guns and my one blade.

'Christ, you scared the hell out of me, old man.'

I put the Nine back in its holster, and the .44 and switch back into my pockets.

'Something wrong?' Garvin asked.

He was a short, stocky Irishman. A pug nose that had landed just below his blue Mick eyes marked his continually sour-looking face.

'Yeah. Something's wrong.'

But I got up before he found out what it was.

Wally Garrity called me on my office phone and asked me to come on over to Computer Services, so I collected Jack Wendkos who had his own tiny cubicle down the hall, and we took the elevator downstairs.

'Been listening in on some interesting chats,' Garrity smiled.

These computers were his world, his work, his playground, his domicile.

'And?' Jack asked.

'What do y'all know about vampirism?' he drawled.

'Not a thing. I saw a Dracula movie once in high school,' I told Garrity.

'This is no movie, Lieutenant. These people are serious. Real serious,' the computer king said. 'Someone's been throwing parties, it seems.'

'What kind of parties?' Jack asked.

'Not the kind with Bud or Miller Lite, I don't think,' Garrity replied.

'Blood ritual?' I asked.

'They never say it in those words. But someone's been doing Black Masses, and apparently they're using real blood in the ritual.'

'Any idea where these things are taking place?' Jack wanted to know.

'They keep on referring to some place out in the sticks. Maybe on a farm. But they're being careful because they know about hackers like me,' Wally grinned.

'Can you give us a guess where these things are happening?' I asked.

'You'll be the first to know if they give us a scent, Lieutenant.'

We turned to walk out of his office.

'One thing.'

'Yeah, Wally,' I said.

'These guys aren't fooling around. I mean it's not like some high school adventure. They sound more mature, LT. They sound like grown-ups. And for the record, Jimmy, Jack, these folks are scaring the shit out of me.'

He tried to smile, but he couldn't quite pull it off.

'You mean for real?' Jack asked him.

'These guys are *wrong*, Jack. As in *evil*?'

Jack looked over at me with a lame grin.

'No shit. These folks come from somewhere other than this planet. I mean, I think I'm going to start wearing my gun to work.'

He blushed just slightly, and then Wally Garrity returned to his station in front of his state-of-the-art computer.

Chapter Fourteen

Samsa was taunting us with verse from Edgar Allan Poe. He was daring us to nail him before he did victim number three. Jack seemed to be taking it even more personally than I was.

'We should've shot him when he took off from the White Castle,' my younger partner said. His voice betrayed his anger.

'You know we don't take pot-shots at anyone when they're running down a street or alley unless we're sure it's clear. It was dark, Jack. We could've burned down some old lady walking her dog.'

He didn't answer because he knew I was right and he knew he wouldn't cut loose on a suspect unless the shot was definitely in the clear.

The phone rang. We were sitting in my office, looking for messages about the Goths or the vampire cults that might show up in the personals. We'd come up empty.

Wally Garrity was on the line. He thought he had something for us, finally.

'They're talking about something special going down tomorrow night,' Garrity told us. He gestured toward his computer screen where he'd hacked into a chatroom with two of the ordinary chatters.

'They ain't talking about sex, Jimmy. They ain't talking about drugs. They're talking about something to do with human blood. They even used those words in reference to what's happening at this gathering tomorrow night.'

'Do they say where?' I asked.

'In fact they do, Lieutenant. Apparently they're outdoors types. The cold evidently doesn't phase them. Fisherman's Slough, way out on the Southwest side. Out in the sticks. No one fishes there anymore. I've been out there. It's more like a lover's lane.'

We watched them converse – they appeared to be a male and a female. The call names were Gothgirl '77 and Bramlover 12.

'Bram Stoker wrote *Dracula*,' Wally told us.

'Yeah. I heard the name before,' I said. 'He was an Irishman, wasn't he?'

'Hell if I know. I don't read fiction,' Wally grinned.

'I know. Computer mags,' Jack smiled.

Wally blushed because Jack had exposed his reading habits.

'I'm just not a well-rounded person,' Garrity shot back at us.

Gothgirl '77 was talking once again about the 'big event' planned for the next evening. It was February, I remembered. Today was the twelfth, a Thursday. So tomorrow—

'It's Friday the thirteenth. How convenient,' Wally smirked.

'You think this Bram guy wears a hockey mask?' Jack said.

'Hockey mask? I don't get it, ' Wally admitted.

'You don't watch horror movies either,' Jack accused the computer geek.

'No, I don't. Sorry.'

'*Friday the Thirteenth* . . . Wally, my man, you gotta get out more often.'

Gothgirl talked about Fisherman's Slough once more. She asked her friend Bram for directions, and he came up with them.

She told him she'd never partaken of the 'real thing' before, and I assumed she wasn't talking about having a Coca-Cola. She was in a high just thinking about her first time. It was going to be like a sort of communion, but not the kind my church practiced. I looked for a mention of Satanism or devil worship or black sabbath, but she never used such terms.

I asked Wally if maybe we were hooking on to a wrong number. Could it be possible that these were two kids who'd killed some domestic pet and used the blood for this big assembly of spooks on Friday night?

'No, Lieutenant. I don't think so. He said it was human blood. He used those words, just before you and Jack got down here.'

'Okay. Then we'll have to crash the party in the woods.'

'This sounds like that *Blair Witch* thing,' Jack said.

'What?' Wally asked.

'Faggeddaboutit,' Wendkos replied. 'Keep reading your fucking magazines, Junior.'

Wally blushed and then returned to his video screen.

It was still very cold. Spring never really seemed to break through in Chicago until the latter part of April, if it arrived that early.

We had arranged for the County Sheriff's deputies and the Park District Police to accompany us on this bust. We were out of Chicago proper, so we needed their okay to deploy our own guys in the event of arrests.

We stood behind a small copse, watching the parking lot of Fisherman's Slough. It was too cold for the lovers to park tonight. It was in the low teens, the radio had told us. The Sheriff's people and the Park District cops were sitting in the warmth of their patrol vehicles in another lot a half mile away. We couldn't scare anyone off with copper rides visible by the Slough, so Jack and I and six Chicago uniforms walked the four blocks from where we parked our cars and spread ourselves out in the woods that lay just beyond the parking lot.

It was eleven-thirty. We'd been standing out in the cold and in the remaining three inches of snow that still lay on the grass. Winter wouldn't seem to flee. It lingered, maddeningly.

A car pulled into the lot. It idled, but no one got out. In another few minutes, three more vehicles pulled into Fisherman's Slough. I reached into my leather jacket's pocket and retrieved the .44 Bulldog. Luckily I was wearing thermal underwear and a navy stocking cap. Natalie told me I looked like the Boston Strangler when I left the house to do this roust.

A van pulled up, finally, and dark clad people came out of the five vehicles. I beeped Jack twice with my hand-held radio. It made an almost inaudible chirping sound, but I was far enough away from our new arrivals that I was confident they couldn't hear it. It was Jack's job to beep the other uniforms, then.

They gathered in the parking lot. They scoped the surrounding area very carefully, and then they made the move toward the woods. They were heading toward Jack Wendkos's post, it appeared. When they'd moved out of the lot, I whispered into the radio.

'Your spot. Incoming.'

'"K",' Jack replied.

When they were far enough away from me, I talked to the other patrolmen on my hand-held. We would begin to converge on Jack's location.

I tried not to make any sound, but the snow covered left-over leaves and brambles, and I could hear a slight crackling from time to time as I progressed through the woods toward my partner and his new party guests. There was no alternative. I had to keep on going. We weren't going to alert the Sheriff and his deputies and the Park District cops until we were sure we had grounds for an arrest. In other words, not until we saw the blood.

The least we could do was bust them for being in the park after closing hours – 10:30 p.m.

I saw an opening before the Slough itself. There was a campfire site just at the edge of the water. The other cops had to be coming in. We'd have them with their backs toward Fisherman's Slough. There was no escape route that I could make out.

A fire burst forth from the campsite. One of them must have used charcoal starter or gasoline, because the flames jumped toward the cold, black February sky.

A male was dressed in a ceremonial black cape. It had a red interior, I saw, as he raised his hands skyward. There was a collective groan that emanated from his 'followers', if that's what they were.

I moved as close as I could get without leaving the cover of the trees and foliage that surrounded the campfire. There appeared to be six males and six females – the clown with the cape made thirteen. I wasn't a fan of numerology, and I wasn't a believer in the bad-luck aspect of that number, but I had never taken any chances at wearing that numeral on my various game jerseys in baseball or football or softball.

I was no expert on the black mass, and it really didn't matter to me if that's what they were up to. I just wanted to catch them dirty with human blood. Their answers about the source of the serum would prove to be very interesting. And we might even get lucky and get some information about Samsa. There couldn't be that many entrepreneurs in the gore business, I didn't think.

There was only a pine tree between me and the thirteen spooks all dressed in their finest black apparel.

The guy with the cape was wearing a mask. It was one of those Halloween pullover types, so I couldn't see any of his real face. This mask was the usual rendering of Lucifer, with the horns and the Vandyke beard and mustache. I could see that much from the illumination of the still-flaming fire they'd started.

The moans increased, until the caped figure pulled out what looked to be a glass vial. It was too dark to see what color the fluid was.

The caped devil-lookalike uncorked the vial and brought it to his lips – very theatrically. Then he passed the vial on to the other members of his cult.

They took a sip and passed it along, and as they did so, the moaning turned into a chant.

I took Latin in high school, but I remember little to nothing of it. We read about Caesar crossing the Rubicon or some damned thing—

'Let's go!' I said over the hand-held. It was loud enough

111

that the black-clad men and women jerked their heads toward me as I emerged from behind the tall pine. My fellow cops began popping out from behind trees and bushes as well.

I had the Bulldog palmed. I wasn't planning on using it. Jack had his Nine pointed toward the ground as we trotted up to the group by the campfire.

'Just stand very still,' I ordered them.

They were all wearing black masks that covered only their eyes – like the Lone Ranger's mask. Everyone but the honcho with the scarlet and black cape looked the same.

'Why don't you take off your Halloween finery,' I told the thirteen.

Everyone removed the black masks. Except the head man.

'You too,' I told him.

They had nowhere to run from us. The Slough was at their backs.

The caped leader slowly began to tear off the rubber Satan mask.

'Hello, Lieutenant,' Maxim Samsa said.

He was smiling brightly, as if he were pleased I'd shown up.

I took just one step toward him, and then he bolted around and shoved aside three of his co-worshippers, and before I could lay hands on him, he dove into the murky, black waters of Fisherman's Slough. By this time we could see the flashing lights of the Sheriff's Deputies and the Park District Police.

Jack dove into the Slough after him.

'No! Jack! No!'

I ran to the water's edge. The other patrolmen were converging on the remaining twelve worshippers.

I saw my partner freestyling out toward the middle of the Slough, fully clothed. He hadn't had time to throw off anything before he dove in. But Jack was the only figure I could just barely make out in the water. When he reached almost the halfway marker in the Slough – the opposite bank wasn't more than a hundred yards away – he was treading water and looking all about. Then he grudgingly turned back toward the rest of us and swam back to the muddy beach.

One of the patrolmen with Jack and me ran to a Sheriff's cruiser and found a blanket and put it over Jack's shoulders.

Wendkos was quivering by now, uncontrollably.

The Sheriff's deputies arrested the twelve remaining black-clad freaks for trespassing the park after closing hour. We would have to interview them all after the charges were filed.

'Son of a bitch just disappeared, Jimmy. I swear I was right behind him . . . '

He shivered.

'Then he went down and disappeared. The son of a bitch just vanished.'

I went over to the Park District Police and asked them to scour the entirety of the Slough and the woods that sur-rounded them. They didn't appear happy about wandering about the premises on a night as cold as this, but when I told them this guy Samsa was wanted for the murders of the two young women they'd read about in the papers, their eyes widened in recognition, and they took off after the caped Count.

Janet Meyerson was one of the black-clad attendees. I saw her being questioned by the Sheriff himself. I told the head county copper I wanted to see Meyerson first, once we'd transported the twelve of them to the county lockup.

'Hello, Janet. Nice to see you again so soon,' I smiled at her.

She flipped me off, but I didn't say anything more to her. Jack was trembling. He had to get some dry clothes. We would have to let the Park District people come up with The Count.

'He's not supernatural,' Wendkos said with his teeth chattering on the ride downtown. We had arranged for Meyerson to be transported to our headquarters in the city as soon as County was through with her trespassing beef.

We had not come up with the vial. Either The Count had it or one of the others tossed it before we could lay hands on them. We'd have to search the Slough in the morning. I had to know if the blood belonged to either of Samsa's victims.

'Of course he isn't. He just swam under while you were on the surface and he made his way to shore and then he took off.'

'Where's he going to go? That place was crawling with us, cops every goddam place. How's he going to slip through all that manpower?'

'Maybe he won't.'

'You don't sound very confident, Lieutenant.'

He'd sliced me to the bone and had avoided two shots from my miniature howitzer, the Bulldog. He took off down the street when we had him for sure at the White Castle, just after he had 'communed' with his female followers – if indeed they were followers.

This guy was very lucky. Or he was supernatural.

And he had taken off with the blood. He'd be the one to make sure he left no evidence behind. The rest were indeed just followers. Samsa was sly. He was slippery. But he wasn't the devil or Dracula or anything else unworldly. He was a stealthy murderer. Likely he was very intelligent, even without the formal education.

I was not looking forward to explaining to our mercurial Captain why Maxim Samsa had once again eluded capture. The Captain had no sense of humor about escaped murderers or about the cops who allowed them to do so.

I could've thrown another blast from the .44 his way, at the Slough, but Jack popped up in my line of fire when he took off after him. Samsa wasn't worth any bodily harm to my partner, so I knew withholding fire was the right thing to do.

Samsa got away again, regardless of the circumstances. That was the bottom line. Whether I got reamed out by my Boss or not, I was the senior investigator, and the weight fell on my shoulders and no one else's.

'Maybe the prick's got real batwings under that fancy cape. But now he'll have to really go underground,' Jack lamented.

114

'Not necessarily,' I countered.

'Why, not necessarily?' Jack asked.

'He's got three more vics to bleed. Three more stanzas from that Poe poem to copy. He enjoys the work, Jack. We got a real live sociopath on our hands, this time. He enjoys what he does, and he thinks he's getting better at it all the time.'

Jack Wendkos had finally stopped quaking, once he got into dry clothes.

'Just be thankful this cheesedick didn't jump into Lake Michigan.'

'Why, Jimmy?'

'The water's a whole helluva lot colder.'

Chapter Fifteen

The Count left tracks on the mud beach where he got out of the Slough. The Park District Police found the vial of blood. It was tossed about thirty feet from where the campfire had blazed. All the members of The Count's 'blood cult' had been arrested for trespassing, but we didn't have anything else on the twelve of them unless we found out that the blood used in his ritual belonged to one of the two women he murdered. We were still awaiting the results from the Lab and the forensics people.

We went after Samsa in every way we could. We checked DMV and found that there was a Honda motorcycle under his real name. We had his plate number, and every copper in Cook County had his tag by now. I thought he'd change plates or get rid of the bike. He was that greasy, but you never knew. We tossed the apartment where he nicked me with his knife. We found gray duct tape, but not much else we could use to have him prosecuted by the Candy Man, our prosecuting attorney. The Candy Man was his nickname because of the horror films by that name. He *was* a horror to go up against in the courtroom. He just about never lost. And he had the highest rate of death-penalty decisions in the state of Illinois.

The Captain was not as irate as I figured he would be about letting Maxim Samsa slip away from us once again.

'Next time shoot the prick,' the red-haired Captain told Jack and me. I wasn't sure he was being serious, but I knew his military background. He was a member of the Rangers in Vietnam and he'd had some ties to Operation Phoenix – which was all about assassinating North Vietnamese and Viet Cong brass. He never said anything to me about it because I was just a standard grunt in that Lost War. He was no braggart, either, which kept him silent on that piece of American history, so I never asked him about his exploits. Both of us, I assumed, were happy to be done with that goddamned war.

I would've shot Jack if I'd cut loose a round with the .44. There was no clear line, and I was beginning to wonder if there ever would be. I preferred a clean collar. Shootings required vast reams of paperwork, something I was not at all fond of going through. But I knew I'd kill Samsa if the situation required.

The net was out. It wasn't just us in the CPD anymore in this Count business. County and State were involved. The FBI had tossed its hat into this affair. They loved serial or series killers because it meant headlines. The US Marshal's Office had offered its services, which we accepted because they were extremely efficient at finding and arresting people. They were, in fact, much better at it than the famous Federal Bureau of Investigation was. They were much lower key and lower profile than the Fibbies, and they had a great track record for coming up with perps.

We needed to do more canvassing on the West Side. There were sufficient bodies assigned to snatch The Count, so I thought we should turn our attention to the murders of the old guy, Arthur Ransom, and to Dilly Beaumont and the two faceless, dead bangers we found in that alley.

'It's the girl, Jack.'

'Who?'

'Joellyn Ransom. The old guy's granddaughter. There's something she knows that we don't.'

'Why do you think so?'

'Because, junior, she looked like she had more to tell us when we talked to her at her library job.'

'What're you getting out of all that, Lieutenant?'

117

'Body language, Jack. The evasive eyes. She looked right at me when she barreled into the old man's apartment just after we'd arrived on that scene. She eyeballed me with no fear, then. And later she appeared all squirrelly when we saw her that next time. Maybe Abu Riad had a talk with her about the facts of survival in his hood.'

'You mean he's threatened her.'

'Yeah. She knows something, but Abu Riad doesn't want any more heat thrown his way. Otherwise she'd be on a meat wagon leaving the West Side.'

We drove past Rico's crib twice just to make ourselves visible to the killer punk. Then we headed toward the girl's residence.

We found her apartment and parked the Taurus about a half block down. It was a rainy afternoon in mid-February, but at least the temperature was in the mid-fifties. So no snow or ice. But the rain kept the yos and yoettes off these mean streets. And we didn't bring any back-up because the patrol cars would attract too much attention. Two white boys in the hood would be bad enough.

No one was walking that hood when we approached her entranceway. It was four o'clock. She should have been home for an hour by now. The schools got out at 2:30 – at least the secondary schools did. Joellyn was a twelfth grader at DuSable High School. She was a year ahead of my son Mike.

Her educational experience, I was certain, was alien to my son's, at his lily-white Catholic school.

She answered the doorbell on the first try. We walked up two flights to her flat. She was supposed to be living with her father, but I had never laid eyes on him.

Joellyn was dressed in her uniform – which had just become a rule at DuSable and several other Inner City locations.

'Yes?' she asked. I wondered if she remembered us.

'We'd like to ask you a few questions,' I said.

She let us in.

118

'I shouldn't . . . my father's not home.'

If her old man lived here, I couldn't spot any evidence of his male residency. I had the feeling Joellyn lived here alone. She wasn't eighteen, and she wasn't an adult, then.

We sat down on her old but comfortable three-seat couch. She stood across from us. She appeared tired, as if she'd gone sleepless for several nights.

'I think Abu Riad is involved with the murder of your grandfather,' I told her.

The young woman didn't blink.

'I found out something interesting about Arthur,' I told her.

'Yeah?'

'Yeah. He owned that apartment building.'

'So?' she asked. She was becoming a bit more openly hostile.

'So he owned the two three flats right next door, too.'

'And what are y'all asking me?'

'Your grandfather wasn't rich by any means, but he owned property. That's kind of unusual around here, isn't it? For a working stiff like your Grandpa to own real estate?'

'Because he was black?' she accused.

Jack sat quietly next to me. His eyes were on the girl. She wasn't looking anywhere but directly at me, this time.

'I don't mean that, no. I meant that most of the folks around here are poor. How come Arthur Ransom has the fazools to buy apartment buildings?'

She stared at me as if she were trying to laser her way right through me.

'My grandfather worked for forty years at the railroad. When he first moved in around here, he used to tell me, this was a decent place to live. The houses and apartment buildings was kept up. There was whites and blacks here for a while, and then, he told me, blockbusters come around and spooked white people into believing black people was going to run them out of here. And the white people believed it and sold their property for real cheap prices. That was what Grandpa told me. He had some money from the stocks and

119

bonds he invested in – did y'all know he graduated from high school and had a year of junior college?'

'No. I didn't know that.'

Jack continued to watch her. But she never looked anywhere but at me.

'So that's how he bought them apartment buildings. And now they worth about the same as his ashes that we spread at his old job down at the railroad.'

Arthur Ransom had been cremated. We went to that service, also, but Joellyn was the only other mourner at the West Side funeral home that night.

'Who inherited his property?' Jack suddenly broke in.

'That none of your—'

'If you want us to arrest the people who murdered your grandfather, you have to be straight with us, Joellyn,' Jack warned her.

'He left it to me . . . but when I turn eighteen. And that's not until August.'

'So you're the landlord of those three apartment buildings,' I repeated. 'So what is Abu Riad up to? He trying to muscle you into selling those lots?'

She didn't answer.

'Is that man threatening you, Joellyn?'

She looked out the living room window, toward the street.

'I don't know nothin' else. I think y'all ought to come back when my daddy here with me.'

'Daddy doesn't live here, does he,' I countered.

'Yes, he does. He . . . he at work. Now I think it's time y'all left.'

'Don't let him do it to you too, Joellyn,' I warned her.

'Who?'

'You know who I'm talking about,' I said. 'He killed a woman I was in love with – just so you don't think this is all just business with me. He didn't pull the trigger on her, but he might as well have. You see, they shot her little boy – his name was Andres. Shot him all to hell in front of Cabrini . . . You see how wide Riad's territory is? Her name was Celia Dacy. She was a student, but older than you. She was

120

training to be a nurse. She graduated and got a job and she was just about to get herself and her little boy the hell out of Cabrini. Then Andres was murdered and she tried to even things up, but it got her killed . . . I was holding her when she stopped breathing . . .

'So. If you want to tell us what he's got that's biting into you, we might be able to take him all the way out of your world. And out of everybody else's world around here too. You get tired of him yanking your strings, you let me know.'

Jack and I got up off the couch and let ourselves out.

I went down to City Records. My contact there was Danny FitzMartin. He was an old-time member of the Daley machine, but he always talked straight to me when I needed help. He was a politician, like a lot of guys in the city machinery, but I couldn't help liking him for his quick, Irish sense of humor.

'I looked it up for you, Jimmy, boyo.'

'And what did you find?'

We sat in his spacious office that overlooked Michigan Avenue. All the monied shoppers went by his building in never-ending waves. I could see them down those six floors from us.

'Your friend the gangster, Mr Abu Riad, is a very civic-minded banger. He's got a little something going with the Feds about urban renewal on that lovely side of town.'

'The federals are going to sink some money into that territory?' I asked him.

Jack was back at his office, gathering any information we were receiving from the public about the sightings of The Count.

'That's what's brewing, Jimmy . . . but you bloody well never heard any of this from me.'

'So let me think out loud. Abu Riad gets his hands into those federal bucks if he can deliver some real estate in a dead and dying neighborhood. And some of this one-time worthless property lies in the hands of an old guy named Arthur Ransom.'

121

FitzMartin didn't blink or nod or gesture affirmation to me in any way.

'Dangerous stuff, this, Jimmy. You really want to get in the muck with this fellow? No one's been able to hook him for almost thirty years. Maybe that's a message, yeah?'

'Riad didn't order Ransom killed for some chickenshit initiation thing. He wanted him out so he could take the deeds and . . . the girl doesn't legally inherit the lots until she turns eighteen. And Ransom's murder and the killing of his neighbor lady, Dorothy Beaumont and the whacks on those two fifteen-year-olds—

'Things were getting out of hand. It was drawing too much attention from us. He probably figured Ransom was too low profile, that we'd slough it off like a lot of inner city slayings . . . They don't make headlines. They're common-place. But then Jack and I spend all that time on those cases, we make too many appearances in the hood, along with getting in Riad's face at his own house . . . '

'Why're you sharing all this with me, Jimmy? I'm just a minuscule part in this city's machinery and I don't know dick about dick. I just shuffle paperwork all the livelong day.'

He smiled slyly at me, and I knew the interview had concluded.

Chapter Sixteen

The first indication of anything being off key came from a tactical detective named James Burnside. He grew up on the West Side and had lived there until he finally escaped, went to college, joined the Police Academy, and graduated to street cop and later a member of Tactical.

'She's no virgin, Lieutenant,' Burnside explained.

He was a tall black man around 6'2" and probably weighed in at 235. An ex-fullback at Dunbar High School. He had been decorated numerous times. His picture had been in the papers for all kinds of West Side busts he'd made.

'What do you mean?'

He looked at me carefully as we sat in the downstairs lounge at headquarters. We were alone because it was midway through the midnights shift. Almost 4:00 a.m.

'I mean don't let the clean-cut wholesome thing fool you about Joellyn Ransom. She's been into shit, from time to time. Look, I heard you were looking for information on the Arthur Ransom killing, and I heard from some of my sources in that neighborhood that you and Jack had interviewed her.'

'And?'

He took a sip out of his lukewarm-by-now coffee in the styrofoam cup.

'She's no innocent little lamb, Lieutenant. We never had cause to arrest her, but she's a little bit too tight with some very wrong individuals.'

'Like who, for example?' I asked Burnside.

'Like the main man himself. Abu Riad.'

'And how do you know all this?'

Burnside laughed.

'It's like our business, Lieutenant. You know?'

I felt my cheeks being scorched in embarrassment. Of course I knew Joellyn and everyone else in her hood were Burnside's business. It was his *job.*

'I'm sorry, James. That was a dumbass thing to say. But she doesn't come off as—'

'She's a player, Jimmy. That's about all I can get into at the moment. There are things I can't say, now. It's an ongoing thing, you know?'

'Yeah, but she's involved in a murder investigation.'

'I know, Lieutenant. That's why I felt obligated to come get you *into the game.'*

'Jesus Christ . . . you're telling me that this seventeen-year-old kid is playing me?'

'You're not the only cop she's played. She's skipped on three drug raps. Her friend Mr Riad always comes around with a lawyer for her, and she's never been caught holding. But we're not after her on a drug beef. Unfortunately I can't get into what we are after her about. You understand, Lieutenant?'

'Yeah. Sure.'

'I'm not trying to be a pain in the ass and I'm not trying to be uncooperative. We both play for the same team. But the rest is very sensitive.'

He got up from the leather chair he was sitting in.

'If you become, say, aggressive about looking at her? We wouldn't be too disappointed. As long as the right thing happens with Joellyn Ransom, I don't personally give a flying fuck who pulls the trigger on her.'

He nodded my way and then took off down the hall toward the exit.

Wendkos didn't believe it at first either.

'Joellyn Ransom?'

'That sweet little cherry pie. Remember how we both ached for her when she told us she was never getting out of the neighborhood? That was world class. Should've got the Oscar or the Emmy for all that. She had us fooled. Clean. A victim . . . I should've wondered why Riad hadn't burned her. I just thought that he was backing off, since she wouldn't inherit grandpa's property until she was eighteen.'

'She must have known, then. She must have known the old man owned those three flops.'

'And she's close to Riad. I never knew that bald prick liked them that young.'

'How else could she survive alone in that apartment, Jimmy? We thought her old man lived with her, but we've never seen him once in the visits we've made to her place, or by asking around for him. So she's living alone and Riad is picking up the tab.'

'I don't know how else you can see it,' I answered.

'And Abu Riad keeps the bitch in a separate pad because if the media caught wind he was playing house with a teenager—'

'They'd do a Joan of Arc on him. They'd deep-fry the motherfucker, yeah.'

'But we only have Tactical's word about their connection. How do we get her tied to Riad? You can bet he's careful about being seen with her, Jimmy.'

'She'll be almost impossible to tail. We'd stick out like cows' asses if we tried to surveil her in her hood.'

'How about using an undercover copper?'

'I don't know if Tac wants to share their manpower, but I'll have the Captain do his thing with them.'

Cooperation among the various Units in the CPD was not notoriously commonplace. Everybody wanted to make their own busts because that was how you advanced upward in the ranks. But the Captain could be very persuasive because Homicide was considered the most serious of all crimes, after all.

They gave us a young, black Tactical named Earvin Watkins. He went by the street name Blade, and he looked like the actor Wesley Snipes – hence the monicker.

125

'They've been watching her for some time – I'm allowed to share the wealth with you, Lieutenant Parisi. It looks like your Captain is one persuasive dude. She was a big piece of our case against Riad. But the murder of grandpappy now supersedes all the other happy horseshit.'

He smiled some big, white, fierce teeth at us. No wonder he fit right into his underground assignment. He had penetrated the Vice Kings. He was a player. He was a made man, now, for six months. We were very fortunate to have him on loan.

'You wouldn't think she was a yoette by scoping her, would you?' Earvin asked Jack and me as we sat in the Taurus in the downtown parking lot. It was midnight. The shift had just changed and the other policemen were at roll call or already on the street if they were working overtime.

'What is it that you want me to do for you, LT?' Earvin asked.

I was sitting next to him in the backseat; Jack was behind the wheel. We couldn't linger, or Earvin would be made. This department had corrupt cops. It had policemen who were on Riad's payroll. Abu Riad hadn't run loose all these years by not being connected to members of the force.

'I want proof that this girl is indeed tied in with this cheesedick. Photos, audio recordings. Anything you can get that'll get me leverage over her. Rico Perry has gone deep underground, but Joellyn doesn't know that we like her – yet. If we can get her to flip on Riad . . . '

'I'll see what I can do, Jimmy,' Earvin smiled with those wide-screen teeth.

'Thanks, Earvin. Don't get yourself shot,' I grinned.

'Thought never occurred to me. Jimmy, Jack . . . Later.'

Earvin got out of the car and slipped off into the dark.

It all seemed to work. Joellyn inherited the lots with the brick flophouses on top. She sold the property to Riad, her lover. And then he shared the proceeds of a federal renewal deal there, on the West Side. No one would suspect the grieving granddaughter of Arthur Ransom. Joellyn was squeaky clean. No jewelry implanted in various parts of her body, no gang tattoos. No sign of her connection to the evil that came in the package of Abu Riad.

Joellyn was only seventeen. In other areas of this city, she might still be considered a kid. A teenager. But she had already made her bones.

She fooled me. She fooled Jack. She probably did a number on her teachers at the school too.

Where was her father? The guy who was supposed to be living with her?

Maybe Riad had taken him all the way out of the picture, just like Arthur Ransom. There was no family left for Joellyn, so maybe that was why she became snared by the neighborhood chieftain. The Vice Kings were an extended family for these kids in the neighborhood who had no one else.

Perhaps Joellyn wasn't looking for an extended family. Perhaps she was looking for a way out of the West Side. Her grandfather couldn't help her alive, but dead he was her ticket to parts unknown, far, far away from these mean streets and ugly barrios.

We kept an eye on Joellyn with Earvin's help. We also kept an eye on Abu Riad with the help of the now cooperative tacticals.

But The Count still retained all the headlines and the interest of the talk shows, radio and TV. So he kept on dragging us back to his high profile bat's ass.

The Count had no living relatives. His aunt was deceased – the one he'd attacked and bitten.

We were still in the dark about the Goths and the vampire cults that may or may not have been his connection to killing the women and draining all their blood.

The vial came back from the Lab. The traces of blood inside it had matched neither of Samsa's two victims, but it was human blood.

'So where'd that blood come from?' Jack asked as we left forensics and the crime scene technicians.

'He's got someone else strapped to a bed,' I said.

127

We checked the missing persons files for any females in the 30–35 years category. We came up with just six on the computer.

I thought we'd go all out on the chance that Samsa's new blood bank would be on that list of six, so we sent out six pairs of cops to each of the addresses.

Our woman's name was Barbara Gautier. She lived only seven blocks from the Petersen woman.

We knocked. There was no answer. We knocked louder. Nothing. And then Jack put his foot to the door handle, and the door exploded into the living room.

Barbara Gautier had last been seen a week ago. She hadn't checked in at her job at the truck painting outfit on the Northwest side. She did have parents, but they were both in a senior's home with advanced Alzheimers.

'Barbara? You here? Police!' Jack cried out.

We heard a feeble moan. We walked toward the bedroom in this small apartment on the Northwest periphery of the city.

My .44 was in my hand, but my arm was extended toward the floor. I raised the weapon up.

'Barbara?' Jack called as we entered the bedroom.

I flipped on the overhead light.

A woman was in the bed, a twin sized, and she was under a number of blankets.

'Who are you?' she wheezed.

'Police,' Jack explained.

'Police? My God, what did I do?' she pleaded.

'Are you ill, Barbara?'

I asked the obvious question.

'Had the flu all week. Too weak to get out of this bed except to go to the bathroom . . . and I blacked out twice, I think, going there.'

She could barely raise her head.

'Have you eaten anything?' Jack asked her.

'Couldn't keep anything . . . down.'

She would've been an attractive woman if she weren't this deathly ill, I supposed.

'Didn't anyone come looking for you?' I asked. 'Christ, the cops had to have made a visit here by now. You're on the missing persons list, for Jesus sake,' I asked her.

'Thought I heard knocking. Been too weak to get up and answer the door.'

'Doesn't your landlord have a key?'

'He – He's on vacation. Went back to eastern Europe to see his family. Don't know which country.'

Some pair of lazy pricks with badges had knocked on Barbara Gautier's door but hadn't thought to force their way in. Apparently Barbara wasn't a high profile missing person.

I went into her living room and used her telephone to arrange for paramedics to come take her to the hospital. Just as I hung up with the paramedics, my beeper went off. I called the 911 and heard that two of our brother homicides had come up with a winner.

She was barely alive. In much worse shape than Barbara Gautier had been in. At least Barbara had drunk some fluids, or she would've probably been gone by the time Jack splintered her front door.

How could there be this many forgotten human beings in the world? I couldn't fathom all this neglect.

Theresa Meecham was another brunette. Thirty-three years old. No relatives or friends to check on her. But when the police had come, someone had answered. I could guess who it was. Maxim must not have been wearing his make-up. Whatever it was, I wanted to know the whole story when I hooked up with the two lazy bastards who never asked to have a look at Theresa Meecham. I read her file. I saw the names of the cops who'd supposedly investigated her whereabouts. They'd written: 'Subject not at home. Boy-friend met us at the location. Said Ms Meecham was out shopping, that she hadn't called in sick at her job at General Electric plant in Schaumberg because she was angry with her boss and was quitting. No sign of a struggle indicated inside the apartment. Told "boyfriend", a William Wyanet, that we'd be back to see Ms Meecham on the following a.m.'

'They never did the second interview,' Jack said.

'Apparently they had better things to do, and this guy "Wyanet" was very convincing.'

'So convincing that the dumb pricks couldn't check out the bedroom?' Jack asked.

'They came to this address at about noon. They both probably had hot lunch dates. Maybe even a pair of nooners. It's not like this laziness is uncommon, Jack.'

She was strapped to the bed when Sergeants O'Connor and Mendelheim entered the premises by popping the door lock with a plastic card. Samsa hadn't greeted these two detectives, unfortunately.

Theresa Meecham could barely open her eyes. There were several filled and capped vials of what was probably her own blood. We would have to see if Meecham's serum matched what we'd found at Fisherman's Slough.

'So what's our next move, my Lieutenant?' Jack asked as we waited for the paramedics to transport yet another attractive thirty-year-old loner to the hospital.

'He doesn't know we've been here. Why don't we wait around for him to take another transfusion. All right with you, Dr Van Helsing?'

'I can't wait to say hello,' Jack shot back at me.

Chapter Seventeen

We got Theresa Meecham transported to Christ Hospital on the Southwest side. We had the Crime Scene technicians finish their business, and then Jack and I took the first six-hour shift after we'd both been home to change clothes, shower, and say hello to our wives.

Natalie had been exercising at home on the treadmill, and she'd been doing all kinds of other exercises. She did some work with weights, but she liked push-ups and sit-ups and things which did not require barbells. Natalie said she didn't want bulk; she wanted lean and mean. The mean part I never witnessed, regarding my wife.

We had just fifteen minutes to make love in a rush in our bedroom. She was now using the pill because we decided to cease making little Parisis. We were both Catholics, but the pill didn't seem like a sin to us. And neither of us much liked some priest in Rome making our bedroom decisions.

When we finished that outburst of passion, I was sweating profusely and had to take another shower. Natalie, however, simply smiled and hadn't burst forth with a single bead of perspiration. She had just been toying with the old man, here.

Jack was to take the first watch. We had four crews of partners to stay inside Theresa Meecham's apartment. Six-hour shifts. I had already called the Captain and let him know about the screwups on Missing Persons. The Captain said he would take pains to make sure those so-called police officers found new work and perhaps new careers. I almost felt sorry for those poor bastards, but then I remembered the helpless look on Theresa Meecham's bloodless face when we entered her crib.

'You think he'll really come back?' Jack asked.

'He left all his goodies behind. Maybe he didn't see the Crime Scene guys take everything out of here. He might come back – if he's as arrogant as I think he is.'

I was referring to the several vials of blood that the forensics people had taken into evidence from here.

'I don't figure he'd go to all that trouble and then leave it all behind.'

But he had eluded us before when it seemed we had him. I had no great confidence that he'd be bold enough to return, but right now it was all we had. The kid was like a fucking goblin or ghost. He evaporated just when you were about to lay hands on him. I'd never admit as much to Jack or anyone else, but this Maxim Samsa or The Count or whoever he really was had some unusual ability to remain elusive when every copper in Cook County was aimed at his pale white ass.

I missed Doc on stakeouts. Jack was too quiet, too reserved. Doc would make me laugh even when things were supposed to be dreadfully serious. Gibron had the knack for bringing out the silliness in both of us. I liked Wendkos a lot. He just wasn't Doc Gibron.

'I'll crap out first. Wake me after two hours – and this time, Jack, I don't give a shit how sound you think I'm sleeping. You *will* awaken me. Got it?'

He smiled again and nodded. I was lying on the couch in Ms Meecham's front room. Her blinds were all shut so that no one could see in. Jack stood by the window where a table and lamp stood. The bulb was dim wattage, but Jack was standing there trying to read the *Sun Times* sports page.

I started to doze off with the quiet rustling of the pages as Jack turned them.

I was standing on a very narrow platform. It was only wide enough for me to have my heels on top. My toes hung over the edge. It was like a cliff with just the tiniest ledge for

132

me to stand on. And below were alligators or crocodiles – I could never distinguish between the two. They were leaping and snapping at me, and each time they rose toward me, they got just a little bit closer. There was no escape from my ledge. There was no way to climb higher. And the gators or crocodiles were waiting, below.

Then I had a sensation of slipping off that precipice. I tried to turn and grab hold of the side of whatever it was that lay behind me, but I could not establish a grip. All this time I could hear the snapping of the reptiles' jaws. They were leaping higher and higher with each try, and coming closer and closer to me while my precarious position was becoming more and more compromised—

Then Jack shook me. It was two hours later, he informed me by showing me his watch. It was a cheap Timex, but cops couldn't afford better if they weren't thieves.

'The fuck?' I said. I thought that last snapping critter was about to grab hold of my left leg. 'Oh. Sorry, Jack,' I apologized when I realized he'd saved me from my own nightmare.

'All's well, my Lieutenant.'

I got up and let him have the comfortable three-seat sofa. He didn't argue. We both hadn't slept more than three hours in the last thirty-six.

I sat in the straight-backed leather chair by the window and the dim wattage bulb. But I had no desire to read, and I couldn't have anyway because I'd left my reading glasses at home on the nightstand.

I took a quick glance out at the street as I put my fingers between the blades of the blinds. Nobody out there. It was very late. Past two a.m.

Then I heard someone coming up the stairs outside Meecham's flat. The entry door downstairs didn't have a lock. This was a very old apartment building, and the owner obviously didn't concern himself with security. Whoever it was had just walked right in.

I called for back-up, and dispatch said two squads were within three or four blocks of Jack and me.

I walked over to Wendkos and shook his shoulder as he lay on his side.

'Jesus, Jimmy, I just shut my—'

'Someone's coming.'

He sat up like he'd been jolted with a bolt of electricity. We walked over to the door.

But the footsteps had stopped. Maybe Samsa, if it was he, had smelled something wrong. The way you thought you smelled natural gas when you suspected a leak.

We waited another fifteen or twenty beats. I was on the left side of the doorway and Jack was opposite from me. I had my Nine out and aimed chest level at anyone coming in, and Jack had his Nine out also, but his was pointed at head level for a man like Samsa.

The knock on the door shocked us both by its abruptness. I cocked my weapon and so did my partner.

I looked at Wendkos quizzically. Who the hell was knocking on this door at two in the morning? Samsa wouldn't, I knew.

I yanked the entry door open, Jack and I stepped into the opening, and we aimed our pieces directly at the noggin of a Domino's Pizza delivery man.

'*Shit*,' the delivery guy croaked. He couldn't have been far past twenty-one. He was tall and skinny, but he had a very red complexion at the moment.

I looked down and saw the little puddle he was making on the floor of the hallway.

'*Shit*,' he murmured again.

I thought he might faint, so I grabbed hold of the arm that wasn't holding the rectangular pizza box. I helped him into the apartment.

'*Jesus*,' was all that he could muster once we'd lowered our weapons.

'We're police officers,' I explained.

'I hope to fucking God you are!' he shot back. 'I pissed my fuckin' drawers!'

After he'd gone into Meecham's john to clean himself up as best he could, he came back to us in the living room.

'You know who ordered the pizza?' I asked.

'There's a name on the ticket. And an address. That's all I know.'

The kid had sandy brown hair and a full head of it.

I read the ticket. It had Theresa Meecham's name and address and phone number on it.

'How come you didn't call to confirm the order?' Jack asked the deliveryman.

'Because we're busier than hell . . . We're always busy.'

'What fucking time do you close?' Jack asked.

'Four. We deliver late. That's why we're always busy. We deliver up 'til a half hour before closing, at four. They're thinking of going to a twenty-four-hour business because we don't serve booze or beer.'

'We'll need to go talk to your supervisor or boss,' I told the pizza man.

We caught some luck. The Domino's had caller ID. The ticket for the pizza also included the time the order was taken. I called downtown and had them look up the address for the number on the caller ID, and we got an address that was less than a half mile from Meecham's apartment. But the cop who looked up the number gave us the bad news.

It was a corner payphone.

We thanked the pizza man with the pissed-up blue jeans and we thanked the supervisor too. Then we got in the Taurus and took off toward the location of that payphone. We didn't expect that The Count would be sticking around to wait for us—

And then I told Jack, our driver, to hang a U turn and head back to Meecham's.

'He's decoyed us out of her place. He wants his shit,' I explained.

The tires squealed as Wendkos floored the Ford.

We had our weapons unsheathed once again as we tread the stairs toward Theresa's flat. There was no creaking because we walked on the extreme sides of the staircase.

The door was unlocked, as we had departed in haste. Jack

turned the knob and we saw the living room in the exact state that we'd left it.

The Count couldn't know that the Crime Scene people had removed the vials of blood unless—

I switched off the light and peered between two blades of the blinds. The street was empty—

Until I noticed a dark figure that stood in the doorway of the three flat directly opposite from us.

'The motherfucker's playing us again, Jack. He's across the street . . . Get on your cell and have every available squad in the area seal everything off within a three-block radius of us. Give them Samsa as a description.'

Jack opened his cell and made the call. This time we weren't going to go charging outside until the troops had arrived.

I gave them five minutes. Then the two of us walked slowly down the stairs from Theresa's place toward the entry door. I stopped us at the door and looked out of the glass toward the figure that still stood directly opposite us. The troops had been instructed not to use their emergency lights as they approached this area of operations.

I cracked the door open, and then we made our way out and toward the black outline of a man. The dark figure didn't flee. He simply remained in place.

Tall, thin, dark clothes. It had to be Samsa.

But he wasn't running. He didn't flee as he had all those times previous . . .

Then we charged across the street. Blue lights suddenly strobed behind us as we aimed our weapons head high at the man in the doorway.

'Police!' Jack called out as we made it within five yards of the still motionless man.

'Oh! Hey!' he yelled and raised both hands.

He was tall and thin and very pale, we saw, when we got near him. The only illumination out here was the street lights behind us, and also the sweeping blue lights of the four patrol cars that had appeared behind us now, as well.

'The fuck!' the tall man blurted.

It wasn't Samsa.

'Police,' Jack repeated. This time he said it almost quietly.

'What're you doing out here at 3:00 fucking a.m.?' I asked.

'Waiting for my fucking ride – you ain't gonna shoot me, are you?' he pleaded.

We holstered the pistols.

'I asked you what you're doing out here at this hour.'

'Waiting for my ride.'

'Your ride?' Jack asked the tall, pale man.

'Yeah. I work, you know?'

'What shift starts at this hour?' I demanded.

'I'm a fucking baker, officer. I make fucking bread, you know? At the Sunshine Bread Company out on Western Avenue?'

Jack asked him for ID. His name was Vernon Veldt, and he even had an ID card from Sunshine Bread Company.

We apologized, but Veldt wasn't satisfied.

'You guys scared the fucking hell out of me. I ought to report your asses to someone downtown . . . fuckin' cops. You coulda shot me—'

Jack took him by his black leather jacket's collar.

'You don't calm down, I might just shoot you for fun. You know how cops always have an extra cold piece they carry, just in case they shoot the wrong guy. I mean, you watch TV, don't you Vernon?'

That ended the bitch session. Vernon's ride drove up just about one minute later. It was some delicious looking platinum blonde who was a baker herself, Vernon explained as he pouted and walked toward his ride.

The blonde smiled at Jack out the driver's side window of her yellow VW. Blondes and brunettes – all women – seemed to smile at my partner.

I dismissed all the patrol cars that had converged on Vernon.

'He's ten steps ahead of us every time out,' Jack admitted as we walked back to the scene of an attempted murder. 'This prick is pulling our yash, Jimmy. Oh, he's cute, this son of a bitch is.'

'Cute' wasn't quite the word I had in mind for The Count, Maxim Samsa.

Chapter Eighteen

We were on the way to Joellyn Ransom's apartment when I blacked out.

At least Jack Wendkos let me know that I had blacked out when he pulled over to the curb on a West Side boulevard and slapped my cheeks lightly until I came back.

'I . . . I lost some time,' I told him as we sat in the Taurus.

'I noticed . . . What's wrong, Jimmy? You look like an apostle of The Count's.'

I had trouble catching my breath, so Jack handed me some paper bag left over from one of our fast-food lunches. I breathed in and out into the bag until I felt like my oxygen level was back to normal.

He said I still looked white, so he headed us back to the downtown and St Luke's Hospital.

'No heart attack. No stroke,' the ER doctor told Jack and me after he'd examined me.

'Your blood pressure is up too high, Lieutenant Parisi,' the physician explained.

His name tag read Frank Bernard, MD.

'It's one-eighty over one-ten. Not good . . . Are you taking medication for hypertension?' Bernard asked.

I told him I was on three medicines. Something for my cholesterol, and two beta blockers – I thought that was what our doctor called the last two.

'Even worse. My best diagnosis would be severe stress, Lieutenant. I'm the wrong kind of doctor. You need to see a psychiatrist or a psychologist about this sort of thing. I can't find anything else physically wrong with you, other than you seem worn to the rims. You better get an estimate from some other car dealer,' he smiled.

I thanked him. We walked out of Emergency, and Jack drove me home.

Stress-related. I knew those words before they ever came out of Dr Bernard's mouth.

My white face had gone. My natural color had returned, pretty much, Natalie thought. But she had a blood-pressure cuff at home that she knew how to operate, and she read my rate at one-seventy over one-oh-five.

'Still much too high, my love.'

She had worked as a paramedic in the military before she'd gone to college and the Police Academy.

'You need to see the company man.'

She was referring to the Department's shrink. Dr Terry Wilson. I'd seen him before, and I trusted him. We had talked about the death of Jake, my father, and about my hang-ups regarding whether my mother Eleanor had pushed him down those twenty-six steps intentionally.

Wilson told me it was why I had to be a detective. I had to find out if my own mother was a murderer. As it turned out, after talking to Eleanor about it, I believed that she hadn't meant to cause Jake's death. She had been angry with him for coming home drunk yet one more time from The Greek's saloon. She meant to poke her finger in his chest to express her rage, but she had not intended for my father to tumble down those stairs and break his neck.

It took years for me to come to that resolution, however.

Wilson never asked me to lie down on a couch or any of the usual TV shrink business. He never asked me 'how do you feel about *that*, Jimmy?' He had a way of leading me into a conversation about myself that I hadn't thought possible. I was not inclined to do any deep soul-searching. I had no intention of penetrating the darkest corners of my soul. With

139

Wilson it always seemed like sympathetic talk between two brother police. He never sounded like a shrink.

He stood with his back to me, looking out his window at the Loop.

'Your b.p. is not satisfactory, sir.'

'Yeah. I know it isn't.'

'You're going to tell me eventually that all this blackout/ high blood pressure stuff is job-related, aren't you, Jimmy?'

'Sounds like a likely scenario.'

'So let's skip the chickenshit. What's really going on?'

He turned and looked at me. He was tall, perhaps six-three, and he had yellow blond hair that could've secured him a spot on the Beach Boys or some surfer band of the sixties. But he didn't have the California drawl. He was strictly a city kid, raised on the Southwest side. We knew each other's biography very well after all the history between us as patient and doctor.

'I'm sliding down on the downslope,' I told him. I figured I might as well cut to the chase since Wilson wasn't much for polite chatter.

'You think you're burning out?'

'I know I am.'

'And you think it's inevitable, Lieutenant?'

'Isn't it?'

He smiled broadly. Perfect teeth. He would've made a suitable subject for a billboard in LA. He was a handsome forty-five-year-old shrink. The women who worked down-town, here, were mad about him.

'No. It isn't, as a matter of fact. But you've been in Homi-cide for a lot longer than the usual ten years that most detectives spend at your kind of work.'

'I can't even think of what I'd do besides this job.'

'But you feel like you're headed toward some kind of collision with whatever's at the bottom of that slippery slope you're gliding down. Right?'

'That's a fairly accurate description.'

'You have another high profile, big deal case with this guy who drains his victims of blood. And you have another case

140

that didn't begin as high profile with the murders on the West Side . . . have I got all this down accurately, now?'

'Yeah, Doc. I'd say that fairly sums it up.'

'This blood perpetrator. He's making you feel impotent? Incompetent?'

'I've enjoyed higher levels of self-confidence than I am currently. Yes.'

'We both know that some cases never come to closure. We both know that you've been trained – mostly through street experience – to let go.'

'I *never* let go, Doctor.'

'Yes, I know. I think I know you pretty well, Jimmy.'

He looked out his window once again.

'You're fifty-five, right?'

'Yes.'

'You could take a leave of absence. Like your old partner, Doc Gibron, did.'

'I don't think he's coming back. I think he's going to finally do it and retire.'

'You've got enough years to do the same, don't you, Lieutenant?'

Wilson still had his back to me. It was a way interrogators had of making you feel uneasy – by turning away from you as if you didn't really exist.

'I can't. I won't retire. I won't leave with all this shit left for somebody else to clean up. My problem, my responsibility. I won't pass these cases onto anybody. Not even Jack Wendkos.'

'So how are you going to deal with all this stress we've been discussing, Jimmy?'

He had turned back and faced me once more.

'I can't run, Doctor. There's no place for me to hide. Vacation or sick leave won't do it. The only cure I'm going to find is when these two items on my menu are locked up.'

'What if you black out again?'

'I won't.'

'What makes you certain?'

'There's no certainty. A healthy kid just out of the

Academy could do the same thing. Unless you show me that there's something medically wrong with me – and don't give me that stress shit again because there ain't anyone who doesn't deal with that – I'm going to have to walk.'

'I can prohibit you from duty, Jimmy.'

'Then you just take my service pistol and shoot me in the head. Give me the same kindness you'd give to a lame horse.'

Wilson sat on the edge of his desk.

'All right. I won't have your Captain put you on medical leave . . . if you see me at least once a week.'

I knew he could have me pulled off the job if he thought I was burned and gone, so I really didn't have much choice but to consent to his demands.

'Don't take me off the job, Doctor, because then you might as well put me down.'

He looked at me carefully, as if he were making sure he hadn't missed anything.

'One more blackout or similar kind of episode, Lieutenant, and it will be out of my hands altogether. I'm going to give you something for anxiety. Don't take any alcohol with it.'

'I don't drink, hardly.'

'Yes. I know, Jimmy. Take the meds, Lieutenant, and if you don't feel better, let me know and we'll try something else. But most of all remember that if your b.p. doesn't improve in a month, I'm going to yank you in like the world's biggest bass.'

I got up, shook hands with him, and then I left.

We had not heard from Tactical's plant, Earvin, in almost two weeks. He was still trying to find a way to bind Joellyn Ransom with Abu Riad in the killings of Arthur Ransom, Dorothy Beaumont, and the two faceless gangbangers. Joellyn was on the backburner. I was sorting things into piles of priority. Which I didn't like doing because it seemed, then, that one vic's death was more important than another's. It wasn't the way it was for me, but I was certain someone might perceive it as a sign that I was assigning more weight to one case over another. To me, all murders are equal. There's nothing more heinous than stopping someone's breathing for all time.

It's all anyone really owns. So it's a theft of the ultimate magnitude.

The Count taunted Jack and me. He knew we were waiting for him inside Theresa Meecham's apartment and that was why the pizza man showed up. That was why we rousted and scared hell out of that poor fucking baker on his way to work. Samsa thought he could come and go and blend back into the background like a chameleon.

He was still not clear enough in my head. The only time I felt I had an advantage over a murderer was when I thought I could predict his next move. Samsa wasn't like anyone I'd ever sought before. He was kinkier, weirder, and maybe more intelligent. The Count was into mocking me, the police. He would try to do it again. He'd let me come close, and then he'd evaporate like the light fog does over Lake Michigan when the sun burns it away.

Samsa thought he could go on indefinitely, hitting and running. It was guerilla warfare. Something I should have thought about sooner. Something I'd been involved in, thirty years ago in a Lost War.

How would Jack and I nail him before some other police agency caught up with him first? I had to get better acquainted with Maxim Samsa. I had to know what he wanted, what he really desired. What he was after.

There was little to nothing known about that blood ritual we'd interrupted at Fisherman's Slough. The talk had been silenced in the chatrooms, so Wally couldn't help us there.

There were, however, some individuals who were conversant with the occult. I got the information via a phonecall to the relaxed-sounding ex-partner of mine, Doc Gibron.

'There's quite a bit of literature about vampires, Jimmy P,' Doc had said during the call the morning before this April Thursday.

'What? You mean somebody studies these geeks?'

'Generally, yes. There's a splinter of the Psychology

Department that deals with paranormal literature. Ghosts, vampires, werewolves. All the garden variety of horror critters . . . Talk to Dr Joseph Benniman at Northwestern on the Evanston campus, Jimmy. He might be able to help you.'

Benniman worked in a cluttered if not outright messy cubicle of an office at NU in Evanston, a northern township, right above Chicago on the map.

He was short and stocky. He sported a Fu Manchu mustache and long, very dark brown hair. Dr Benniman struck me as a relic and leftover of 'flower power' and the early seventies. But there was a Chopin étude playing as Jack and I tried to clear the junk off two folding chairs in order to sit opposite this paranormalist or whatever he called himself.

'Actually I have an MD and a PhD in clinical psychology. I'm what they used to call a lifetime student. I'm going after a Master's in Anthropology, nowadays . . . What can I do for you two gentlemen?'

We explained about the Samsa case. He was aware of The Count through newspaper accounts.

'You think this killer is really involved with vampirism?' Benniman asked us.

'We caught him and a group of others in the middle of some kind of ritual. I'm not sure, but I thought I heard Latin being invoked.'

All I had was two years of high school Latin, so I couldn't be positive what Samsa and his friends had been moaning and chanting.

'But they were using blood in the rite?'

'Yes,' I told the Professor.

'Sounds like a Satanic cult. Lots of these kids just make it up piecemeal as they go along, after one of them buys a paperback on Satanic ritual. The real cults would probably never have allowed themselves to be observed. They work in strict privacy. It sounds like you were breaking up the amateur hour, Lieutenant.'

'This amateur has murdered at least two women by draining their blood via a needle of some kind. These two young women took about three days to terminate, Doctor. They were so weak they couldn't lift their heads off the pillow. We know that because the third victim didn't die.'

He blushed apologetically.

'Have you interviewed the young woman who survived?' Benniman asked me.

'We can't. She's in critical condition at St John's Hospital in Winnetka.'

'I'm very sorry. I didn't mean to sound flip about all this, Lieutenant.'

'Can you tell us anything about cults in this area, northern Illinois?' Jack asked.

'Yes. I've interviewed Satanists, would-be werewolves and vampires.'

'Are they for-real?' I asked. 'What I mean to say is, do they genuinely believe they're—'

'Yes,' Benniman said. 'They're very sincere about their psychoses, I'm afraid. It is very real to these shapeshifters and vampires and blood ritualists.'

'Do you have any documented material on them?' Jack asked.

'I have the galleys of my book about them. The book is going to be published in New York next month, as a matter of fact.'

'Could you . . . Would you let us look—'

'Of course, Lieutenant Parisi. As long as you don't quote me without permission. You're aware of copyright laws, I'm sure.'

'We won't steal your stuff, Doctor. We just want to have a handle on where these people are.'

'I'll make a Xerox copy of the galleys for you if you'll promise not to re-copy them and return my copy to me in two weeks.'

'It sounds like a deal,' I told him.

We walked out of his office, out of his paranormal sciences wing, and out onto the gorgeous campus that was nestled close to a still-frigid Lake Michigan.

Chapter Nineteen

My son and I walked out of the downtown office after Michael gave his statement to the Prosecuting Attorney's Office. Three other boys from Michael's old grade school were there to make their statements against Father Mark, as well.

'You did the right thing. I admire you,' I told Michael as I started up the family van to take us home.

'Did I, Pa? Did I really?' he asked.

'There is no doubt in my mind,' I returned as I looked over to him.

He watched my eyes and then a slight grin took over his face.

'I wish there were no doubts in my own head,' he said as I pulled out of the headquarters parking lot.

Benniman's galleys were a series of interviews with cult members, self-proclaimed vampires and supposed were-wolves – among an assortment of other mental cases who imagined that they were spawned by 'the dark side'.

All of the interviews were done with anonymous subjects. No one seemed to be very proud of their 'situation' in life. At least not proud enough to give their real names and addresses.

However, it appeared that a number of these self-proclaimed vampires had a loose sort of organization that met from time to time at the various clubs and bars that Jack and I had already visited a few times. The clubs weren't

146

named, but it was pretty obvious that Merlin's was a haven for these wannabe bloodsuckers.

'We need to have surveillance on the bar,' I told Jack.

'We'll need the green light from the Captain,' he replied.

We took a walk from my office down the hall.

When we walked into his cube – the door was always open – he motioned with his forefinger to give him a moment. He was reading some file or other.

'Yeah? What do you need?'

'We need a stake on Merlin's for the next few days,' I told him.

'You want to help me out here, Jimmy?'

'We read that guy Benniman's book. He says these so-called vampires, like Samsa, meet on the full moon at what he called specialty clubs. One of those places is called Merlin's. We've been there before, so we know that there's no lack of monkey-whackers in that joint. I figure it's a good bet that Samsa will try to attend, or he'll send someone who's close to him.'

'What'll you do with the members of this Mickey Mouse Club when they show up, Jimmy?'

'Interview them. Try to get a handle on where this guy Samsa likes to spend time.'

'Those Goth girls frequent the place, Captain,' Jack added.

'You haven't persuaded any of them to talk about Samsa so far, Jimmy.'

'We'll get to one of them, sir.'

'I hope so. How much manpower is involved in this thing?'

I explained to him about two-man, six-hour shifts, round the clock for the three days including the full moon.

'Full fucking moon?' he asked.

'Their rules, Boss. Not mine,' I smiled.

The full moon was to rise in two nights. We had forty-eight hours to prepare. I didn't think Samsa would be dumb enough to appear in a public place like Merlin's. He already knew we'd seen his girlfriends there, so he'd know it was likely that we would be hanging around.

We only needed one talker. Just one who was willing to spill everything he knew about this ex-reformatory punk who had graduated to the big leagues of Murder One.

We eliminated the day watch because we were aware that nothing went down at Merlin's until the sun did. The Captain was relieved at the reduction of coppers it would take to eyeball the vampire hangout.

Jack and I drew the later shift of the two remaining watches – the shifts were 4:00 p.m. to 10:00 p.m. and 10:00 p.m. to 4:00 a.m. We didn't actually draw that later shift – we took it because we figured nothing would percolate until the very wee hours near dawn.

I started to bring headphones and jazz cds on stakeout. It reminded me of Doc Gibron and it passed the time.

'How're we going to know the vampires from the Goths?' Jack asked as we settled in for hours of waiting and doing little or nothing.

'I had a talk over the phone with our friend Leonard Bliss. He acknowledged that these sorts of lovely folks do indeed people the late night hours of Merlin's – usually around three or four in the morning on the date of the full moon. Leonard himself is rather spooked by these vampires. He was reluctant to come forth with any goodies about them until I reminded him of my close relationship with the parole officers in his district. Then he spewed forth with what I just told you.'

'We picked one bar out of a hat, Jimmy. They could be almost anywhere.'

'I don't think so. They might be in a few other joints, sure, but these guys seem to favor places where there's a high comfort level. Most of the other places we scoped out discourage these people from coming in. They run off mainstream business. Most bars want young females to show their tits and the rest of their equipment to entice young males to come in and swill it up before they take their shots at the mating call.'

'Merlin's is definitely not mainstream.'

'They don't have many havens in the public venue, Jack. We saw three or four likely spots in Samsa's hunting grounds – or at least where he's looked for victims to date. Merlin's is as good a place to start as any.'

I put the headset on and let Jack take a nap. I bought a couple of Dave Brubeck cds because Brubeck was one of the jazzmen that I didn't mind listening to when Doc forgot his earphones and played the all-night jazz station out of Evanston on the squad radio.

I watched the entry to Merlin's. They had a sign with a few lights on it that barely illuminated a five-pointed star.

I was midway through the first Brubeck cd when the Goth girls walked into Merlin's. It was eight o'clock – early for these young women. Nothing usually popped around here until after ten p.m., Leonard had explained to us the last time we were here.

I nudged Jack, but he was still awake.

'I saw them,' he said. 'Want to go in and corner a few of them?'

'No,' I replied. 'Let's see if there's any new blood going to join them tonight.'

Jack lay back against the passenger's-side seat. I was behind the wheel.

I returned to my jazz. It wasn't as bad as I thought it would be. I hadn't been a fan of beebop. Not like my partner, Harold Gibron. But the music seemed more appealing, now that I was left alone by my ex-partner. Jack was a rock fan, so there was no use trying to proselytize him.

It was after ten, so I woke Wendkos from a sound snore.

He sat up and rubbed his eyes.

'Anybody new?' he asked.

'No more Goth girls. But some black leather females who look like they know the ass end of a Harley pretty well.'

'Biker bitches?' Jack grinned.

'You ever called them that, your nards'd be ascending via the tips of their steel-toed bootery.'

'I'm sure you're right.'

149

I took off the head set. I'd been through the two Brubeck compact discs more than twice. I got out of the Taurus, pushed the front seat forward, and climbed into the back so I could lie down. It was too cramped in the driver's seat.

I lay down and closed my eyes.

I dreamed the dream about the gators or crocodiles snapping at me while I stood precariously above them on a very narrow ledge.

'Jimmy,' the voice said.

It sounded very far away. The voice was almost a whisper. *'Jimmy . . . I think he's here.'*

I sat up as if I'd been shocked by a naked electrical wire. 'Who?'

'Samsa. Asshole himself.'

'We're not calling for back-ups. Not yet. We're not embarrassing both of us with another false alarm.'

'I know. It's okay. Let's go in after him.'

I pushed my hair back with my fingers. I got up and reached for the front door handle and then I opened the driver's-side door. I pushed the driver's seat forward, and then I crawled out of the unmarked Ford.

Jack was already on the sidewalk, waiting for me. I pulled down my black leather coat, and I checked to see if I had all three weapons – they were in place, the entire trio.

'Don't pull anything out – including your dick – until we're sure it's him.'

Jack nodded, and then we walked toward Merlin's front door beneath the five-pointed, dimly lit star.

When we walked in, no one looked over at us. They were all engrossed in whatever it was that they were talking about. There were several groups of them. The Goth girls were in the far right corner of the room. They were the four that we'd interviewed previously. But if they knew Jack and I were present, they gave no visual sign that they were aware of us.

We walked over to the bar. Bliss wasn't tending the slab tonight. It was an older biker-type. He asked us what we wanted. He knew we were cops. You could smell the wariness

150

all over him. He was bigger than Leonard also. They had to have a gun stashed somewhere behind the bar – these kinds of saloons always did. I wondered if this guy was packing a sawed-off shotgun in a wooden slot, back there.

'Where's Leonard?' I asked the biker-bartender.

'Who the fuck's Leonard?' he shot back.

'The guy who used to tend bar here, ' I said. 'You know, the parolee who looks just like your younger fucking brother.'

'You're a cop, ain't you,' he said.

'What's your name, genius?' Jack asked.

'Wiley. Wiley Stokes.'

'Wiley Stokes and Leonard Bliss. All in the same profession,' I laughed.

'Look, you don't have to get a hard-on at me. What do you want?'

'We want to talk to some of your patrons, that's all,' I explained.

'Which one of my . . . patrons?'

'The ones who think they're nephews of Count Dracula, Wiley. The loose motherbrothers who think that this full moon's going bring out the fangs in their faces, Wiley.'

'I don't know nothin' about—'

'This is a murder investigation, my man. And I'll bet you share the same PO with brother Leonard Bliss. No?'

'Man, you don't have to yank my schwantz that hard . . . They're over there in the back. On the left. They're the fry-outs who think they can turn into fuckin' bats.'

I nodded at Wiley. Then I slowly reached inside my jacket for the Nine. Jack put his hand on his weapon, also, before we turned away from the bartender.

'Oh man, you ain't gonna shoot—'

'Not unless it's *you*, bro,' I warned him.

He took a step back from the bar.

'Just relax . . . Nod your head toward the artillery you got behind the bar,' I told him.

He nodded toward the middle of the wooden slab. Jack walked slowly around the bar toward Wiley, and when my partner reached the barman, he looked, found the sawed-off, double barreled weapon. Then Jack cracked it open and removed the two slugs inside and pocketed them. He put the shotgun back where he found it, and then he circled back to me. His Nine was still in his palm, as was mine.

'Keep very still, Wiley,' I whispered loud enough for him to hear and nod in affirmation.

I peered over to that far left hand corner. This place was murkier than just 'dimly lit.'

Jack and I walked over to a trio of young men sitting at a round table. There were no drinks on that surface of wood before them. The one that Jack thought might be Samsa was sitting with his back to us. Jack gestured with his right thumb toward the black-clad man just as we neared them.

'Why don't you turn around very very slowly,' Jack said softly to the figure with his back to us.

The other two vampires started to rise, but I gestured for them with the barrel of my piece to sit back down.

The unseen member of the trio didn't turn as Jack had ordered him to.

I took hold of his chair and yanked him around.

It wasn't Samsa, but I could see how Jack thought it might be The Count. In this dark, from a distance, out in the street, this guy could pass for our boy. He stood up when I took hold of his arm.

'If you're holding, don't even think about it,' I warned him. 'I will shoot you dead, right in front of your boyfriends.'

'What do you want?' the pale-faced Samsa lookalike wanted to know.

He was the same height and the same build. Even facially he could've been Samsa's younger brother. This guy wasn't twenty-one, but I wasn't here to card anyone for Wiley.

I patted him down and found that he was clean – no weapons. Jack did the same with his two partners.

'Let's take a walk outside,' I told them.

The Goth girls were now fully aware of our intrusion into their domain.

'Hello, ladies. Sorry, but we're not on your dance card tonight. Maybe some other time,' I smiled over at them.

152

They weren't even a little amused with me.

'Let's go outside, gentlemen.'

'Why? We didn't do anything,' the Samsa clone complained.

'Either you take a walk outside with us for just a few minutes' pleasant conversation, or I will roll you three fucks up for the drugs I know you must be packing on you somewhere. You still want to stand here and bitch, motherfucker?' I told him, my nose maybe an inch from his white snotlocker.

He backed off with his next 'face'.

Jack and I walked them outside, past a relieved Wiley who wouldn't get to blow any of these young wannabe vampires in half tonight.

Outside Merlin's the night air was dank, even though we were deeply into April, now.

'You guys know some guy named Samsa? Maxim Samsa?' I asked the three.

No one even blinked. Jack stood behind them. Neither of us was displaying firepower. My Nine and Jack's were back in the holsters.

'I know at least one of y'all is under age. I'm not here to roust you on a beef like that. I'm here trying to get some information on a series of homicides – and one attempted murder. You know this guy, if you're part of his crew, I want you to know you're going to go down with Samsa. You're on his crew, you're at least an accessory to murder. And that means very serious time. You won't be able to go play Count Dracula on the full moon anymore. Instead you'll become some inmate's bitch for a very long stretch in a public hellhole. I know Samsa never explained to any one of you the downside of associating with a murderer. I don't give a shit if you're in this for laughs or because you're getting even with mommy, I don't give a fuck what your story is . . . If you are not an 'associate' of Maxim Samsa, then you can spread the word. Ain't going to be no safe port or harbor for Count Fuckface. I'm going to have him, and if you don't speak up now and I find out later you were running with this prick, I'll send you down. Serious down.'

They didn't answer.

'Let me see the IDs,' Jack demanded.

They knew the next thing to happen was that we'd pat them down for funny pharmaceuticals.

The deadringer for The Count's name was Matthew Brine.

'All right . . . Fucking okay,' the Samsa lookalike blurted out.

We looked over at him.

'But these two don't know dick. Get them outta here, all right?'

I nodded toward the door of Merlin's, and his two pale-faced, associate undeads walked back into the bar.

The lookalike turned to Jack and me.

'Samsa ain't got no associates. He does his thing on his own. Look, I ain't no partner to what he does about the blood. He does that solo. When someone wants a vial to do ritual – he's the guy you see.'

'How do you contact him?' Jack asked.

'You ain't gonna use my name about any of this, are you?'

'Not unless you start stuttering, asshole,' I told him.

'Look. There's this underground newspaper. Real small. Basement publishing, you know?'

'Yeah? What's it called?' Jack demanded.

'*Legion of the Undead*,' he answered.

'Where do I get my copy?' I asked.

'You got to go to a 'zine store on Algonquin and Wright. It's called Tatters and Rags.'

'When do they come out with this newsletter?' I asked.

'Every Friday night. After midnight. Only a few people even know about it, man, so don't go using—'

'We'll keep you anonymous, Junior – unless I find out you've been lying to us or passing bogus information. How well you know Samsa?'

'I spent some time with him at St Charles. Nobody really knew that motherfucker. He was way beyond the buoys then. Now, Christ, now he's mid-Atlantic.'

'You be on your way now, young bloodsucker,' I smiled. 'Fly. Fly away.'

There was genuine hatred on his face. Some blood had entered his cheeks, and for a moment, just before he turned from us and joined his brethren, he almost looked like just another member of this sad-assed human race.

Chapter Twenty

Earvin the Tactical cop had his eye on our girl Joellyn.

'She been keepin' her distance from the main motha-brotha, Lieutenant,' Earvin smiled. 'She been playin' it real cozy.'

'That's because Riad's got someone on the pad downtown, here, with us,' I answered. We were sitting in my office, but Earvin was standing by my window. Someday when I retired, I was going to rent an apartment right on the Lake, and all I was going to do all day long was watch the sand and the water and the sky and the people who dotted all that landscape.

Earvin nodded. It was well-known by all the cops on the CPD that some of our brethren were dirty. It was that way on any big city force.

'I ain't talked to no one but you and Jack, here,' he nodded at my partner. 'I didn't even speak of it to my own Boss, Lieutenant McMahon.'

'If she's his teenaged, virgin squeeze, he won't be able to keep her at arm's length for long,' I said. 'Keep an eyeball on the two of them. He'll have to get his root wet, sooner than later.'

'I hope you're right, Lieutenant. Because I think your Captain is gonna pull the plug if something don't happen in the real near future.'

Earvin took one more look out of my window, turned to us, smiled, and then departed.

'He's been running loose all these years, Jimmy,' Jack reminded me. 'He isn't free because he's careless.'

I nodded in affirmation.

Jack watched me.

'I know. Doc told me about Celia Dacy before he went on leave. He said you might take this case a little too personally.'

'He's right.'

'Don't you think we ought to cut ourselves loose from it?'

'No. I don't. And I'll tell you why, Jack. It's because of the very thing we just got done reminding Earvin about. There are more than a few motherfuckers with their hands slimed with Riad's blood money. I know all about that shit because my family owns some of the members of this police force. You know the Ciccios?'

Jack nodded. Everyone knew them.

'There are some people around here who don't care if the money is guinea or black or fucking Bulgarian, Jack. They'll get on their backs, spread their legs and squeal like a porker for a couple of fazools. So I'm telling you we can't *trust* anyone else to speak for Arthur Ransom and Dilly Beaumont. And all the other stiffs Abu Riad's put on our meat wagon.'

He watched my eyes. He never looked away. It was one of the reasons I had complete faith in Jack Wendkos. Call it body language. I call it character. Something my young partner wasn't deficient in.

'He still better reach out to her pretty soon, Jimmy, or the Captain will short-circuit the whole fucking scenario.'

It was my turn to look out the window at the Lake.

We checked out the bookstore where they sold *Legion of the Undead*. It was a magazine – they called them 'zines in this oddity of a bookstore called Tatters and Rags – that I was unaware of. I'd never seen it next to *Time* or *Newsweek*, but then my knowledge of periodicals was severely limited. I read the newspapers and not much else that wasn't case-related.

The owner's name was T. Johnson. I asked him what the initial stood for.

'What initial, man?'

He was skinny and pale, just like many of his clientele. He was over six feet with very bad posture. It seemed as if he had a spine problem, but I didn't ask him. He'd probably answer, 'What spine problem, man?' His face was pocked by old scars from acne, it appeared. He hadn't practiced hygiene in some time, by the ripe odor emanating from his stained, black T-shirt. There were salt stains under the arms. He was a real charmer.

'When does *Legion of the Undead* hit your stands?' Jack queried.

'Never heard of it,' the ripe stinker lied.

Jack went across his counter and grabbed a handful of black T-shirt. There were only three or four customers in here with us, and they were all entranced by something on T. Johnson's shelves in the back of the store.

'You don't have to get like physical, man,' the stooped shop owner complained.

'I'm becoming very angry with your responses, *man*,' Jack smiled at him with a handful of grungy T-shirt still clutched in his right hand.

'Okay, okay. Let me go, huh?'

Jack released him.

'Yeah. We carry that mag.'

'When's it due?' Jack continued.

'Like tonight . . . but it comes out real late. Like after midnight. There aren't many copies – three or four in here – and someone always buys them out in like a half hour after they arrive.'

'These customers . . . they're a bit unique in lifestyle?' I asked.

'Oh, they're vampires, man.'

He said it so off-handedly that I nearly laughed in his face.

'Vampires?' Jack scoffed.

'No joke, man. These dudes are not to be fucked with. They're like a cult . . . and I could get fucked up just telling you about them.'

'No one's going to drop a dime on you, Tee,' I told him.

'I'm not worried about you, Officer Sir.'

He looked at a few of his spooked-out customers toward the back.

'The fuckin' walls have ears, as they say,' the proprietor said.

'They ever hassled you?' Jack asked.

'No . . . but I just sell their rag. And it's hardly worth it, man, because like I said, it only comes down to a couple copies a month. It's not like these motherfuckers intend to go mainstream, like *Playboy* or *Screw*. You know, the slicks, man.'

'What are these 'zines about?' I asked.

'Vampire shit. Don't look so amused, man,' he told me. 'These people take it for real. Blood rituals and shit.'

'I know. The guy we're looking for supplies the blood,' I told him.

'They can't, like, use animal blood or even blood from the Red Cross, say. It's gotta be fresh shit, from a real victim.'

'I know. You have any idea what a pint of that kind of blood goes for?' Jack asked.

'I'm just tellin' you what the magazine's all about, man. I'm not a member of their fuckin' tribe, dude.'

Jack grabbed him by the filthy T-shirt again.

'How much does a pint of the real thing go for, jackass?'

My partner was literally in his face.

'Five. Five "K",' he answered.

'Five thousand a pint?' I asked as Jack released him.

'That's the word. From the 'zine. I wouldn't know from experience. I ain't into that shit, like I told you.'

'Who's got money like that for a drink of the *real thing*?' I asked.

'These are bored, upper-crust motherfuckers who have odd tastes, Officer Sir.'

'You call me Officer Sir one more time and your nards are gonna ascend back where they were before all that crap on your face came into bloom.'

T. Johnson put a hand on his acne scars.

'That's kind of insulting, Off . . . *Lieutenant Parisi*. Sir.'

'Who are these upper-crust folks?' Jack asked.

'I don't know their names . . . but they'll be in tonight for the 'zine. After midnight, like fuckin' clockwork. I never see them, other than when that rag comes into the store.'

'How many?' I asked.

'Two, usually. A man and a woman.'

'And how do you know they're wealthy?' Jack asked.

'Their ride. It's a Beamer one time and a brand new black Jag, the other times. Come to think of it, the Beamer's black too. Everything about them is black. Except for the color of their skins.'

'What do you mean?' I asked.

'The guy . . . he's like an albino. Think he has like pink fuckin' eyes. Scary son of a bitch, man. She's not a lot less strange, neither. Platinum blonde. Good dye job. No fuckin' roots, you know . . . but they dress in nothin' but black. Top to bottom. All fuckin' black.'

One of T. Johnson's customers made her way to the counter toward the three of us.

The proprietor rang up about six sales. They were all magazines that seemed to be about the black arts – Satanism, blood ritual, shape-shifting and vampirism.

When she looked up at me and Jack, I saw she wore black eyeshadow and black lipstick. Her face was covered with white powder to enhance the bloodless appearance. Her fingernails were painted the same black as the rest of her cosmetics. She smiled, and I saw the extraordinarily long canine teeth she sported.

They were fangs. You could see the slight bulge in her lips when she stopped smiling or growling at us, or whatever it was she was doing.

She turned away quickly, and then she walked out the door.

'No blow jobs from *her*, man,' T. Johnson declared.

I had to laugh, and Jack couldn't refrain either.

'She's not the type who'd be lookin' for the usual body fluid, if she went down on you, man.'

'You have a very extensive vocabulary, you know that, cheesedick?' Jack retorted.

'Thank you, man,' he smiled.

160

When we saw what was left of his teeth, I was sorry he ever lifted his lips to give us a peek.

'It's the same two every time this *Legion of the Undead* comes out?' I asked.

'Yeah. The same two. Every time . . . I get the feel that the two of them are very connected people, Lieutenant. I don't just mean their big bucks. I got the impression they were tight with important people. I don't know how they could be livin' that kind of lifestyle without someone like you pullin' their plugs – unless they were joined at the hip to some players.'

'What kind of players?' Jack asked.

'You are gonna keep me out of this, no?'

I nodded, and I gestured with a roll of my right hand for him to continue.

'From what I heard . . . I hear shit that I should probably forget around here . . . I hear that they come from families with big political connections. You know. Well-heeled Gold Coast motherfuckers. Like that.'

'The 'zine arrives tonight,' I repeated.

'Not until after midnight. But they'll appear almost the minute I lay the copies on the shelves. It's like they know exactly when to blow through that front door.'

'Who publishes this thing?' Jack asked.

'Nobody anybody'd recognize. It comes out of a basement, man. It's like extremely crude. Some fucker does it with a computer and a printer and a stapler. No copyright – comprendo?'

'Personal publishing,' I said.

'That would elevate the quality,' T. Johnson explained.

'If these two don't show tonight,' I warned him, 'I'm going to think someone informed on us, Tee.'

The blush accentuated his pock scars.

He raised his hands in surrender.

'I always cooperate with the gendarmes, man.'

'If I think you dropped the silver coin on us with the albino and his lady, I'll sick Lady Dracula on you. You know. The sweetheart with the fangs who just left,' Jack grinned.

161

'You cops like to fuck with people's heads. Don't you.'

'It passes the hours, braindead,' Jack replied.

'You wouldn't really put that bitch on me, would you?' he begged.

'We'll be back tonight, Sparky,' I told him.

'What the fuck's a sparky?' T. Johnson moaned.

'It's the old nickname for the electric chair,' Jack told him, with a smile.

Chapter Twenty-One

We were waiting outside the 'zine store. Jack and I were in the Taurus, and I was once again emulating Doc Gibron by listening in on the jazz station from Evanston with earphones I stole from my eldest daughter Kelly's room.

I was starting to appreciate the jazz pianist Ahmad Jamal. I thought I heard he was from Chicago, but I always confused Jamal with Ramsey Lewis, another piano player I was learning to admire.

Before we arrived out here by the underground magazine store, I had done some phoning to Tactical about Joellyn Ransom. She had not been spotted anywhere near Abu Riad in at least three weeks. In fact, Tactical hadn't eyeballed Arthur's granddaughter for a month. I made a mental note that Jack and I were going to have to have another face-to-face with the young lady I was convinced had been involved in the demise of her grandfather.

And I received a call a few hours earlier from the Prosecutor's main office that Father Mark had indeed been indicted for child molestation. They seemed confident that my son Mike would have to take the stand if there were a trial. I called Mike after I spoke with the Prosecutor, and my son never blinked when he told me he was ready to serve as the state's witness against the priest. I almost choked up during the conversation with my boy because I don't think I had ever been as proud of him as I was when he responded as he did.

'You sure you want to see this through,' I told him.

'Yeah. I'm sure, Pa.'

'If he's got a good lawyer, he'll try to make you look like you were compliant.'

'I know, Pa. You already warned me.'

'It's no holds barred in a courtroom, Mike. That's all I'm saying.'

'You don't need to protect me, this time, Pa. I got it straight in my head.'

'You certain?'

'Pa.'

'Mike ... I ... '

'I can do this thing, Dad.'

My chest swelled, and I wanted to hold him, but he was too big for public embraces.

It was well after 1:00 a.m. We were still awaiting the albino and his lady friend with the great root job. The radio station I was listening to was doing a tribute to The Modern Jazz Quartet. Just when they were about to play the Quartet's Greatest Hits, a black Jaguar pulled up to the curb in front of the 'zine store.

The albino had long, platinum blond colored hair – just like the tall, willowy female creature who got out of the passenger's side of the black Jag.

We let them both enter the building. I wanted to give them time to grab a copy of their favorite vampire periodical. When I figured we had waited long enough, Jack and I got out of our copper ride.

They had just been rung up by the proprietor of the mag shop. We had our IDs in their faces as they turned to see who was behind them. The white-haired albino showed us both a pair of no-shit fangs and he *hissed* at Jack and me. Before I could control my instincts, I saw my own right arm and hand with the .44 Bulldog at the end of them both extended and pointing right at the fangs the albino had flashed us with.

'Jesus, man!' the male blurted.

He'd closed his mouth very quickly.

I could see the protrusions beneath the skin of his girlfriend's cheeks. She opened her mouth and bared her set of false fangs for Jack's benefit.

The woman didn't hiss when she bared her over-large canines. But the effect was still a bit discombobulating, to say the least, because the next thing I saw was Jack's Nine in the lady vampire's face.

'Shit, man!' she protested.

'We don't bite, for Christ's sake,' the albino exclaimed.

'Funny, you had both of us fooled,' I told the two.

Jack lowered his piece, and then so did I. When we saw that they weren't going to employ their unusual choppers, we put the weapons back in our holsters. I could hear the two children of the night huff out some air of relief.

'What is it you want?' the blonde she-vampire asked.

'We'd like to know all about that special little publication you're both palming in your cold-blooded hands.'

The female didn't flash any of her teeth at me.

We brought them down to headquarters in the Loop for questioning. They both protested before we drove them down to our offices, but after they'd seen us react to their fang-baring, they were still a bit in mild shock. So they remained passive and quiet on the ride down here. .

They sat close together, across the table from me in the interview room.

'We know that you know Maxim Samsa. If you deny it, I promise I'll have you here for hours – especially if you try to lawyer-up on us,' I told them.

I was seated, but Jack stood in the gloom of the corner behind me. His arms were crossed in front of him.

'We haven't done anything—'

I looked into his slightly pink eyes.

'There have been two women murdered and another almost made it a trio. If you don't tell us where we can find Samsa, I'm going to make sure you both wind up as accessories to murder.'

The last threat was effective. They both sat up attentively.

These were a couple of dilettante vampires. It had become a little too real, now that their asses sat in a copper building.

'Look, I didn't know—'

'Where'd you think he got that five-thousand dollar vial of blood from?' Jack queried from the dark of his corner.

'He told us he got it from a hospital where he was working,' the woman told us.

'That's right. We had no idea—'

'You read the newspapers?' I asked them.

'No,' the albino retorted.

'So you never heard that Samsa was wanted for these killings?' Jack shot at them.

'No,' the woman replied.

'You're lying,' I told her.

Suddenly there was a trace of almost human color in her ghastly cheeks.

'But that's not what I asked you. I want to know where we can find your blood supplier. You better move this along, or I'll have you both in a cell, waiting for your very high-priced attorneys.'

She looked at the albino, and then their glances locked. He drummed his fingers lightly, and then he transferred those pink eyes onto mine.

The apartment was a part of an old warehouse that was in the process of being transformed into living quarters for up and coming yuppies on the near north side. Our two favorite shape-shifters had spent very little time abstaining from squealing on Samsa. The albino had given us Samsa's new address just after I threatened them both with accessory to murder again.

Samsa was on the top floor. The entrance to the building had no security system, so we just opened the door and entered. There was no elevator, so we had to ascend the four flights of steps. Two uniforms accompanied Wendkos and me, and six other patrolmen were surrounding the perimeter on the outside.

When we got to the top of the steps – I was first, and then Jack and the uniforms – I banged my .44 against the door to Samsa's crib.

166

No one answered the loud blows against the entryway. I slammed the handle against the door four more times, and when no one responded, I moved over and Jack laid a powerful foot to the handle. The entrance exploded open, and the four of us rushed in.

The living room – at least I supposed it was the living room – was black. No light at all, not even from the window that overlooked the street outside. I flashed the window with my flashlight, and I saw that Samsa had painted the windows black from the inside. I turned and found a switch for an overhead. It illuminated the room where the four of us stood, but only faintly. The bulb must have been a forty-watt job.

No one home, it appeared. So we walked toward the bedroom. There was no bed inside, just a mattress on the floor without any sheets or blankets.

'I'm surprised it isn't a coffin with his native soil inside,' Jack cracked.

Nobody was in a laughing mood.

One of the patrolmen cried out as if he were in pain, and we rushed out of the bedroom toward the bathroom. We saw the whiteness of the uniform cop's face because he had already flipped on the bulb inside the john.

It was in the bathtub. Blood. Quarts and quarts – perhaps gallons of it. The officer who'd found it had to rush past us out into the living room. The other patrolman couldn't hack it in there either, and he made his way out, as well.

The tub was two-thirds filled with blood. I knew it would be human without the ME or some MD telling me what it was.

We found a syringe that an undertaker might have used lying on the floor next to the tub. In the medicine cabinet were vials filled with the same scarlet serum. It had to be human, I was certain.

We searched the kitchen and found no clue as to where Maxim Samsa might be floating on his vampire batwings. We would have to stake this location out for a while, but my heart was descending downward because my policeman's intuition was telling me Samsa wouldn't be coming back to his blood warehouse. He was still one step ahead of us. He was living like a man on the lam. Samsa never planned on staying at any location for more than a few hours, I understood. He would be jumping squares ahead of us on the chessboard, always maintaining a distance between us.

We made the call downtown to set up surveillance, but I knew this tree would never bear fruit.

'He's too clever,' Jack murmured.

'Yeah. He's sly, all right. But no killer's uncatchable, Jack. This guy's no Jack the Ripper. We're not going to let him become a legend.'

I was driving back downtown.

'So how do we nab this prick?'

'We keep an eye on the albino and his playmate. They figure they're off the hook now that they gave us an address for Samsa. They think we'll move on, away from them.'

'They are just buyers, in this blood delivery business. No?'

'They had those goddam fangs made custom, Jack. They're not the dabblers I thought they were. They're into the ritual. And Samsa wasn't collecting all that gore for himself. He was peddling his goods for those big profits. I think we tail the albino and his high-maintenance old lady, and we'll spot the other members of this cult or whatever it is, and eventually we'll find Maxim Samsa lurking somewhere very near them all.'

The surveillance came up with nothing on the warehouse location. Jack and I tailed the albino and his girlfriend, whose names were Richard Cooley and Agnes Dickinson. They were both wealthy offspring of big money on the Gold Coast, as Jack and I had surmised because of their expensive automobiles and addresses.

The two never went out during daylight hours. We had round the clock eyeballs on them, and the dayshift never saw them emerge from the expensive penthouse they cohabited on Michigan Avenue. They moved around at night when Jack and I were on them.

They played it cozy for the first few days we were behind them. Maybe they were frightened that the police were indeed watching. But about one week after our interview, they took a ride in the black Jag to Highland Park, one of the elite suburbs of Chicago. It was three in the a.m. as we cruised north on the Outer Drive.

They arrived at an estate in Highland Park that lay on at least ten acres of wooded property. Whoever lived here obviously didn't have to worry about mortgages and his kids' orthodontia. This was an *estate*, not just some lavish home.

'We're out of our jurisdiction,' Jack warned me.

I took my cellphone and called the local police via 911. They put me on hold.

But not for long. I talked to a Lieutenant Jorgenson of the Highland Park Police, and he offered to send out a few patrol cars as back-up – which I accepted for political reasons – it was his turf, not mine, that we were treading on. You didn't want to make enemies among your own brethren when you were on the job. So it paid to be polite.

We waited until the Highland Park cruisers pulled up next to the Taurus. We were parked at the entry gate. There was a security system.

'We go over this expensive fence and your department's getting a call, no?' I asked the sergeant in the first squad car.

'Yessir, Lieutenant. Their system sends out a warning to our office. Right.'

'So can you ignore the warning call, this time?' I asked.

'We can respond very slowly, Lieutenant Parisi,' the sergeant smiled broadly.

'These very wealthy folks may be engaged in a very strange rite, Sergeant.'

'Really? What kind of rite, LT?'

'Satanic. Black arts. Something to do with vampires. Paranormal shit, I'm afraid.'

'Is that illegal, sir?' the sergeant asked.

'No . . . but the blood they're using in the ritual may very well be the stuff they acquired from Maxim Samsa.'

The sergeant perked at the mention of Samsa.

'He's the guy who—'

'Yes, Sergeant,' Jack affirmed.

'You two go on, then. We'll charge in if you think they're using goods from a murder scene. That'll be our grounds to come help break up their little get-together.'

Jack and I walked down from the main entrance to a less conspicuous stretch of chain-link fence. It was safe to assume that the security system would pick up on our ascent over the six foot fence, but the Highland Park cops would give us some extra time to assess whether or not there was just cause for entering the estate.

Jack bounded over the chain-link easily. It took me a great deal more effort than it took the junior partner. We walked as quietly as we could toward this mansion on the north shore. I could only hope the owner didn't let dogs roam his compound.

The night was quiet. It was only a few hours before dawn. The near-dawn air was humid and sweet.

The living-room windows were uncovered since the house lay well back from the road and any prying eyes like ours. Jack and I stood about fifteen feet from that same window, but we were concealed by a large thorny elm. I recognized the tree by the sharp pain I received when I nudged the thorny trunk.

'Shit!' I whispered loudly enough for Jack to hear.

I showed him my tiny wound on the tip of my right thumb.

We looked into the window and saw all we needed to see in order call in the cavalry. I called the Sergeant from Highland Park on my cell. Their communications center patched me through with the number he'd given Jack and me.

'They're in the middle of some ritual, all right,' I informed the Sergeant. 'They're using what appears to be blood. There's no way of telling if it's human, however . . . What do you think, Sergeant?' I asked in a very soft voice.

The chanting of a dozen people in black robes was audible, coming through that big picture window in the front room.

'I think we've got just cause for inquiring about the nature of this little get-together, Lieutenant.'

He broke off, I assumed, to call in for more back-up.

When I was nudged by my partner – the two of us still partially concealed by that murderous thorny elm – I turned and saw the dimly lit sight of a nude female lying on a table which was surrounded by the rest of the black-cloaked cult.

I couldn't make out faces. If Samsa was among them, the large hoods over the cloaks hid him from my line of sight.

Now an apparent priest held a scabbard above his head. Only the light from a fireplace behind the cloaked figures illuminated the room very dimly. The priest withdrew a curved blade from the stone-encrusted scabbard. He raised the blade above the midsection of the naked female lying on the table before him and the other cult members.

Jack and I didn't wait any longer. We tore around to the front entrance as the flashing blue lights strobed the grounds of the estate. Highland Park Police arrived in four more cruisers.

Jack didn't need to kick in the front door. The door was barely open, but it was indeed already cracked inward.

When we entered the hallway past the entryway, a dark brown pitbull stood in front of us. The dog bared its teeth. Jack raised his Nine toward the growling canine. I heard my partner cock the hammer.

And then a hooded figure appeared behind the dog.

'Fritzy! Sit. I said sit!'

The pitbull plopped its ass on the carpeted floor.

'Police,' I told the figure in black.

My hand held the .44 against my right thigh.

'Really?' the cloaked figure asked.

We rushed toward the living room, past the robed figure and the nasty-looking, but now quiet, pooch.

The other robed figures had their hoods down, now, and the well-endowed naked 'victim' was sitting up on the table.

171

'Are you guys really cops?' she smiled.

She got up off that same table, and as she did, Jack and I watched as her melon-like, perfect breasts bobbed like buoys in the ocean.

Chapter Twenty-Two

The night, tho' clear, shall frown –
And the stars shall look not down
From their high thrones in heaven,
With light like Hope to mortals given –
But their red orbs, without beam,
To thy weariness shall seem
As a burning and a fever
Which would cling to thee for ever.

The third stanza of Poe's 'Spirits of the Dead' was attached by tape to the toe of Marilyn Gurk, another drained-to-almost-the-last-drop loner who had just yesterday appeared on our updated list of missing women, aged thirty to thirty-five. We hadn't even had the chance to go to her apartment and check on her. The smell from her small studio attracted the nostrils of the building's superintendent, and he called the police. The uniforms who broke down her door telephoned homicide.

The small studio apartment was where Jack and I entered Marilyn Gurk's final chapter. She was attractive, had no immediate family in the Chicago area, and was generally known at her place of employment – August Realty – to be a very private person. She didn't date, didn't seem interested in relationships.

How did Samsa find her? She wasn't a member of the health club where our vampire-killer worked and where Samsa found his first two victims. He might have stalked her randomly, out in the street, perhaps, following her about to and from work. He might have observed she was on her own, almost always. Whatever it was, I didn't think we'd get a break like the health club connection because Samsa was too bright to leave us another pattern to connect his dots.

We'd had too many close calls with this guy. He was becoming a sort of legend in his own time to some of the homicides downtown. I'd get these sad headshakes from a number of my homicide brethren when I encountered them at headquarters, from time to time. It was almost as if they were suffering with me, because everyone knew what those rare kinds of cases felt like – the unsolved cases. The killers who remained free from incarceration. They were a definite minority, statistically, but they hurt like hell. It was like an incurable ailment, something no MD could diagnose. There was no cure for that depression that came with an unsolved jacket. You carried it around like a cancerous lump that no chemo or radiation could touch and cure. It was worse than ulcers that ached without remedy. It was a pain so deep inside that no surgeon's knife could extract it.

Samsa was already legend, as far as the media was concerned. There was something on TV almost nightly regarding him or other self-proclaimed vampires. Sadly, teenagers were beginning to see Samsa as some kind of renegade anti-hero. The next thing would be the movie and its sequel.

The coverage on him was almost nightly. I hadn't heard as much material on the occult since *The Exorcist* movie came out. Samsa was a colorful Satan, the way they on the tube portrayed him, and he was only slightly less romanticized in the newspapers and mags.

Kids were mimicking him with Dracula masks, and it was far from Halloween. The Easter Bunny had been supplanted by this supposed shape-shifter. His legend grew daily. He was becoming Chicago's version of Charles Manson. All Samsa lacked were the murderous female acolytes.

Maxim Samsa had emerged from the minors, all right.

174

He'd gone from bush league killer to the *show* – the major leagues of murder.

His fifteen minutes of fame had extended beyond all of our expectations. He wasn't high 'profile' any longer. Maxim Samsa was full frontal, and his face never left the palate of the media. He was their fair-haired renegade bloodsucker, and Chicago now *belonged* to him.

We drove to Joellyn Ransom's apartment building. She had appeared on a missing person's list just two days previous, so she wasn't our case – yet. Not until she turned up dead, that was.

We knocked and there was no answer on the ground level entry door. Jack rang the second-floor apartment, they buzzed us, and we went inside. Jack flashed his badge at the middle-aged black woman who scowled when she opened her door and saw two white guys in her hallway.

'*Po-lice*,' she spat as she slammed her door shut.

We went up to Joellyn's flat and knocked, but there was no answer, as we expected. We tried the knob, and the door was unlocked.

We drew out our weapons, and then Jack pushed the door open wide.

'Police!' we announced ourselves.

Not a sound from inside.

'He's done her, Jimmy,' Jack declared as we stood with our guns pointed at nothing we could see.

'Just because she's a missing person?' I smiled.

We both knew that the longer she was missing, the better the chance that Joellyn Ransom was dead.

The electricity had been turned off, so the only light we had came from our flashlights. We made our way from room to room, but the place was bare. There wasn't a piece of clothing or a remnant of a tenant to this apartment. The place had been stripped to the bone marrow, from what we could see.

'If Riad killed her, we won't find her unless he wants her found. He performs pretty much the way the Ciccios do their thing, when it comes to killing.'

Jack knew the Ciccios were the renegade side of the Parisi clan. He'd been with me for two of the encounters I had with my family on the sinister side. We'd gone for information a couple of times, and the Ciccios had obliged.

'There's nothing here, Jimmy. It's as if she just evaporated. Vanished.'

'That can't happen. Someone knows. Someone saw her after she left this place. The two yos missing their faces in that alley wouldn't have seen it. But their remaining partner from the trio might have seen something. He's always somewhere close to Abu Riad, our guy in Tactical said.'

We made one last sweep of Joellyn's residence. It was a place where a seventeen-year-old girl became a partner in murder. It was where she learned about betrayal, something not on her course lists in high school.

Her schoolmates might be a place to begin looking for her, I thought. But I didn't say anything to Jack. We had both been reminded, numerous times, that Arthur Ransom and Dilly Beaumont were not considered high profile; they weren't prime-time players. Just two more statistics from the West Side. The West Side was not a source of highly solved cases. These were jackets that never found frequent closure, as it was called. You had to learn to let go, in these barrios. *Nobody knew nothin'.*

And now Joellyn Ransom had disappeared before we could tie her to the murders of the two oldsters, and perhaps to the two de-faced gangsters we found in an alley. Low profile. Negative recognition from the public as far as the media was concerned and as far as some of the upper echelon in the CPD was concerned, as well.

We kept our pistols in hand until we had locked the doors of the Taurus and pulled away from the curb.

Writers called it writer's block. The everyday mope called it constipation. Guys with limp johnsons called it impotence. It was a feeling of helplessness. Which I had never thought would overtake me. I couldn't go soft on the streets. I couldn't hit brick walls and bounce off without making a fragmentary impression.

But it was the way it actually was. No shrink could soft talk it into something else. No one could explain it away by telling me I was delusional. Every time I walked by my board, the board I shared with Jack Wendkos, I saw those red names. The unsolved murders. The uncollected perpetrators. The red words gnawed at me and kept me awake at night. Kept me awake so often that I had to sneak out of the bedroom and lie sleepless on our front room's couch. I couldn't roll around all night and keep Natalie awake. The Redhead had to go to work too. And she had no red names on her board, the one she shared with Terry O'Mally.

O'Mally was her age. Just recently divorced. Very attractive. Very popular with his male and female counterparts.

I thought I was beginning to hate O'Mally for being as attractive as he must seem to my wife. Being married doesn't make you go blind or deaf and dumb. Natalie came home nights telling me all these hilarious tales of her partner's lightning sense of humor. Women loved men who could make them laugh, and frankly I'd become an absolute drag for the last several weeks. Natalie noticed it, but she tried to avoid the conversation about it. My son Mike asked me, at breakfast the other day, what the two-ton monkey on my shoulder was doing there. This from a kid who was about to lay the wood to a pedophile priest in open court.

The black dog was becoming more like a black elephant. I could hear the creature scampering about when I tried to lay my head on the pillow to go to sleep at night.

Natalie caught me when I moved to the couch, one evening.

'What, Jimmy? What?' she demanded.

'I can't sleep.'

'Why? Because that phony bloodsucker is still on the loose? Come on, lover. You need to be a little more of a pro about this, Lieutenant. You know all about the occasional big fish that never wind up in the boat. It happens to everyone, and you know it.'

'It's not just him.'

Natalie sat on the couch next to me and began to stroke my head and hair with her gentle, thin fingers.

177

'Then who is it, Jimmy? *What* is it?'

'I'm too old for my job. I'm not competent at it anymore. This fuckin' goon is playing with me, and I got the feeling that ten years ago I would've hauled this piece of shit by his cheesedick balls into the lock-up. He wouldn't have slipped away, Natalie. I wouldn't have fucked things up. I wouldn't be running a lap behind this prick, the way I am now.'

'You want to retire, Jimmy?'

She kept stroking my hair softly.

'I could, in six months. I'll have my thirty years in, then.'

'Do you *want* to, I asked you.'

I took hold of her hand, and I kissed it.

'No. I'd die if I didn't have the work. You know me, Red. No hobbies, no sidelights. And you're on the job and the kids – except for the two girls – will be on their own soon. Hell, in a few years the little guys'll be in pre-school. Shit. What'll I do? Watch fucking television?'

'Get a security job. Lots of cops do when they retire.'

'I don't want to be a retired cop. It's like getting sent to the minors, Natalie, it isn't police work. It's . . . '

She bent down and kissed me.

'Then you answered your own question, Lieutenant. Retirement is definitely not on your agenda.'

'It's all cut and dried, the way you put it.'

'Are you going to sit around and troll for pity, Jimmy? Well you're trolling at the wrong fish, bub. You're not a pity person. Self-pity or pity from another source. So fagged-daboutit, guinea. This is a temporary setback. You're going to nail this bad guy, Jimmy. I can feel it in my bones. And you know about us Gael women and our natural intuition about things like this.'

'You won't even give me the courtesy of an "Aw, Jimmy, I know how you must feel"?'

'Hell no, Lieutenant. Getcha ass up and back into our bed.'

She took me by the hand and pulled me to my feet. She led me back to the bedroom, got me in the horizontal position, closed and locked the bedroom door, pulled off the T-shirt that covered all by its lonesome all that lovely flesh,

178

and then she started to perform her magic act on my tired but willing body.

Doc returned to work that following Monday. Without warning, without calling me on the phone. Nothing.

'What are you doing here? Thought you were definitely retired.'

'Ran out of vacation days, accumulated sick and personal days, and I got lonely for the view from your office.'

'No. Come on. Tell me what really made you come back.'

'Loose ends.'

'Like what loose ends, Doc?'

'Arthur Ransom. The little old lady across the street. I hear you were looking at his granddaughter as a possible accomplice to Mr Riad.'

'Where'd you get all that intelligence?'

'I talked to Jack in the lounge before I came up here . . . They're going to keep him with us on Samsa and all the other unfinished business on our board. I convinced the Captain I'd make him miserable if he didn't assign me back to our terrible trio.'

He stared out my window toward Lake Michigan.

'I never get tired of seeing that water. I tried a dozen times to get started on that novel I've been avoiding for the last twenty years, but I just don't have it in me, Jimmy.'

'Sure you do. It's just coming out slow. Sometimes it takes years. You always told me that story —'

'Maybe. But I do know that things aren't finished with me and you and those little fellows on our unfinished business list.'

'So Mari kicked your lazy ass out of the house? Is that the real picture?'

He pointed his finger like a gun barrel right at my face, and he snapped his fingers.

The family doctor made clucking sounds.

'It was one-fifty over one hundred, Jimmy. Not good. And don't tell me it's the pain from your sinuses driving that bottom number up. I think I can smell stress in these nostrils.'

He upped my dosage on one of my beta blockers, but I never told him about the black spots I'd begun to see from time to time.

The spots were getting bigger and bigger. And one day I figured they'd cover all the landscape before my eyes.

We interviewed the entire crew from that little black magic get-together in Highland Park. No one had a clue about the current whereabouts of Maxim Samsa. No one knew where he hung out, now that every cop in northern Illinois was looking for him. Nobody knew nothin' – it was remarkably similar to the response we received on the West Side.

But this was the big-time case. This was the magna profile jacket that everyone talked about. It was the source of pressure that Jack and Doc, now, and I felt pushing us along, like the cold hawk blustering off the Lake in January. It drove you from behind or it pelted you in the face, but that force was always there.

No one mentioned Arthur Ransom except for our friends in Tactical, but those guys didn't give two shits about who or what made headlines. The Prosecuting Attorney's Office never gave us heat about Ransom's demise or about the disappearance of his granddaughter, Joellyn. It was Samsa. Always Samsa.

He had delivered his third slice of Edgar Allan Poe, and the newspapers were filled with it. The paranormal, the supernatural, always sold newspapers, even if Samsa was nothing but flesh and bones. It grabbed the city's attention. They couldn't get enough of vampires and vampire cults and shape-shifters in general. The book Chicago was reading was Bram Stoker's *Dracula*, even if it had never been featured on *Oprah's Book Club*.

My son Mike was asking me questions about how the Samsa case was going. The Redhead knew better than to inquire. I was fielding phone calls and e-mails from all the slick magazines and talk shows in the United States. I refused them all.

The Captain had to get cops to work security around me when I went out in public, otherwise a dozen microphones would be pointed at my chin while a dozen remote TV cameras followed close behind.

'We need to find Joellyn Ransom,' the regenerated Doc Gibron pronounced in my office while Jack Wendkos stood sipping at a can of lemonade.

'The West Side'll be the only goddam place these assholes from the media will leave you and us alone,' Doc grinned.

Chapter Twenty-Three

Doc was back with a vengeance. His earphones and jazz collection was now, once again, a staple of CPD equipment in the Taurus. Where we went, his bebop accompanied Jack and me and him. It seemed to lift me, having him back. I wondered if he had talked with my wife before he decided to return to the job, but it seemed like I never had a chance to ask him.

'Rico Perry. He's the odd man out,' Doc pronounced as we drove toward the West Side. This time there were no accompanying uniforms. Doc called it 'security.' It seemed Riad knew all of our moves before we made them, so we weren't going to announce our visit to the hood by letting one of Riad's ears on the CPD catch wind of our visit.

Rico was the guy we needed to squeeze, Doc told Jack and me. Rico was aware that two of his fellow yos had had their faces removed via a street cannon and that Joellyn Ransom was now missing in action. We wanted to see if Rico felt the heat of his being on scene when Arthur Ransom bled to death, along with his unfortunate cat.

We found him walking down the block where he lived. We pulled over to the curb.

I rolled down the window. I was riding shotgun, Jack was in the back and Doc was behind the wheel of the Ford.

'Rico!'

'Oh!' he answered.

'Talk to us here or talk to us where it'll be a lot more secluded. Your call, Rico.'

The tall, thin black looked up and down the block. No eyes to see him talking to us, he observed.

He got into the back seat of the car with Jack. It was dusk and it was too dim for anyone to observe him talking to five-oh.

'We're taking you to a special place, Rico,' I turned and told him.

'Y'all tryin' to get me waxed?'

'No. Not at all . . . You're a made man anyway, aren't you?' Jack smiled.

'You five-oh always fuckin' wid me. Why?'

'You mean why would we be bothering a stone fucking killer like you, Rico?' Doc laughed.

'I ain't done no—'

'Please. Save the bullshit for the grand jury,' I told him. 'We're trying to offer you a way out.'

'Way outta what?' Rico Perry demanded.

'Life in prison, asshole. Whatta you think the Lieutenant means?' Jack hissed.

'I told you I ain't—'

'Whole fuckin' block knows you and those two now-faceless motherfuckers burned Arthur Ransom and Dilly Beaumont down. You think we're stupid, Rico? We know you're dirty, dirtier, dirtiest. Shit, we got two of your bro yos in the lock-up now who can't wait to roll over and squeal on you just for a reduced sentence,' I told the black kid in the back seat.

We pulled into a White Castle at the periphery of this West Side. We parked the Taurus, got out and sat at the bar inside.

'Ain't this special, Rico?' I smiled. 'Dinner with the five-oh at the Castle. Fuckin' sliders for everyone, mah man.'

I grinned at him, but there was no joviality on his hand-some African face.

The girl took the order from me. I asked for a dozen cheesesliders and four Cokes.

'Get me a order of them french fries,' the banger blurted at the girl. When she looked over to me I nodded in affir-mation.

183

'Did you kill Joellyn Ransom too, you piece of shit?'

I took him by surprise. I had him by the collar of his black leather, thigh length jacket, and he was shocked at how close and in his face I had suddenly become. The White Castle was deserted at this hour. The Castle did their main business at lunch and late at night. It was too early in the evening for them to be jammed.

'What the fuck you talkin'—'

'I'm through talking, Rico. I'm gonna pull your fuckin' plug. I'm gonna let your bossman know you squealed on him and that you said he burned Joellyn Ransom down because the bitch got greedy and wanted a real share in all that fed money Riad's gonna claim with that urban renewal shit right under Arthur Ransom's old crib. Riad was poking that little bitch, wasn't he.'

'I don't—'

'How long you think you're going to last when I spread word that you dropped the dime on Abu Riad for Arthur Ransom. We offered you a sweet deal and a reduced sentence on Arthur if you'd implicate the head banger. And how could you pass up a sweet deal like that?'

'You ain't got shit. You bluffin' and bullshittin' me!'

'Try me, you punk-ass motherfucker. Just try me!'

I let go of his collar just before our food appeared before us. The three of us cops went right at the cheesesliders that I divvied up by four. But Rico sat with his eyes planted on the cheeseburgers and Coke and his hands flopped at his side.

We made haste at cramming all that wonderful cholesterol down our gullets. Rico sat still. As if he were a stone image planted next to me at the White Castle counter.

'You ain't got shit.'

'Deon Jackson,' Doc said softly.

That got Rico's attention.

We didn't have Deon Jackson, who wasn't related to Charles (Abu Riad) Jackson, in our hip pockets, but it was a calculated maneuver on Gibron's part. He knew, as the other two of us did, that Jackson had been feuding with some of the younger members of the Vice Kings. Rico and his more newly blooded brethren had been at odds with some senior gangsters – Jackson being a part of that senior faction. This was all gathered information from our Tactical cops who had penetrated the Vice Kings for intelligence.

'I don't believe y'all,' he retorted.

'You can sing the same song to us as you wave bye-bye from the paddy wagon that'll ride you to the cell you'll be sharing with some buttfucker for the next forty years, Rico,' Jack told him.

Rico stood up.

'I want to go back. You ain't gonna charge me, then I want to go home right now.'

'Wait 'til I finish this last cheeseslider,' Doc told him.

'You ain't gon' pull this bullshit on me.'

'You're right. You're too smart, Rico. Charles Jackson, aka Abu Riad, will be tickled ebony to hear you had this modest repast with the Chicago Police Department.'

'Go on. Tell him. I ain't buyin' you bullshit, man.'

'We already got a pool on you at work, Rico,' I told him.

'You got what?'

'A pool. On who guesses the day you turn into ground chuck, motherfucker.'

Rico stared at me with a glance of genuine hatred.

'I want to go home. Now. Or I call my attorney.'

'Okay. Just let me finish this Coke,' I told him.

I sipped at the soft drink slowly. I knew the kid's eyes were burning into my back.

Finally I rose, paid the waitress for the full bill, and then we escorted Rico Perry back out to the parking lot.

'You think he'll roll?' Jack asked after we'd deposited the teenaged gangster back onto his home soil.

'I think he's got some serious thinking to do. He might really think we're trying to bullshit him into a corner, but if we have any luck at all, he's going to get into Deon Jackson's face, just to find out if there was any truth to what we told him.'

'Jackson isn't going to let this young punk make any accusations. If we have any luck at all, this'll light the fuse that's been begging to be lit between those two factions in the Vice Kings. We just might start a civil fucking war,' Doc grinned.

'Or he finds out that the three of us are really full of shit and that we made up the whole scenario with just the slightest bit of truth behind it,' I suggested. 'Either way, the way things were going, we got nothing to lose. Maybe we'll get a real special sideline seat for a little internal *humbug* among our favorite group of murderers.'

'It's not personal with you and Mr Charles Jackson aka Abu Riad, is it, Jimmy?' Doc sneered.

'It sure as hell is. Always will be.'

'Good. Now it sounds like you got your hard edge back on.'

I was going to ask him what he meant, but he walked out of my office abruptly.

Then I knew he had talked with Natalie before he decided to return to our thing, homicide.

A few days passed, but we heard no rumblings from the West Side through our Tactical contacts. I really thought that a kid like Rico Perry might flip on Riad, but you never knew, with these bangers. Sometimes their fidelity was as true as the Corps or the Outfit's, here in Chicago. Sometimes it was a race thing; sometimes it was just a perverse matter of honor, or what passed for honor in the barrio, in the hood.

Doc wanted to re-interview every 'vampire' from the mini orgy in Highland Park. He said he wanted to check out the nude, especially, because he'd felt left out, having missed the whole bust.

'Great tits,' Wendkos informed the now-senior partner. 'But not monumental. And how're you going to get her to flash you in the interview room?'

'*Ve haf our vays*,' Doc grinned slyly, doing his best movie-Nazi impression.

My wife's career was flourishing. If I lived long enough, she would probably wind up running Homicide. But the Captain was my age, and like me, he never planned to give up the ghost or the ship. All we both had was this job. The Captain didn't even have the family. He was what we used to call a lifetime bachelor. It seemed that no one knew anything about his personal life. And no one ever seemed to inquire.

Natalie had made three homicide busts in the last three weeks. All of which were considered very high profile cases – none of them were no-brainers or slam dunks. They were difficult investigations, but she and her partner Terry were on the inside track, going up rapidly.

If I weren't so proud of her, I would have certainly been jealous. The Redhead was on a hot streak, and I was still on my treadmill, treading nowhere fast. The set-up with Rico Perry was desperation. It was doing something when you couldn't do anything. My life was inertia, just then. I was the giant rock at rest.

Samsa was my burden. Arthur and the West Side killings were jobs. It wasn't because of that same old song about profiles. Samsa prodded me – like that white leviathan in *Moby Dick* plagued Ahab. Call it an obsession. Call it a burden or a fixation or whatever it was. But it haunted me.

Not because there was anything supernatural about Samsa. I knew he was just a man. Just a very evil individual. And he'd had the better of me in every encounter to this point. He had me reeling and ready to retire. I'd been on the verge of quitting, and Samsa was the reason. He was the match that met my tinder.

Then Doc had returned. He got us rolling toward Abu Riad – even if it were an outright longshot. But he had taken action. He was what I needed. Natalie couldn't provoke me as he had because Gibron knew where all my buttons were. Jack was too young and polite to kick me in the ass and tell me to get on with it, but Doc knew just where to aim his big front toe.

We brought in the vampires from Highland Park. The list included financiers, lawyers, psychologists, two beauticians, and an undertaker.

'He's the guy we hang out to dry,' Doc said to Jack and me before we entered the interview room.

The undertaker's name was Gregory Corso. He was thirty-eight and single. Short, fat, balding, he looked like a lifetime loner.

He had his own mortuary on the Northwest side. He'd inherited the place from his father.

'So it was you who supplied Samsa with those mortician's needles,' I said even before we sat down.

The balding man was already sweating heavily. His brow was pocked with droplets and there were gray stripes beneath each armpit on his long-sleeved white shirt. The cufflinks were gold with diamonds set in their middles.

He looked taken back. He had agreed to talk to us without a counselor because he knew he had nothing to hide, he'd told us.

This time I had made a fortunate guess.

He colored deeply and the sweating seemed to accelerate. I would soon need to hand him a bath towel.

'We saw evidence of your "gifts" to Samsa at each of the crime scenes, Mr Corso.'

'Jesus,' he whimpered. He couldn't seem to get his mouth to work.

Doc looked over at me with a smile of encouragement. We were down big in the bottom of the ninth, and he and Jack and I were aware of it. It was time to pull something out of our collective asses.

So I continued to take my shot at him. I could see that I had guessed right. He and Samsa were not strangers. His was not a one-time chance occurrence wherein his life and Samsa's intersected by chance.

'You're an accessory to at least three homicides, Mr Corso. I once more want to remind you that you may ask for an attorney at any time during this interview, and then we have to immediately shut down.'

'But I never knew . . . He told me he was studying mortuary—'

'How'd you figure he acquired that human blood for your little club meetings?' Jack asked.

'I told you! He told us he'd been robbing blood banks at several hospitals. Surely you don't think that we—'

'Think that you innocent bloodsuckers would resort to murder to procure the essence of your ritual?' I asked.

The blood drained from his face altogether, then. I thought he might become physically ill.

'You had no idea that he might be the Maxim Samsa that all the newspapers and media were talking about. You want us to buy that scenario, sir?' Doc demanded.

'*Yes*!' he cried.

'All right . . . okay . . . ' I said. 'Maybe you really weren't aware. But you got to believe that a jury would have difficulty believing that someone involved in a group, a cult, like you are . . . You do understand that it wouldn't cast you in a very favorable light.'

Corso was on the verge of hysteria. I thought he might lawyer up, but he started to weep, instead.

'If you can help us as at all, Mr Corso. If you can direct us toward Samsa with any information that could help us in apprehending him. It would go a long way in promoting good will between you and the police. We'd be inclined to lean your way, if you understand what I'm saying, sir,' I told him.

Doc handed him a handkerchief, and Corso mopped his brow.

'He's a coke freak. I mean big time. I have an acquaintance, he supplies me from time to time – do I have to implicate him, too?'

'Everything you tell us is in confidence. If we have to collect your connection, he won't know it was you, Mr Corso, who dropped on him.'

'Matt Cabrero. He's a Mexican dude with Colombian connections. He works for the Outfit too. You know, the Italians.'

Jack looked at me and smiled.

'Don Vito,' he grinned.

189

'We don't have time to fuck around with you, Corso. Where is this guy Cabrero?' said Doc.

Corso looked over and answered.

'He hangs in Old Town. Makes a lot of bread off kids. You know, tourists and teenagers. Likes to hang out in head shops. He won't be hard to spot.'

'Why?' I asked.

'His hair is white. White as snow. He's got a slow eye. Lost the real one in a knife fight . . . He can be very violent. I never saw him that way, but I always paid in cash.'

'A snow-white-haired Mex with one for-real eye,' I repeated.

'Yes. And he always wears a Texas Rangers ballcap. I think he's from south Texas, somewhere.'

'You've been helpful, Mr Corso . . . But tell me,' Doc asked. 'How the hell did you ever get hooked up with a bunch of self-proclaimed vampires?'

'I was . . . I was lonely. There were women . . . I was . . . lonely.'

Doc watched Corso's sad green eyes. Then my partner gently tapped his fingers on the walnut surface of the table in front of us.

Chapter Twenty-Four

The call from Tactical came just twenty-four hours after we'd interviewed the mortician, Gregory Corso.

The three of us drove the Expressway to the West Side and found three patrol cars surrounding a smoldering Chevy Cavalier. It was parked on the street next to a vacant lot. Someone had set the car on fire the previous night, and when the firemen arrived on scene to put out the blaze, someone smelled the terrible stench rising from the trunk. When the fire had cooled off sufficiently, they raised the trunk and found the body of Joellyn Ransom. The fire hadn't raged long enough for her body to be consumed, and they found a purse with her ID in the trunk along with her remains.

The body was in bad shape. She looked as if she'd been dead for several days, but the ME and the coroner would determine how long she'd been deceased, as well as whether or not she'd died in that trunk or had been killed and moved there. I assumed the latter case to be a lot more likely.

'She appears to have been manually strangled, Lieutenant,' Dr Gray pronounced after he'd taken a long look. 'Ligature marks on her throat suggest as much. We'll give it a much more thorough look when we have her on the table, of course. But it looks like someone shut off her air, Jimmy. Someone with very strong hands. The marks are very pronounced. She was no match for whoever it was.'

Gray moved back to his vehicle and then took off.

'This all started as a simple gangbanger initiation, as I

recall,' Doc said as they put Joellyn Ransom in the body bag and removed her from the Chevy's trunk.

'Just an old man and his cat. Just one more killing on this West Side and no big deal,' Doc lamented.

He had a far-off look on his face. Doc looked gray today. Much grayer than he had before he took off on his sabbatical. He was thinking about the two young black girls that he'd investigated long ago. It was the drive-by shooting case of two pre-teen girls that had nearly driven him off the job then.

His eyes met mine.

'It is our old friend Abu Riad, Jimmy. Isn't it. We know he did it or had it done, don't we?'

He was becoming increasingly agitated as we stood on this broken West Side sidewalk next to a still smoking vehicle that had hidden the corpse of yet another West Side youngster.

'We know it's him. He knows we know. And all we can do is . . . '

His voice dropped off.

He raised his hands.

'Hey! I'm all right. It's part of the business that we do. I understand. I've resigned myself to it, Jimmy. Haven't you, Jack? There are things which are never resolved. Cases that stay open. Wounds that never seem to heal. And you have to get your mind settled about it. There is no justice for some victims. No one speaks for them because they're simply the voiceless dead. I know that. Hell, we've all conceded. It happens. It just happens, and you have to go on as if all this made some kind of sense.'

He put his hands up once more, but then he dropped them. He walked back to the Taurus, alone.

'Jesus, he sounds depressed,' Jack whispered.

'Yes. He does,' I replied.

I walked toward our vehicle. Doc was sitting in the back seat, looking out the window toward the still-smoking Cavalier. The firemen were still on scene. They doused the vehicle with more water now that they were certain there was nothing to fear from a gasoline explosion.

Jack got in the car and started it up. He was the driver again. Doc and I liked him to do the wheel. It gave us a chance to relax and to think, between destinations.

No one spoke on this ride, all the way back downtown.

Matt Cabrero was underground, our Narcotics cops told us. The word had slithered out that we knew about him and one of his notorious customers, Maxim Samsa. It became more and more frustrating to have to worry about watching who you talked to at headquarters or even on the street. Abu Riad had ears among us and so did the Outfit. And Matt Cabrero didn't do the volume of cocaine trade that he did without the blessings and involvement of the Outfit, Chicago's branch of the Mafia. The Ciccios were one of the multiple families in the Outfit. They were connected to the Parisis by blood – they were the offspring of my father's (and my Uncle Nick's) sister Rosalee. She had married a Ciccio before the Korean War. I had gone to family dinners and graduations and funerals with the Ciccios. It wasn't something we looked forward to, but they were *familia*, and my dad, Jake, and his brother, Nick, did not disavow blood, even if the blood had become tainted. They were very traditional Italians when it came to family ties. We didn't shun them even though we knew the business they were in.

One of my cousins was murdered by The Farmer, a recent series killer that Doc and Jack and I resolved with a boost from my wife, Natalie. The Redhead shot him in our living room, and I made it there just in time to shoot him myself.

Because of that cousin's death, I felt I owed something to my sinister side of the clan. My head told me it wasn't a debt and I owed them nothing, but my heart and my gut told me something very different.

Jimmy Ciccio was a distant cousin of mine, but I hadn't seen him since grade school. He was the blackest of sheep on the Ciccio side because he dealt in narcotics. Prostitution and gambling were crimes, but they didn't have as much slime associated with them as drugs did. The old time mustache Petes wouldn't do drugs or sell them either. The modern Outfit crews made huge profits off cocaine and heroin and other street drugs, so it became commonplace to deal in the illegal pharmaceuticals sometime after World War II.

I hardly recognized Jimmy Cheech. He had become totally bald – the aftermath of a bout with cancer. He was thin, almost skeletal. And he had piercing gray eyes that reminded me of a fierce wolf on the prowl. I called him first to set up the face-to-face.

He met me at one of his Italian restaurants on the North-west side, not very far from my home. I didn't tell Jack or Doc that I was meeting Jimmy because I'd said before that I never again wanted to reach out to the Ciccios for infor-mation or help of any kind. But we were in that mode of desperation on Samsa, so I made the call.

'Jimmy? Jimmy, is that you?' he smiled.

His teeth were white and perfect, a complete, porcelain set.

I shook his hand. It was out there and I could hardly refuse it. We were family, I told myself.

We sat at a table at the back of his restaurant called 'Little Italy'. It was one of the restaurants that served as a front for his real business interests. He knew that the Parisis were aware of his real profession. He didn't make any excuses for what he did, and he never asked any favors from our side of the family.

I ordered the lasagna. Jimmy ordered nothing but a glass of some very expensive burgundy.

'Got no appetite, Jimmy. Not after this last batch of chemo. But they say the shit's in remission or whatever, so I'll get my weight back up when this shit gets out of my system . . . I haven't seen you since we were kids.'

'I'm here to try to get some help on locating a murderer named Maxim Samsa.'

'Yeah, I read about this little vampire prick in the papers. Very dramatic, no?'

'He supposedly does business with Matt Cabrero, a Mexican who's in sales in Old Town. Sells to kids and tourists.'

'And you want to locate this beaner so you can grab Samsa.'

194

I looked at his gray, wolf's eyes, and I wanted to get up and bolt.

'Why do you think I'd know where to find this guy?'

'He can't do volume unless he's got your blessing, Jimmy.'

'And why would I want to cut off one of my own fingers for you, Jimmy?' he smiled.

'If he's connected to a killer like Samsa, that brings a lot of heat where you don't need it.'

'Very astute . . . but if I flip the Mexican, then I become a fucking squealer, no?'

'It's just good business, Jimmy Cheech.'

'You're my namesake. But the Parisis and our clan were never tight. You had your road and we had a different boulevard, but you never asked anything of me before. I know you had dealings with some of our family, but you never tapped my shoulder. And I respect you for it, Lieutenant Parisi.'

The lasagna arrived with his second glass of wine. The restaurant was dark, but not so dark you couldn't make out the red and white squares of the tablecloths. We were the only two patrons sitting at the tables. It was early. His business came in after six.

'I'll keep out an eye for the beaner. I'll let you know . . . Aren't you going to eat?'

'I'll take it home in a bag, thanks. I've got to get to work,' I explained.

'Fuckin' vampires. This guy takes their blood, no? I thought only those Polacks from east Europe pulled that kind of shit.'

He got up and sent his piercing, gray stare at me again. I knew Jimmy Ciccio didn't have long. He was among the walking dead, too. But not because he drained anybody's vital fluids. His people killed you the old fashioned way, with a .22 slug in the back of your head.

'Been good seeing you, namesake. You take care, Jimmy P.'

I didn't hear from my cousin of the same first name for three days, so the three of us decided it was time to tour Old Town.

195

It was a tourist trap, a place where teenagers and out-of-towners came to find the ambience of the Windy City. There were head shops and titty bars and jazz joints that used to headline some well-known musicians, but now the neighborhood had become seedier, more run down. It became more common knowledge that these joints ripped off rubes who didn't know where the real action might be in this city.

But people still came here and the merchants still did business and uninitiated young people came down here to see what their parents had searched for when they were young. You could still catch whiffs of the doobies being lit in the alleyways and on some of the darker corners. This was Chicago *noir*. This was the dark side of the city in a way unlike the West Side and the Southside. The west and the south were the barrios. Old Town was still a hub for the hipsters and the wannabe hip. T-shirt shops, shops that sold bongs and pipes. Pornography palaces. Back alley joints where you could get a massage and a blow job for fifty fazools. It depended on how well paid off the cops were in order for you to find illicit delights in these establishments.

We weren't wearing suits or blazers or the usual detective attire that was expected downtown. We were dressed casually – polo shirt and blue jeans for Jack. Sports shirts and khakis for the two old men, Doc and me. Our weapons were secured in ankle holsters or beneath the light cloth jackets Doc and I wore.

It shouldn't have been difficult to sight this white-haired dealer with the Rangers' ballcap, but we didn't spot anything remotely similar to Cabrero's description. The streets were full of kids on this Saturday night. The music blared from the shops and saloons and discos and jazz joints. It almost envigorated me a bit because the sights and sounds and smells were the same as the ones I'd experienced when I was nineteen and twenty, before I went to Vietnam.

'This place doesn't change. It just gets a shade grungier every time I return,' Doc said.

'I kinda like this neighborhood,' Jack admitted.

'That's because you don't have to get up and pee seventeen times every night yet,' Doc cracked.

'Well I'll always have that to look forward to,' Jack grinned.

Doc slapped him on the shoulder.

'I'd give my pension to be your age again. So many women and so little time.'

It was one of Doc's familiar lines. As far as I knew, Gibron had been married twice and had been and was faithful to both spouses. He never even joked about adultery.

'Hey,' Jack whispered to us.

There was a man standing in the doorway of a strip bar just thirty feet in front of us. I couldn't tell if he was just hanging there or if he was some kind of doorman who encouraged clientele to partake of the flesh inside.

We kept our stares purposefully away from the guy in the ballcap. It was a blue hat, but I couldn't see if it had the Texas 'T' on it.

The three of us kept walking slowly toward the man in front of the titty bar. A few customers weaved their ways in and out of the place, but then two college-aged boys stopped in front of him. Then the trio turned and walked away from us. Jack and Doc and I picked up the pace and followed them. They took a left into an alley, but we were closing in. We began a trot to try and catch up. As we made our way into the gloom of an alley with a burned-out street light, we saw the three men huddled together. A transaction was obviously underway.

We found our pieces and took them from their ankle holsters and shoulder holsters.

'Police!' Jack called out.

The college boys whipped around and raised their hands. The man with the blue ballcap spun around and began sprinting down the alley. Jack took off after the runner.

The college boys appeared to have loosening sphincters.

'Relax, gentlemen. No one's going to shoot you if you behave,' Doc smiled.

Jack was on top of the ballcapped runner in less than a

197

block. Wendkos had been a boxer and he still trained and kept in excellent shape. The running drug salesman was no match for our guy. No contest. Jack could've caught Samsa too, all those months ago, but he slowed down because I stumbled and almost flopped. His weakness was his loyalty to the senior partner – me.

Wendkos walked the runner back at gunpoint. The drug dealer had his hands up on the way back to us.

'Go,' Doc told the college boys.

They looked at Gibron as if he were speaking Russian.

'I said go, girls!'

Suddenly it registered, and the two young men took off.

We looked at Jack's collar. He wore a blue Cubs' baseball hat and he had black hair. He was a Mexican, it appeared – a mestizo, an Indian. But he didn't fit Matt Cabrero's description.

We took him back to the Taurus anyway, and then we drove him downtown.

'You know Matt Cabrero?' I asked.

We sat once again in our interview room in the downtown headquarters.

He was a dark-complected Mexican Indian. You could picture him in the mountains fighting with Emiliano Zapata. Fighting with a machete.

'Never heard of the motherfucker,' he said in perfect *Ingles*.

We had caught him dirty. He was packing a load of cocaine and crack cocaine. The cocaine was for the rich college boys, and the crack was for the poorer 'heads' on the street. He had some heroin, as well, for the more well-heeled clients in Old Town.

'I guess you win a free pass straight to narco, then,' Doc concluded.

He looked at the three of us around the table.

'You all are homicides, right?' he asked.

'You win the bunny rabbit, yo,' Doc smiled.

'What do homicides wanna do rousting me?' he asked.

198

He watched us, but we remained quiet.

'You want Matt Cabrero bad, no?'

We continued to watch him.

'What's in it for me?'

'Let's go, tiny dick,' Jack said and stood up.

'All right, all right! Don't get no hardons! Maybe I know this guy. Maybe I know where he can be . . . located.'

'You have exactly one minute, asshole,' I told him.

'Don't get all huffed, Lieutenant . . . I know this man you want. You go blind on what happened tonight if I point you in his direction. Is that what this is?'

'You win yet another bunny rabbit, braindead,' Doc grinned.

'Maybe I can help you, then,' the Indian said.

He looked up at us and smiled like he'd just copped all five numbers on the lottery.

Chapter Twenty-Five

It was time to put some heat on Abu Riad. Doc loved to call him by his 'pre-slave' name, Charles Jackson.

We called him to come downtown, this time, because I felt he was a bit too comfortable in his own neighborhood, in his own home. He was accompanied by one of Chicago's finest ambulance chasers, Robert Geldman.

We sat in the interview room, the four of us. Jack was out chasing leads on Matt Cabrero from the information the Indian had given us in exchange for not arresting him on drug possession and sales. Doc and I sat opposite Abu Riad and his attorney, Geldman. Geldman looked the part. Well over six feet, graying sideburns, and a suit that cost the better part of my remaining mortgage.

'Let's begin by saying this is nothing more than harassment on the part of the Chicago Police Department, and more specifically the Homicide division,' Geldman smiled. Perfect choppers, courtesy of thousands of well-spent dollars on orthodontia, I was certain.

'We're here regarding an ongoing homicide investigation. You're here because you told our Captain you were happy to be cooperative. Now that we've done the perfunctory bullshit, can we get on with it?' I asked them.

Neither man was smiling. Only Doc showed me some facial amusement or bemusement.

'We've got a body, as you both know. Seventeen-year-old Joellyn Ransom. We know that this young woman had a relationship with your client—'

'That's a lie,' Riad hissed at me. His face was somber, maybe even angry. I began to wonder just how personal his connection was to the late Ms Ransom.

'Can't keep secrets in the hood, Charles,' Doc smiled at him. 'Everybody knows you were planting the turnip with Joellyn Ransom.'

Riad leaned forward toward Doc.

'You are a vulgar man, sir. I find it strange that a man with an advanced degree like yours—'

'Ah, cut the crap, Charles. Save it for the NAACP and the reporters. You're a common criminal. The only thing uncommon about you is the cooperation you get from the people you're sodomizing in your area of operations.'

'None of what you're saying has ever been proved in a court of law, and if you don't get down to direct questions – rather than personal attacks, Detective Gibron – we shall have to terminate this discussion,' the gray-sideburned lawyer demanded.

'You're almost as slick as your client, Geldman. When I want to smell some more fertilizer, I'll let you know,' Doc said. There was a slight hint of authentic anger in his words.

'Yeah,' I continued. 'We know you had some kind of a connection to Ms Ransom. We know she was strangled and dumped in the trunk of a car some local punks decided to light on fire just for grins . . . You didn't torch the car yourself because you wanted the body found. Joellyn was a message, just like Dilly Beaumont and the two gangbangers who lost their faces in that alley. And I know you don't know anything about any of this, Mr *Riad*, but bear with me for a moment. You're being investigated by the Federal Bureau of Investigation and the Internal Revenue Service.'

Riad's face showed just a blink of surprise.

'None of that has any foundation—'

I looked at Geldman, and he shut up.

'What's the matter, Charles?' Doc grinned. 'Didn't know that the IRS was looking at you too?'

'If we could stick to questions about Ms Ransom?' Geldman interrupted.

The glare between my partner and Riad was palpable. There was a thermal presence between the two of them. I had my personal thing with Riad regarding the murder of a woman I had loved. But Doc had gone beyond my private vendetta with this gang lord.

'Did you have a sexual relationship with Ms Ransom?' I asked.

He shifted all his venom toward me now.

'No. I did not.'

'You're certain? Because if we find any remnants of your DNA in her autopsy . . . Well, it'd be embarrassing for you, no?' I queried.

'You aren't going to find anything,' Riad said. His face had now gone to black stone.

'You must've used rubbers, huh?' Doc cracked.

Riad came up out of his chair and tried to get his hands on Doc's throat. I jumped up, came around the table and wedged myself between their clutching hands.

'*All right! Everybody sits back down!*' I yelled at them. Geldman was sitting like a petrified hunk of wood in his seat. But they finally let go of each other, and Doc and Riad sat down.

'It was that deep, huh, Charles?' Doc grinned at Riad.

'You don't know what you're talking about,' Riad fumed.

'And why is that?'

'Because . . . because Joellyn Ransom was my daughter.'

Doc was still in a state of near shock an hour after Abu Riad and his lawyer left.

'Where'd that fucking curveball come from?' my partner asked as we sat in my office.

'We can check it out, but I have the nasty impression his story's true.'

After Riad laid the bomb on us about Joellyn being his daughter, he explained that he was the girl's biological father. Donald Ransom, Arthur's son who had vanished into the woodwork of the barrio, had married Ophelia Johnson, the biological mother of Joellyn. Ophelia and Abu Riad had been lovers just prior to the marriage between Donald and

Ophelia, but mommy was carrying a one-month-old surprise in her oven when she married Arthur Ransom's son.

So Joellyn was Riad's daughter and had no blood tie to Arthur Ransom. She was still tied in to the old guy's death with the same motive of monetary gain via the old man's West Side property—

But our entire notion of Abu Riad being her lover and her murderer had just flamed out. We were back to nowhere. We knew Riad had Arthur burned. And Dilly and the two faceless gang members. But Joellyn's demise was now a bit more than shrouded in West Side mist.

'Who's left?' Doc said.

'You got me by the shorties, partner.'

'Did she have a boyfriend?' Jack asked. He had returned from scouting out Old Town in search of Cabrero.

'What boyfriend? We thought she was punching her daddy, remember?' Doc reminded him.

'So she might have had a boyfriend. Maybe the boyfriend thought the same way we did, that Riad was her sugar daddy, not her for-real daddy. Maybe he was jealous. Maybe he got carried away and squeezed a little too enthusi-astically,' Jack told us.

'A boyfriend?' Doc thought out loud.

'Why not? A crime of the heart,' Jack said.

We arrived at DuSable High School where Joellyn was a student. We talked to the principal, a man named Robert DeMarco, and he directed us to Joellyn's senior year counselor, Brenda Shea. Brenda Shea was a thirty-one-year-old African-American beauty. She had dark skin and a natural hairdo that wasn't long enough to be called an 'afro', like the seventies hairstyle. She had brown eyes and a tall, thin, lean body that grabbed anyone's attention. It certainly took hold of our focus as soon as we walked into her office.

When we were finished noticing her obvious charms, I finally re-acquired my speaking voice.

'Did you have any contact with Joellyn Ransom?' I asked Brenda Shea.

'Yes. I was her counselor, this past senior year. But she never finished out the year – as I'm sure you already know. It was tragic. She was an excellent student.'

'Did she ever talk to you about personal problems? You know, romantic issues?' I asked.

'From time to time.'

'Was there any particular boy she was fond of?' Doc asked.

'There were a few.'

'Anyone special?' Jack asked her.

Brenda smiled at Wendkos the way young women of any color always did. I didn't see a gold band on her finger, and Jack never wore his marriage ring to work.

'There was one boy who wanted to be her significant other . . . but she kept him at arm's length.'

'Who was he?'

'Another dropout, I'm afraid. And he was a year younger than she. She thought he was just infatuated with her. She kept turning him aside, like a puppy—'

'What was his name?' Jack smiled warmly at her.

'Oh, I'm sorry. I was babbling! His name was Rico Perry.'

She watched our faces transform from casual pleasantry to a far more somber mood.

We received the tip on Rico from Tactical just two nights later. He had a new crib just six blocks from his old apartment where he was supposed to be cohabiting with a mother and two younger brothers. The new flat was in an abandoned apartment building. He was living on the top floor.

We arrived at the West Side location with four patrol cars full of uniforms as back-ups. The kid was a killer, even if he hadn't burned Joellyn down. He'd done Arthur and probably Dilly and his two bros who got gunned down in the alley. We didn't know what his true body count was.

Jack led the way up the stairs. There was no lock on the entry because the building had been condemned and awaited demolition. The whole block was ready to undergo the steel ball.

We got up to the top floor and Jack banged on the door.

'Police!' he bellowed.

There was no answer, so Wendkos put his foot to the entry. This door still had a functioning deadbolt.

The door blew inward, and as soon as we were inside, we heard someone racing toward the back door. We ran after the fleeing figure, and as soon as we got to that back exit, we saw Rico Perry flying down the stairs toward the alley.

But the patrol cars were covering that escape route. Blue beams of light lanced the backyard where Rico Perry stood like a cornered coyote. There was no place for him to run.

'Up!' Jack shouted.

Perry raised his arms skyward, toward the black, night heavens.

Doc walked around behind the young man.

'You wouldn't be thinking of cutting me, would you, Rico?' Doc asked.

The boy reached into his black leather coat's pocket.

'Whoa!' Jack warned him. 'Use your left hand . . . slowly.'

Rico changed hands and went into that same pocket with his left hand, this time. Out came a long switchblade. He dropped it on the scraggly grass of the backyard.

'You carrying? You strapped, Rico?' Doc continued before he patted him down.

'Left hand . . . gently,' Jack again warned him.

He reached inside his coat toward the waistband, and he drew out a nine-millimeter automatic. He held it daintily by the handle, almost as if the weapon had a disease on it. Then he dropped it to the ground.

Doc handcuffed the boy, and then he patted him down to make sure he was indeed disarmed. The kid was clean, then.

'You had a big thing for Joellyn Ransom,' I told the handsome, athletic-looking black teenager.

'Naw.'

'Bullshit. We talked to your teachers, to your counselors. Everyone in that school and in your hood knew you had it bad for her.'

205

'They lyin'.'

'But she belonged to Abu Riad. She was untouchable, no?' I asked.

'I doan know what y'all—'

'You thought she was Riad's bitch, didn't you,' I shot back at him.

'*She wadn't no bitch, mothafucka*!' he shouted as he snapped himself upright from his chair at the interview table.

'No. She wasn't. You loved her, didn't you? You didn't think a badass like you, Rico, could ever let a girl, a woman, get to you because you're a stone killer. Right?'

He glared at me as if he was mentally cutting my throat. Doc and Jack stood in either corner. They were letting me handle this show.

'You let a bitch get to you and then you found out that she belonged to the head motherfucker. Yeah? But you didn't know, just like we didn't, that Joellyn Ransom was Abu Riad's daughter . . . not his bitch, not his lover. His blood daughter.'

Rico Perry couldn't hold back the change in his hard face from vehement anger to authentic surprise.

'Naw. She wadn't none of his . . . '

Then he settled back into his chair and the tears began to flow freely.

'You thought he was taking her away from you because he wanted her for himself. You were afraid of Abu Riad – everybody is. But you saw her on the street. You got into it with her and then you convinced her to come by your crib. You knew it'd be just the two of you. Maybe you used the piece or the blade to help her make her mind up, but you got her inside where no one could see and you put it to her. She was an old man's kept bitch. She didn't want you even though you were more her age, more her kind of lover. She kept putting you off. The other young bitches never said no because you were a big man in the crew, in the barrio. You always had a wad of bills from doing the man's dirty work, but you weren't good enough for his woman, and you couldn't handle it. She stuck in your head, in your throat, in your very guts. And you got angrier and angrier. She wouldn't have you. And then she disappeared for a long time – until you saw her on the street. What? Near Abu Riad's crib? And you stuck that Nine under her ribs and told her to come along. Because you were going to straighten this ho out – right? Am I right, Rico? Did she spit in your face even when you had the piece stuck in her side? Did she, Rico? *Did she?*'

'*Yes! Yes, goddammit!*'

I expected him to break down and sob, but he didn't.

He looked slowly at each of us. The heat of his hatred had raised the temperature in the interview room.

'She wouldn't have none of me. And yeah, I took her back to the crib. And yeah I had to put my piece upside her too. You got it all just right, Lieutenant. That make y'all feel big? It make you feel large? And I was gonna put a cap in her ass too, when she tole me how small I was. That what she kep' sayin', over and over. How tiny, how little I was. And I knew she was puttin' me next to him . . . but I thought she was his . . . not his *daughter*, man. Everyone thought they was . . . not his own blood daughter . . .

'So she kept sayin' it again and again, about me bein' little, small, just a goddam kid, and I took her by the throat and I squeezed and I squeezed and I squeezed until all that smile was gone from her face. The harder I went at her, the less of a smile she was showin'.'

'Then you dragged her downstairs and dumped her in the trunk of that car,' I said.

He nodded.

'You going to write me a statement or do you want that lawyer I offered you when we started all this?'

'I doan need no goddam lawyer. I just wish you'd stayed away until I could've killed that son of a bitch who—'

'You can still get him, Rico,' I offered.

'You . . . you offerin' me a *deal*?' he asked.

'No deals. But you can take Riad down with you.'

'How? How I can do that?'

'Confess to killing Arthur Ransom, Dorothy Beaumont and the two boys whose faces you blew off.'

'How do that get at *him*?'

'You tell the Prosecutor that Abu Riad, also known as Charles Jackson, ordered all those whacks. You say all that, and you can torch that motherfucker permanently.'

Jack and Doc stood quietly in opposite corners.

I looked at the young man – he was barely out of boyhood – across from me.

'Aw right,' he said.

I handed him the pad and gave him a pencil.

'Write it down, Rico.'

'Aw right . . . why not?'

He began to scribble out the beginning of the end for the man who had murdered, Celia Dacy. And for the man who had ordered the shooting that had killed Celia's innocent young son, Andres, out in front of Cabrini Green on a frozen winter's night with the hawk howling in from the east off Lake Michigan.

Chapter Twenty-Six

Now are thoughts thou shalt not banish,
Now are visions ne'er to vanish;
From thy spirit shall they pass
No more – like dew-drop from the grass.

Just when I thought I was on a roll with getting a confession out of Rico Perry and a deal in the works for him to flip Abu Riad, my worst nightmare came back with body number four. This time it was a black nurse who lived by herself on the near north, not far from the other three victims. Samsa left his by-now usual stanza from 'Spirits of the Dead'. There was only one stanza left to go in the poem, I saw, as I picked up Doc's copy of *Collected Poems of Edgar Allan Poe.*

I didn't know if it meant that he was planning only one more murder with the use of his mortician's needle, or if it meant he was moving on to some other poem with multiple stanzas. I was looking for some key, some clue, in the first four victims and the stanzas attached to each killing, but nothing registered.

Martha Daniels was victim four. Recently received her RN from the University of Illinois Chicago, and like the others lived alone with no immediate family in the Chicago area. We found the name of an aunt in Corpus Christi, Texas, listed on a page in Ms Daniels' file at St Edward's Hospital in Cicero, where she worked. We were in the process of contacting the aunt at the moment.

'He's just fucking with you, Jimmy P. He wants you to be all caught up in these little verses he leaves behind. This is an uneducated killer. He's sly. He's very very clever. But he's not used to thinking or speaking metaphorically – as we say in the academic world. He just picked out some morbidity from Poe. Any tenth grader would know about Poe's big fling with death – especially the death of a young woman. Samsa probably picked it up in some remedial literature class at fucking St Charles. Don't spin your wheels, Jimmy. He's got you dangling, he thinks . . . but we'll get him. I guarantee we'll have him, at the end of the day. He's not that bright. He keeps on killing on the same grounds with every cop in the northern half of the state after him. He's going to get caught in the thorns just like that bad old red fox always do, bro.'

Doc and I were standing outside the headquarters in the Loop. Neither of us smoked. Nor did Jack Wendkos. There were several other coppers out here with us who did, however. The three of us were in the minority when it came to tobacco use. Smoking had been forbidden in our offices for over a decade now, so the nicotine addicts had to take their breaks out on the street. We were so used to cops smoking that it didn't seem to bother us when the clouds of carbon monoxide breezed around us.

Jack Wendkos was looking for Matt Cabrero, as we all were. He was the connection that might draw Maxim Samsa to us.

What did we know about this murderer? We knew he was bright but not formally educated. He was clever enough to have avoided arrest for all these months, now, and it was mid-May. He had eluded the CPD, the State Police, the Cook County Sheriff's Police, the FBI and the US Marshal's Deputies. Not bad for a dropout from St Charles.

He made no lasting attachments to anyone. His detachment was in his favor. Cabrero wasn't a friend, just a business connection. Doc and I and Jack figured Cabrero was in the middle of his sales of human blood. The kind of blood that was taken from unwilling female donors. That was what made it attractive to these incredible spooks who'd gone far enough to have false fangs implanted in their jaws. The illicit serum made the ritual – Satanic or whatever division of black arts that these geeks were involved in – a rush, a thrill, a high. Whatever it was that motivated what appeared to be human beings into this kind of bizarre misbehavior.

I didn't think Samsa did it for the money. He watched those women fade from this life for his own reasons. Not gain, money-wise. He was getting even. When you had someone this cruel, then the crimes were about cruelty. Someone had abused him, but I didn't really care who it was, at this point. I wasn't going to spend time developing a profile of my own on him – the FBI had already sent theirs to us and it didn't tell us anything we didn't already know.

Maxim Samsa was a shadowy creature. That was the persona he was creating. He was inventing himself as he went along. His unpredictability was now a pattern in this killer. You could expect the outrageous in him.

Which meant to me that he wasn't going to stop killing with a fifth victim. He thought of all of this as a first stage. Perhaps there were other poets he'd use. Other verses to tape to his victim's cold toes.

All of the above I thought was true. That was why we had to get him now. Before he changed his MO in order to confuse us and throw us off the scent. We had to find Samsa before he invented an even crueler, more sophisticated version of himself.

'If you ever use my name, Jimmy P, you'll never see my face or hear my voice again. You know all that, going in.'

My cousin, Jimmy Ciccio, sat in the same booth he'd shared with me before in Little Italy.

'You ever think of retiring from the cops, cuz?'

'Yeah. Sure. On occasion.'

He looked at me with the wolf's eyes.

'This motherfucker has you so angry that you want to quit?'

'You should've been a psychologist.'

211

'Dead-end racket, Lieutenant. You have to talk to goofy fuckers all day. It doesn't pay good enough. The goofs I listen to either bring in income or they don't get their tickets stamped. You know how it works . . . '

He watched me. I supposed he thought he could cow me into lowering my eyes from his, but I locked on and didn't let go.

'The cops I know wouldn't let this prick bother them the way he does you. They'd figure "fuck it" and move on to something less frustrating, you know?'

I nodded, but I kept my eyes on his.

He wouldn't blink either. I thought the match might become a stalemate, but he finally dropped his glare onto his outstretched fingers on the table before him.

'Your guy Cabrero is going to be available tonight at the Priest's and Priestess – it's a titty bar in Old Town.'

'Yeah. I know it.'

'But you never patronized it, eh, cuz?'

'No . . . but I've been there for professional reasons.'

'Cabrero is going to be there at 4:00 in the a.m. – on the dot, when they're supposed to close. He's supposed to do a fifty K trick for some "h" that's just arrived from a crossover in south Texas. It's high grade skank, expensive heroin, all the way from central America. This is his big sale, and I'm supposed to get twenty-five per cent.'

I looked at him and smiled.

'You want to know why I'm dumping a profit of this magnitude, Lieutenant? It's because this guy Cabrero is into that blood shit with your laughing boy, that cocksucker Samsa. Which means that every law enforcement swinging dick in the Midwest is looking for these two motherfuckers. And the faster we take Cabrero and his girlfriend Samsa out of the picture, the sooner I go back to business as usual —'

'Don't tell me about it. I told you. I'm cutting you no deals. I'm not in Narco anyway, but don't tell me anything you don't want me to hear.'

'Fair enough, Jimmy P. You're a balls-up guy. You never shit where I ate. And we are blood, hard as it is for you to swallow.'

'What can I tell you?'

He laughed, and the lupine eyes suddenly went humorous.

'I remember your old man. And your Uncle Nick too. They were balls-up and straight, like you. I don't know how the genes on your side of the family went wrong, but what the fuck. I'm no biologist. Four a.m., Jimmy P. If I was you, I'd make sure there are no fuckups. You want to land Cabrero now. It was difficult for me, even, to find out where this Mex fuck was floating. You nail him, you'll nail your big fuckin' tuna, Samsa. I guarantee it. They been doin' business without paying tribute to me, and that's another reason I'm handing this white-haired dick over to you. You better collect him while you can, cousin.'

Everyone on scene around Priest's and Priestess was in plain clothes. We were a half block down, but our troops were everywhere in the vicinity. If Cabrero showed, he was inside the net. Jack and Doc and I had already informed Narcotics that we were looking at one of their hottest topics. Murder overrode drug sales, I figured, and Narco went along with us. Samsa was the highest of the high profiles, so they didn't want to muddy our path.

It was 3:30. I had been listening to Nancy Wilson on my headphones, and I asked Doc and found that he was tuned into the same all-night jazz thing from Evanston.

'You're finally seeing the light,' Gibron grinned. He was in the front seat shotgun. I was behind the wheel, and Jack was fully alert and awake in the back seat of the Taurus.

All the other cops on the stake were sitting in more elegant rides. There were black Mustangs, red Hondas, yellow Cameros, a couple black Lexuses – we'd gone all out on trying to use vehicles that players would drive – everyone except us in the Ford, of course.

'Son of a bitch,' Jack whispered. 'He's early . . . look.'

Walking into the front door of Priest's and Priestess was a male with a blue Texas Rangers ballcap and flowing white hair that reached his shoulder blades. He was wearing a blue blazer over a pair of faded bluejeans, and when he turned I

213

saw he was wearing a red T-shirt under the blue blazer. It had some kind of picture on the chest that I couldn't make out from almost a half block away even with the use of field glasses. There was enough light in front of this strip club for us to see him clearly.

Everyone let him walk right in. Then we began to tighten the noose. The three of us in our vehicle were going to take the point and enter the bar. We got out of the Ford and proceeded toward the entry.

There were no bobbling breasts to peruse as we walked inside. There was the sound of a low-volume juker in the background, and the bar was bathed in a red glow. It was like walking into a submarine.

This joint also employed ex-bikers as bartenders. Somehow all that hair and all those facial scars gave the owners a sense of security. Which was why they were constantly being robbed blind at their tills. These dicks were criminals, not employees.

The Mexican sat at the bar alone. It was closing time and all the patrons had gone elsewhere – home, likely. It was an early Thursday morning.

Our guns were drawn before we walked inside. But we had held them at our sides.

The first shot from Cabrero knocked Jack backwards, his arms extended to the ceiling. His Nine clanked on the bar's floor as I let loose with a round from the .44 Bulldog that tore into Cabrero's right thigh and turned him around as if he were doing a ballet pirouette. Doc's round caught the white-haired drug runner in the sole of his left foot as he flopped horizontally and bounced as if he'd hit a trampoline.

Cabrero screamed out: *'Don't! Don't fuckin' shoot me again!'*

I rushed toward him as Doc went back to our partner Jack, who lay on the floor of this saloon with his arms and legs akimbo.

I put the tip of the barrel under Cabrero's chin as I picked up his .22 Saturday night special. Even the grip was taped to make it cold and untraceable.

214

'You aren't going to die tonight, shitbird,' I warned him, the barrel still wedged under his chin as he lay flat on his back.

'Doc! What's the story with Jack?'

'I'm . . . I'm a little bit hurting, Jimmy. These vests don't stop it from feeling like the world's best right hook to the chest.'

Doc was helping Wendkos to his feet. We all wore the vests tonight. It had become standard for forays into the field like this, but you always feared a headshot or a blast to the family jewels. Your vest didn't prevent those catastrophes.

We were lucky Cabrero didn't have enough time to foil the vest by planting one in Jack's forehead or his crotch. Wendkos would feel like he'd been pounded by a heavy-weight, but he wasn't going to wind up in a bodybag.

I hadn't had time to be terrified for my partner. It would be a delayed response thing, like in the old lost war I fought in.

'Get up, you and your microscopic little pecker,' I told Cabrero.

'I'm *bleedin'*, man,' the drug dealer begged.

'How about I shoot you in the other leg?'

By now the titty bar was overflowing with law enforcement. County, State, Federal – we had a quorum from everybody.

'You can't do—'

I cocked the .44 under his chin again, and he struggled to his feet. Someone had called the paramedics, so they took Jack out first.

'I'm *bleedin'*, goddammit!'

'Then bleed, asshole.'

I cuffed him, and then the next batch of paramedics put Cabrero on a gurney – his hands were cuffed on top of his belly so they could transport him before he went dry on us. The medic pressed a wad of bandage against his gaping thigh wound from the .44's blast, and Cabrero screamed loudly. The scarred badass biker behind the bar, who had only just now emerged from the floor behind the bar, blanched, passed out, and hit his noggin on the oak slab and knocked himself cold.

'Medic!' I yelled out. It was out of habit, yelling for the doc, I figured. A habit I thought I freed myself of over thirty years ago in Southeast Asia.

Chapter Twenty-Seven

Jack Wendkos took a ride to Emergency at St Luke's with Doc and me for company. We rode in the back next to our stretched-out younger partner. The vest had saved his life, but no one particularly enjoyed wearing them, lightweight as they were, because they reminded us how vulnerable we really were on the streets.

'I'm sore,' Jack moaned.

He was a tough guy, an ex-Golden Gloves second place finisher in the middleweight category, so if he was sore, he was truly hurting.

'Better sore than the other thing,' Doc laughed and patted his shoulder.

Matt Cabrero was in another ambulance with three of our brother Homicides in attendance. After we saw Jack into the hospital, and after he was released, we'd see about Cabrero – who was likely going into surgery for the two gunshots he'd taken. I was certain that my round from that squat Bulldog did the most damage. I hoped that I hadn't severed anything major in his leg because I wanted to get at him as soon as possible.

'I never saw him pull the piece,' Jack admitted.

'It was dark in that fucking hole,' I told him.

'Dante's ninth concentric ring, young man. You arrested the devil himself tonight, so be proud of yourself,' Doc told him.

'He's no devil. He's just a punk dealer with an overly large legend,' Jack tried to grin.

'He must be an important punk. The Outfit uses him,' I reminded Jack.

'He better come up with Samsa. I think the little joint broke a rib or two,' Jack again groaned. This time he put his head back down and we rode the rest of the way in silence.

Jack Wendkos had indeed broken a rib – and bruised another. I was surprised that a .22 could do such damage to a vest and the body behind it, but Wendkos would be walking gingerly for a week or two, the ER surgeon told him as he released our partner.

The report on Cabrero came to us as we drove, the three of us, back downtown. My shot hadn't hit anything critical, and the shot to his foot was superficial, and we would be able to talk to him in the morning.

The Mexican squinted as if he'd just awakened. He had his eyes on us every step of the way into his hospital room.

'Give us Maxim Samsa,' I told him as we sat in folding chairs about his bed in this private room guarded by two uniforms outside.

'Why don't you ask for Emiliano Zapata, too?' he cracked.

'He's dead. Fuck you. We haven't got time to play with you, jackass, and here's your alternative. You talk, right now, or when the doctor says so, I'm going to let you walk.'

He studied my face.

'Let me walk? I'm supposed to buy that cart of shit?'

His white hair was shoulder length. It lay in clumped strands, next to his weatherbeaten Indian face, on his pillow.

'I let you walk out of here and you'll be dead inside twelve hours,' I smiled.

He tried to smile back at me, but he couldn't pull it off.

'You know who I'm referring to, don't you,' I told him.

'Yeah. I guess.'

'They'll put a .22 short into the back of your brain in half a day, partner. You didn't pay tribute to the man, and you know how that works out.'

'You put them on me,' he said.

218

Doc and Jack were seated on either side of me. They watched the Indian.

'How much is Samsa really worth to you?' Cabrero asked.

'How much is continued breathing worth to you?'

He looked over at my two partners as if to ask was I for real.

They didn't blink, but Cabrero finally did.

'I've got his cellphone number and his beeper ... you won't find them because they're both stolen, of course.'

'Here.'

I handed him a pad of paper and a pencil.

'You'll be staying here until we have him. So these better not be fictional. See that phone next to you? Get him on the blower now. Fix a meet. Make it somewhere public so he won't be suspicious. Tell him you have an order – double the fee – for some fresh female blood. You know? His kind of thing. What was your percentage?'

'Ten per cent. He still owes me for ... Look, you ain't going to take me down with him, are you? I mean, I'm handing him over to you —'

'You're all out of negotiations, Cabrero. But maybe we can keep you away from the hangman – in this state he uses a needle, though.'

'Christ, I—'

'Get him on the phone now,' I told him.

'Where do you want the meet?'

I looked at his white hair and creased face.

'Oak Street Beach. Five a.m. Tomorrow morning.'

He looked at me, smiled, and then he picked up the phone.

Jack wasn't making this trip. He was to go home and rest his broken rib for a few days. He wasn't happy that he couldn't go along with us early in the morning.

No one knew about the meeting at the beach except for Doc and me and Cabrero and Samsa. We heard him tell Samsa the particulars. My first reaction was to have massive manpower surround him until his back was to the water, but I remembered how often information leaked through

219

our department because some ears were on a payroll in addition to the CPD. I wasn't going to have a leak. It would be Doc and me and that was all.

I had Cabrero's phone removed from his private room. His cell and beeper had already been impounded. I sent the two uniforms away and had two new cops placed outside the Mexican's door. No one was to enter Cabrero's room except for his doctor and nurses – and they were required to display their IDs for my cop sentries.

I tried to think of any other avenues for foul-ups, but I couldn't come up with any. Security was as tight as I could make it.

Three in the a.m. I was home and awake. Natalie was in bed. So was the rest of the Parisi clan.

I had been on Samsa for more weeks than I could remember. He had slipped me in multiples. He'd contributed to my sense of incompetence and he'd almost convinced me to retire. He'd almost made me believe all these killers were younger and faster than I was. Perhaps they were younger and quicker on their feet, but I tried to remind myself that it was who was there at the end of the contest – who was the last man standing.

'Jimmy? Aren't you up early?' Natalie asked as she came into the kitchen. I had the dim light over the stove on and nothing else. She was in shadow. I could see only her outline. Then she snapped on the overhead light, and when it came on, we both blinked.

I had the .44 on the table, along with my Nine in its holster and the switchblade none of us was allowed to carry.

'Weapons check?' she grinned.

I nodded and took her hand as she sat at the kitchen table across from me.

'Samsa? Finally?' she queried.

I nodded again.

'But you can't tell anyone until it's done. Only Doc and I are going to meet up with him. On the beach, right before dawn."

'Jesus, how melodramatic!'

'We wanted him to feel safe. Somewhere in public, out in the open. You know how he is.'

'Yes. A sly little rodent.'

'A free rodent, Natalie.'

'Everybody's string runs out. Jesse James, Doc Holliday —'

'He's no legend, Red.'

'I know, honey.'

She put her warm left hand over mine.

'No one knows but Doc and me.'

'I know. You already told me.'

'Oh. Yeah. But it's important nobody else—'

'You'll take him this time. His luck's depleted. He's through, Jimmy.'

I felt the warmth of her palm. I didn't want her to take that hand away. But the doorbell rang and it startled us both.

'It's Doc with the car,' I explained.

She went out to let him in.

'Ready to roll, Occifer?'

'How can you crack wise at this hour of the morning?' I demanded.

'Never went to sleep. I've been gearing for him all night long.'

Doc sat and Natalie went to get us all some instant coffee. I wasn't a coffee drinker, but I figured I could use the caffeine.

When the coffee was ready, she brought it over.

'What if this guy runs before you can get close enough to cuff him?' Natalie asked. 'No offense, but neither of you are exactly in sprinter's condition.'

'He cannot outrun that,' I nodded toward the squat .44 on the table.

'Jesus, Jimmy. It's a good thing you're a good shot and it's even better that you've still got perfect vision,' Doc grinned. 'That street cannon. Jesus Harold Christ.'

'Let me go along,' said the Redhead. 'Michael can watch the kids. It's Saturday.'

I looked at my wife. My first reaction was the macho refusal. Then I remembered that she was all those years younger than I, that she had burned down The Farmer right here in our own home, and that she was a black belt in karate – she'd won more trophies than I and my son Mike combined.

'All right.'

She shot a look at me that displayed her surprise.

'Boy, that was a quick reversal of the Jimmy Parisi I know and cohabit with.'

'We can use your help. I just wanted to keep this as simple as possible. No chances for ears to pick up intelligence. You need to wear your vest. I don't know what Samsa will be bringing with him, but I wouldn't trust the Mexican if I were Samsa.'

Natalie went into our bedroom. Doc and I sipped the instant coffee. I threw my cup down the sink, and I went into the fridge for my standard Diet Coke – the no-caffeine variety.

She returned in just a few minutes, dressed and vested.

We arrived at the parking lot for Oak Street Beach at 4:30 a.m. We parked the Taurus, however, a block away from the lot. That Ford would be an advertisement for the Chicago Police Department.

The cold wind blew in off the Lake from the northeast. We wore jackets over the vests, but the chill penetrated our coverings. We walked toward the concession stand that Cabrero told Samsa would be the meeting place.

The beach was deserted, as we knew it would be. We walked up to that concession building to make sure Samsa hadn't arrived early. When we circled the concession stand, we saw that no one was here yet, so we retreated to the sidewalk above the beach. We could see the stand clearly from our position behind a copse of trees just beyond that sidewalk. I had my night vision starlights, in case it was too dark to see, but the dawn was graying already, and we could see well enough from where we stood, hidden by a group of tall oaks.

Doc looked at his glow-in-the-dark watch dial.

'Five minutes til,' he whispered.

I looked over to my wife. I was in the middle of our trio, and we each occupied the backside of an oak tree. She wore her CPD windbreaker, just as Doc and I did, over the vests. The .44 was still in its ankle holster, the Nine in my shoulder contraption, and the switchblade knife sat in my jacket's pocket. We had hand-held radios, just in case he took off on the three of us. We could get some patrol cars here in just minutes, but I didn't want the outsiders in this scenario. If they were called in, I thought, we'd lose Samsa again.

It was on the stroke of five on my own watch that a figure appeared at the edge of the water behind the concession, perhaps a hundred yards north of our position.

'Let him reach the stand,' I whispered to Natalie and Doc.

They both nodded in agreement. Natalie was to flank left and Doc to the right. I was going to beeline it straight at Samsa when we rushed him. It was only twenty-five yards to that structure on the sand before us.

The figure stayed at the edge of the water. It continued on, never veering toward the brick building. Pretty soon, the figure kept going beyond our station. Now I could see it was a young woman and her dog, going for an early morning stroll. She kept going, right down the beach, away from us.

I looked at Doc, and he shook his head. Natalie just shot me a glance that attempted to convey encouragement.

It was 5:06.

My legs were getting stiff from standing in this upright position behind my tall oak.

Another faint figure appeared at the edge of the Lake, perhaps 150 yards north of our location. The figure seemed to glide over the sand in some odd fashion. It seemed to float—

But I knew it had to be something of an optical illusion in this dim pre-dawn light.

It came straight toward the concesssion stand, and this time I knew it was Samsa. This was The Count. The syringe-bearing killer of all those young women. The object of all my obsessive nightmares for all of these long months.

I raised my right hand to signal Natalie and Doc to swoop down on him. But we had to wait until he reached the building so my two partners could indeed get their angles in order to flank him. When he was in position, he'd have only the lake to retreat into.

I let my hand down when he disappeared behind the concessions. Doc and my wife and I trotted out onto the sand, but Samsa didn't emerge from behind the building.

When we arrived and circled behind . . . We found no one. It was as if he had disappeared.

'He's in the water, Jimmy!' Doc yelled.

I looked out and saw a thin young man freestyling it out toward the middle of Lake Michigan. He was out about 100 feet, it appeared.

I ripped off my shoes and my vest and my shoulder harness, and I took the .44 out of its ankle holder and then I charged toward the water.

'Jimmy!' Natalie called out.

Doc ran behind me, but he knew he'd be no help to me in these cold waters. Doc couldn't swim, and Natalie was a novice. I motioned for them both to stay put before I bolted and ran out into the shallow, frigid water. When I couldn't run any farther, I dove in.

He was about fifty feet from me, then. He wasn't exactly Olympic caliber and his freestyle was awkward. I was a capable swimmer, but nothing near gold medal level. But I kept pumping away with my methodical stroke, and slowly I was on him.

I grabbed him by the back of his hair when I reached him. He thrashed his arms wildly and tried to connect a blow to my head, but I had him from behind and then I dunked him. When he went under, his mouth had to have been opened, gasping, because he was spitting water and choking when I brought him up. I was able to stand in the water. It was perhaps five feet deep here, where we struggled.

I dunked him again and held his head down. This time I held him under a long time. I could hear him gurgling beneath the surface. I brought him up again and made

224

certain that he was Samsa. There was no mistaking his pale, gaunt visage. I dunked him yet again, although he was weak and the submerging wasn't necessary.

I could save Cook County and the City of Chicago perhaps a half million to a million in court costs if I held him down long enough. Drowning would be a just way for Samsa to disappear. It was slow and painful, just like the deaths he'd perpetrated on all those young women.

The sound of his gurgling grew fainter and fainter. It was light enough to see in the cold lake water that his oxygen was about used up – the bubbles decreased in number drastically. I could be his judge and executioner. Think of all the pain he had caused me, I remembered. Think of the humiliation this murderer had dished out to me and to my partners.

He was a high profile killer. The newspapers loved him. I thought of all the publicity he'd generate from all the media. I'd have to endure his picture every day – in the newspapers and on television.

I had his hair at the crown and it took little to no effort to hold him under.

Then I hoisted him up. He gasped for air and then spit out more lake water. When he had his air back, he looked at me as if he wondered whether I were going to put him under yet again.

I had him by the hair with my left hand. He stood up straight. He was a few inches taller than I was, so my left hand elevated higher. He looked at me and I thought he was trying to show me his teeth. As if he were attempting to snarl at me like some cornered dog.

I smacked him with my free right fist, and his head jerked back. I stood him straight up again, and it appeared that some blood ooozed down his oversized canines. I could see that I had broken one of his fangs. He spit the shattered tooth into the water.

I wanted to smack him again, but he didn't show me any more teeth. He almost fainted. He went limp on me, so I had to drag him back to shore. The water made his body more buoyant than if I'd had to drag him across the sand, so we made it back to shore quickly.

Doc grabbed hold of him and lugged him onto the sand. He flopped him down on his face, flat on the beach, and then he cuffed Samsa.

My wife read Maxim Samsa his rights.

Samsa turned his head toward Natalie and gave her a weak snarl. You could see the blood and the remnants of his ruined fang.

'You say a word,' I told him. 'Any word at all. And I'll take you back into the lake and finish the job.'

Doc and I hauled him to his feet. Natalie walked behind the three of us. And then we escorted our prisoner toward the Ford Taurus, down the block.

Chapter Twenty-Eight

The trial of Maxim Samsa was due on the docket in about three months. I interviewed The Count in our well-used interrogation room downtown.

Doc stood outside the famous one-way mirror and watched as I talked to the self-proclaimed vampire by myself.

'You're aware of your rights,' I said.

'Sure,' he grinned. He showed me only one whole fang – the other I'd broken.

He wasn't quite so pasty-faced without his Goth make-up. But he was pale enough to look unhealthy. Creepy. Spooky. Whatever it was that he wanted to cultivate with his appearance.

The gray Cook County jumpsuit didn't add to his vampire persona, however. He looked like just another slick, headed to the joint.

'You have not confessed to the murders you're accused of, so I assume you're pleading not guilty.'

I had asked him again, before we sat down, if he wanted an attorney to be present. He said he was going to be his own counsel, even though the judge warned him that it wasn't wise to be your own lawyer.

'We don't have much of a case history about you, Mr Samsa. We have plenty of your DNA from the tape you used to keep the vics quiet. We have a few hair samples from the last two murders. And we have the testimony of Matt Cabrero – who can't wait to flip you. He's trying to cut a deal with our Prosecutor, but he'll be doing a long stretch.

And he'll probably get life for the shit he's done. You, on the other hand, are looking at lethal injection. Personally, I'd prefer hanging, in your case. But the Supreme Court doesn't agree with me . . .

'Nobody seems to really understand what it was that provoked you to kill these women the way you did. I mean, you didn't make all that much money on draining them, did you?'

He was manacled at the waist and on the ankles as well. His long thin fingers drummed the table top, and the handcuffs clunked a bit as he drummed. Doc thought we should have muzzled him like they do biting dogs, but I refused to allow it.

'You don't know me,' he began. 'I ain't anybody you ever knew. I didn't do those killings. You can take your DNA and . . . '

He smiled weakly. Then he looked up at me again with that broken-fanged, snaggled smile.

'There's more under heaven and earth than—'

'I read *Hamlet*, too, cheesedick. You're not going to startle me with your jailhouse intellect. You're a poorly educated piece of white trash who's garnered some notoriety because of the terrible things you did to a bunch of women who didn't have it coming. You watched them die slowly and you didn't show any pity. That's why I'm going to be there when they put you to sleep like the diseased mutt you are.'

'They can't convict me if I'm crazy.'

'The court psychiatrist doesn't think you're legally insane, and neither do I.'

'I'd have to be crazy to do what I done, wouldn't I, Lieutenant Parisi?'

'You've been watching too much TV. Old movies, Maxim. Insanity, temporary insanity, is past its prime. Juries like to burn down killers like you. You should've turned off the cable and read the newspapers. You're going to die, my man. You planned each of these killings. They weren't spur of the moment or heat of passion numbers. They were cold blooded. Like the snake you are.'

228

'I been around people like you all my life, *Lieutenant*. Parole officers, cops, social workers. All those pricks from St Charles. They all wanted to know about my sad-assed childhood. I didn't have no childhood. Been on the streets since I was twelve, and I ain't looking for any understanding, from you or nobody else. I looked out for myself. You had to be the meanest dog or you didn't eat. Course you wouldn't know about that kind of life.'

'I've seen meaner sons of bitches than you. But not many as pitiless.'

'Pity is weakness. You ever become someone's street bitch, Lieutenant? I'll bet you haven't. Livin' in boxes, in sewers, in terminals – wherever it's warm. Then you finally get caught by some bigger, meaner son of a bitch who likes to do you in the ass in some public toilet. He tells you if you try to run off he'll catch you and cut you so your manhood ain't going to be an issue no longer. He'll castrate you if you run. So you bend over like the bitch he thinks you are and you take it. You take it til the day he goes to sleep before you do, and then you use the box opener you found in the street, and you stab him where the big ole jugular vein is, and when the blood jets up outta him you cut his throat from ear to ear and finish him. You waited six months to do him. Gettin' up the will to cut him open like some fish.

'And then the blood ain't as terrible as you thought it was gonna be. You watch in fascination as the red shower covers his face and chest and puddles on the ground underneath him. You want to do to him what he threatened to do to you, but you can't bear to touch that thing he's used on you again and again . . . you just squat in front of him and watch him try to stanch the flow by grabbin' his neck. But it don't do no good. The blood sorta pulses out between his fingers, and he reaches out toward you with his other hand, but you don't make a move. You let him squirm. You let him wriggle while it's all leakin' out of him onto the blacktop. You're in an alley with dogs and cats and rats. They come on up to him once he's still. A few of them dogs lap his blood, but I shoo them off because I want to watch his eyes. They're still open. When somebody bleeds to death they just look tireder and tireder until the lights go out in their eyes. You oughta see it. It's like nothin' else in the world, Lieutenant.'

'So you got an excuse. You're going to cop that plea? Poor little abused street orphan. Took his vengeance out on a bunch of helpless women—'

'They wasn't helpless. They was alone. Just the way I was. And along come someone who was stronger than they was. Of course I didn't kill none of them . . . I'm just talkin' hypothetical, you understand.'

'You were incapacitated because of the trauma you endured in your youth. Is that about it?'

Samsa smiled.

'And you tormented the vics' relatives with the verses you left behind.'

'Boy, whoever did do them. That was a nice touch, dontcha think?'

'You may not get the injection after all.'

His face went serious momentarily.

'Say again?' he asked.

'They're talking about suspending the death penalty. They've made numerous mistakes that DNA has overturned – but sometimes they were too late.'

'You sayin' that I might get life after all? Even though you know I'm not your man, of course.'

'Yeah. It's possible . . . But if you think about it. If you use your imagination. Think about being confined in a relatively small cage for, what, sixty, maybe seventy years? You're pretty young. Healthy enough. You might live a long, long time.'

His eyes focused on his drumming fingers.

'You won't qualify for parole. See, that's the little twist, recently. It'll be life without parole. You can make book on it.'

He tried to show me a grin, but he wasn't up to the effort.

'Why'd you mess around with those kids? Those Goths? They weren't your kind of people, were they?'

230

'They're a bunch of phony little suburban white kids with too much money and time on their hands . . . I would've done a couple of those cunts. But I never killed nobody, like I told you.

'It would've been sweet to take a few of them out the way whoever it was did those women you're accusin' me of burning . . . yeah. Gold Coast cunts. Cunts in training. I let a few of them blow me, but I never planted my wick in any of them. They thought they were . . . special. I had nigger and spic whores who were better on their backs than any of those white bitches. From the rich hoods. Bored bitches. Lookin' for a rush. That's why they went and did them "alternative" lifestyles. I just dressed up for them because it was good for business. I admit that I supplied them the blood, but I was just the middleman, Lieutenant.'

'You're a really incompetent liar, sweetheart.'

He tried to jump up at me, but his chains kept him seated.

'Don't never call me that,' he hissed.

'How about I unlock you, tell Doc out there to take a walk, and then you can jump out from that chair at me again?'

'You think you bad, huh, Lieutenant?'

'Want me to get the keys?'

He looked at me carefully, and then his smirk slowly dissipated.

'I should've drowned you when I had you under.'

'But you the man, boss. Good guys don't do none of that executioner stuff. Am I right?'

I watched his eyes, but they glanced away from me.

'They said you were a pretty fair student, at St Charles.'

'That what they said at that chicken factory?'

'Chicken' was a euphemism for the prison slang word 'bitch.' Bitch as in the unwilling male mate in a homosexual pairing behind bars.

'They said you scored very well on your aptitude exams.'

'I shoulda taken the SAT and become a real lawyer, huh?'

'You were pretty good in math, especially, they told us.'

'Count all that fuckin' money in some dude's multimillion dollar company. Become a king of fuckin' white collar crime.'

'Do you have any idea, any clue as to the misery you caused those young women, Samsa?'

'Oh, I see! You lookin' for admission of guilt again. You wanna know if I feel regrets for what I already told you I didn't do. Y'all are big on remorse, huh? You want to know if I feel sorry for what I done, but I can't, now can I, since I ain't did what you say I done. That seems simple enough to a under-educated homeless man like me.'

'We found thirty thousand in cash in that flop you were using on the near north just before you went wading in the water.'

'Yeah, but I was all dressed up with nowheres to go since you police officers made up your minds that I was the perpetrator of these terrible deeds which I never did.'

'You can spend the thirty K on some quality reading materials while you're doing life in high security somewhere.'

'Thirty K. That was just chump change to those Goth twats I hung with. They got all hung on blood rituals and black sabbaths. I read up on that shit so I sounded – whattayoucallit – conversant about the devil shit, and I tell you what, Lieutenant Parisi, that shit kinda gets into your system after a while. It's kind of a turn-on. They'd take the vials I brought them and they'd drink the shit and pour it all over themselves, you know their titties and everywhere . . . Hell, I always came home with a sore and depleted dick after a few of them black sabbaths. Drawing pentangles on some stone floor in some deserted farmhouse or wherever it was that they'd located a place to meet.

'But they weren't really serious about the ritual. I mean I don't think they ever really expected Satan himself to appear among us. It was just a nice excuse to get wild and suck a few jalones and ball some of their boyfriends near an altar laced with some fresh blood from the murder of a beautiful young woman.'

'That's what the poetry was about. The Poe.'

'Yeah. They all read him. Poe kept saying the most poetic subject was the death of a young bitch. I started to read him. Some of the stuff wasn't bad. But he had a bad habit of fucking babbling. Fucker died in the street. Some son of a bitch lays a flower on his grave once every year—'

'I know. I read it somewhere.'

'I didn't kill any of them women. And if I did, I was crazy at the time and didn't even know I was doin' them. You see? Either way, I wasn't *responsible*. So if you're lookin' for any kind of statement about me being the guilty party, Lieutenant, you're rattling the wrong door knob.'

He showed me his teeth.

'Why'd you bite them?'

'I don't know what you're talkin' about. These big canines was for show. For my little white-faced Goth gashes. That's all. I never used them like that.'

'We've got your saliva. It's part of the DNA package.'

He tried to appear unconcerned, but it looked like he was weakening, just slightly.

'I think your quarter's spent, Lieutenant. I'm tired. And I gotta rest up for my big trial. I'm my own counsel, you know. And you know what a formidable intellect I got, by now, so if you don't mind—'

'You're a stupid man, Samsa. Anybody who kills a human being is stupid by definition because the odds are truly rotten you'll get away with it. Most of you killers are brain-deads. But then you watch TV, maybe the movies. You see the brilliant killer do his thing in multiples and you see him baffle the cops, and only a miraculous twist of fate gets these TV geniuses caught. You think you're a player, but you must not know the odds against players on the Strip. The house wins, asshole. You don't beat the house. That's why you're living in a hovel, running like a jackrabbit, not knowing the hour and day that you wind up right where you wound up. Shitty odds, Maxim.

'You'll get your picture in a few magazines and daily newspapers, and in three months no one'll remember your

233

fucking name. You'll be behind big gray walls, and it'll be the highlight of your week to see blue sky and yellow sun. That's where you're headed, dumb fuck, and it couldn't happen to a nicer guy.'

'Vampires can't die. They're immortal. How can you be so sure that I won't rise up from the grave and suck the blood out of you and your whole fucking family?'

I smiled brightly at him.

'Because I'll be the guy who pounds the wooden stake through your fucking heart before they bury your sad, lame ass.'

I got up, called for Samsa's escort, and the interview/interrogation was over.

Of all possibilities, the Redhead and I sat on our couch long past midnight watching the original *Dracula*, with Bela Lugosi.

'This poor prick was buried in that cape,' I told my wife.

Natalie jumped when I interrupted her concentration on the archaic horror classic.

'Goddammit, Jimmy! You about gave me heart failure.'

She went back to watching the movie, chomping occasionally on some semi-burned microwave popcorn.

'Jesus God, you about loosened my bowels.'

'You scared?' I asked her with a smile.

'Of course not,' she said. Somehow it lacked conviction.

'There are no vampires,' she said.

'No werewolves, fairies, goblins or ghouls either.'

'That's right. Now shut up.'

'I would've shot Drac with a silver bullet from my Bulldog. Blown his heart right out onto the Carpathian Mountains.'

'Jimmy! *Shut up!*'

'Yes, my love.'

I sat silent while Bela Lugosi as The Real Count hovered over one of his victims. The sights of the crime scenes from Samsa's murders did a slow rerun inside my head.

Then I re-focused on the movie.

'It's just a movie. There are no vampires,' I whispered.

The Redhead shivered and moved closer to me.

'Not anymore, Jimmy. You found him and you put him away.'

I blinked, and then Natalie turned her face toward mine.

Chapter Twenty-Nine

A month after we'd grabbed The Count, Abu Riad went to Federal Court. The trial lasted only four weeks, and he received twenty years for fraud and for income tax evasion. His next appearance in court would be for the murders of Arthur Ransom, Dorothy Beaumont, and for the two gang members he had ordered executed in an alley. The chief witness against Riad was going to be Rico Perry – who was going to get a minimum of twenty years with a chance for parole because of his age and because the murder of Joellyn Ransom was deemed 'a crime of passion'. That was the deal Rico received from the Prosecuting Attorney's Office.

So Riad was finally going away for the rest of his life. It had been a lot of years since Andres Dacy had been gunned down in front of Cabrini Green as his mother Celia Dacy looked on in horror. I didn't know if any of this was payback, but it did feel like some kind of closure, some kind of ending to a long period of suffering. It didn't bring Andres or Celia or any of the other victims back to life, but it spoke for them, somehow.

The Redhead, Natalie, worked homicides. They wouldn't let us work together, but our paths crossed occasionally. As they did on a Tuesday night around 8:30 p.m.

I took her to Garvin's tavern in Berwyn. Doc was home sick with the flu and Jack was downtown finalizing the paperwork before Maxim Samsa went to trial. I would need to get back from this dinner break pretty soon in order to help him finish.

The Garvin's Comeback Inn was located next to a pair of unused railroad tracks. The weeds grew profusely all over those bars of iron, and only a spot for parking was mowed to keep the greenery from devouring his patrons' rides.

Natalie had been here before, but she didn't relish the place the way Doc did. I simply found the bar comfortable – like a torn-up recliner that you can't seem to throw out.

There was talk of renovation in this Berwyn neighborhood. Talk of tearing down Garvin's to find room for a mini strip mall. The Berwyn bigshots promised Garvin a spot for a new place in the strip mall, but like most old guys, John Garvin resisted change. He was vintage World War II, he had fought with Patton at the Battle of the Bulge, and most of the politicians didn't want a brawl with the old man. But John was playing their game against them. He really had dreams of a new joint – without sawdust on the floor. No spitting in the new bar. He just didn't let them know his real plans. In that way, he figured, he'd up the price of the demolition of the current Comeback Inn. I knew all that because he had confessed it to Doc and Jack and me a couple of weeks before.

'How can you stand the smell?' Natalie asked, her nostrils pinched in disgust.

'The place has what Doc calls ambience.'

'You and Doc are full of it,' she declared.

'Yes. We are.'

I smiled at her and she squeezed my thigh.

'John doesn't allow public displays of affection in here,' I warned her.

'Nobody's ever gotten lucky in one of those smelly bathrooms?'

'Well . . . '

'The Count goes down tomorrow,' she said.

'Yes. The trial begins tomorrow morning.'

'He's still his own counsel?'

'Yes, Natalie.'

'You have to be there, of course.'

'Of course, Red.'

'It'll be a media circus, I'm sure.'

'You're right.'

'Jimmy.'

I looked over at my beautiful wife.

'Are you any better, now that this guy is in the lock-up?'

'Yeah. Yes, I think I'm all improved.'

'No more thoughts about retiring?'

'No, Natalie. Not recently. I'm sure something'll come along to provoke those same thoughts all over again.'

'You're not over the hill, my love.'

'You don't think so?'

'I know it. Absolutely. I'm sure you're not decrepit and all used up, sweet.'

'Well, thank you. I'm happy for the vote of confidence.'

'This guy was just difficult. Everybody in the division was aware of that. You didn't make bad moves. He—'

'I'm all right, Natalie. I'm okay. Really.'

This time I squeezed her thigh.

'Was that an indication of things to come, Lieutenant?'

'We could always sneak into one of Garvin's smelly johns.'

'Not in this lifetime, Jimmy.'

'Maybe when he opens his new place, then?'

'Anything is possible, no?' she grinned.

Then she winked at me brazenly, in full witness by John Garvin himself, limping toward us with our brats and Diet Sprites.

The trial of Maxim Samsa went the way the columnists and the journalists and the rest of the media people predicted. It was short, it was no contest, and Samsa was convicted of four counts of first-degree murder. All that was left was for the judge to pronounce sentence.

On a Wednesday following the trial, the judge pronounced Samsa's sentence. Death by lethal injection. The justice explained that the nature of the crimes showed a lack of mercy, of human pity, by its perpetrator, Maxim Samsa. Samsa may have deserved life without parole, and the State of Illinois might overthrow the sentence because of the conflict about the death penalty, but the judge, Alfred Carrigan, said if anyone deserved to be put down like an animal, it was Maxim Samsa.

The Count had his teeth fixed before the trial. The unbroken fang was removed and his crushed canine was fixed. He wore a brown three-piece suit, he'd had his hair styled, and he'd managed to get enough sun somewhere in jail to appear a bit more brown than he'd ever appeared before.

None of which swayed the jury. They were out a total of forty-five minutes. Guilty on all four counts. No brainer. Samsa had stuttered and bumbled his way through, but it wouldn't have made any difference if he had obtained a first-class defense lawyer for himself. The evidence was overwhelming, and The Candyman, our Prosecuting Attorney, was magnificent. He would've nailed O.J. Simpson with the legal attack he threw at Samsa.

Before The Count was taken away in cuffs and shackles – they were slapped on him after he was pronounced guilty – I walked up to his defense table.

He turned and looked at me as if he were afraid I was going to beat him with my fists. He almost flinched.

'Here. This is for you. Keep it close 'til you feel the prick of that needle.'

I handed him a piece of eight and a half by eleven typing paper with some verse typed on it. But I didn't wait to see if he read it. I found Natalie at the back of the courtroom and we walked out together.

'What was that all about?' she asked as we descended a flight of stairs.

'Here. I've got a copy of it. Wanted to keep it for myself.'

We stopped at the landing so she could read it.

> The breeze – the breath of God – is still –
> And the mist upon the hill,
> Shadowy – shadowy – yet unbroken,
> Is a symbol and a token –
> How it hangs upon the trees,
> A mystery of mysteries!

'What is it?'

'Poe's "Spirits of the Dead".'

'Oh. Yeah! The poems that were attached to his vics, right?'

I nodded.

'But why—'

She looked at me, stopped her query, and smiled.

'Which one of you's the real *devil*, huh, Jimmy?'

She kissed my cheek, and then we continued our descent to the main floor.

My son had done his duty. He got on the witness stand and he told the jury what Father Mark had done to him. There were four other witnesses who followed, saying much the same thing that Mike said before them. It was a brief trial. A waste of the diocese's money, trying to defend a priest who had no defense.

The priest got fifteen years in prison.

Michael was still seeing a counselor, but it wouldn't be long before the therapist released him. I had my son back, it appeared. His demons were becoming impotent. Mike was too busy with school and sports and a new-found interest in females to spend much time revisiting the horrors he'd endured with Father Mark.

I wondered if any old mini devils would descend upon me in the near future. I hoped not, but there was never any way to predict their reappearing. I'd have to deal with it if they showed up again. That was what you had to do. There was no place to evade them or escape them. They dwelled somewhere in the dank dungeons of the soul, waiting to break their bonds, waiting to fly upward and at you.

But I wasn't going to spend any time anticipating their re-emergence. I was going to try to enjoy every minute I had with my beloved wife and with my equally beloved children. I could deal with the terror of the street. That was my profession. And whatever it was that still attached itself inside me – I'd confront whatever it was when that time came. For now, I was going to breathe. Breathe until my lungs ached with all that fresh air.

I felt something akin to a high. I felt light, lighter than air. Like a balloon wafting away with the fresh western breeze.

Michael asked for the car keys. I tossed them to him without an interrogation.

'You okay, Pa?' Michael smiled.

'Yeah. I think I am. How about *that*?' I smiled at my son.

He didn't argue. He looked at the keys to the van with something short of astonishment, and he took off.

Epilogue

I knelt on the kneeler. I was alone in the church. It was after the sole eight o'clock on a weekday, so the place was empty.

I saw Father William on the altar. I got up after I crossed myself and I approached our parish priest.

Father William looked over at me and smiled.

'Can I help you, Jimmy?'

'Father . . . I'd like to make a confession.'

'It's not the usual . . . '

Then he looked at me and smiled.

'All right. You know where the confessional is.'

He put the flowers he had in his hands before the altar.

I walked over to the box, opened the door, went in, and I kneeled once again. Father William entered from his side and opened the little door that we talked through.

'Father forgive me for I have sinned. This is my first confession since . . . It's my first confession in more months than I can remember.'

'Go ahead, my son.'

'I was afraid I lost my faith. I was afraid I lost my hope. I was afraid . . . I was afraid I'd lost a lot more than that, Father.'

'God will forgive you. You know that. You know how it works, Jimmy.'

'I was angry at the Church because of what a priest had done to my son.'

'I know. I read all about Mike and the trial. I'm very sorry he had to be hurt so badly by a man who . . . I'm very sorry, Jimmy.'

'I wanted to kill Father Mark.'

'Yes. I understand . . . but you knew that another sin would only compound the first sin.'

'Yes. But I almost killed him anyway. I am a police officer. I'm not supposed to execute anyone . . . I almost drowned a criminal I arrested, a few months ago. And I have to confess, Father, that it felt good, holding him under the water.'

'You are a human being, just like any other. Vengeance seems to taste sweet.'

'I felt that way when I envisioned killing that priest. I am ashamed that I could feel that way. I know better. It isn't the way I really am . . . but sometimes I'm afraid that the guy who enjoyed almost drowning Maxim Samsa and who got a real electrical jolt out of fantasizing about putting bullet holes in a priest – I'm afraid that's the real me.'

'I'm not a psychologist, Jimmy. But it's pretty obvious, even to us laymen, that you reacted the way an outraged policeman would react when he was repeatedly frustrated . . . it took a long time to catch up with this Samsa, didn't it?'

'Yes, but—'

'And it was a long time coming with the knowledge of what had happened to Michael.'

'Yes.'

'Jimmy, anger is natural. It's what you do with it later that really matters. And you didn't murder Samsa and you didn't shoot Father Mark. I don't know any other way to judge a person than to look at the final result . . . Do you, Jimmy?'

I felt the beginning of tears at the edges of my eyes.

I began again.

'Father, forgive me for I have sinned.'